D0438245

MECHANICS' INSTITUTE
*MECHANICS'*
MERCANTILE LIBRARY

Also by Penny Mickelbury

*One Must Wait*

*Keeping Secrets*

*Night Songs*

[A Carole Ann Gibson Mystery]

# *Where to Choose*

## *by*

# *Penny Mickelbury*

*simon & schuster*

SIMON & SCHUSTER
Rockefeller Center
1230 Avenue of the Americas
New York, NY 10020

*Simon and Schuster* and colophon
are registered trademarks of Simon & Schuster Inc.

Designed by Jeanette Olender
Manufactured in the United States of America

1   3   5   7   9   10   8   6   4   2

Library of Congress Cataloging-in-Publication Data
Mickelbury, Penny, 1948–
Where to choose / by Penny Mickelbury.
    p.   cm.
    I. Title.
    PS3563.I3517W47   1999
813'.54—dc21          98-47703
                  CIP
ISBN 0-684-83742-0

*For Joan Garner, Dianne Houston, Jane Murray,*

*and Sally Purvis. You have shown me the true nature*

*of love and friendship and I am grateful.*

## *Acknowledgments*

There is no Jacaranda Estates in Los Angeles, nor is there a community even remotely like it. But that doesn't mean there couldn't have been. I'm grateful to native Angeleno Crystal Cooper, among others, for sharing her memories and insights with me. If there's any error to be found in my make-believe, it belongs to me and not to any of the Angels who encouraged me.

*The world was all before them, where to choose*

*Their place of rest, and Providence their guide,*

*They hand in hand with wandering steps and slow,*

*Through Eden took their solitary way.*

John Milton, *Paradise Lost*

# ✇ *one* ✑

He couldn't understand why he could not walk. First, he stumbled on the cobblestone walkway, and then staggered into the tight, thick grass. He wasn't drunk, though he wanted to be. And darkness was not the problem; this night was brightened by moon and stars. Nor was it the fact that he was in unfamiliar surroundings. He was not the kind of man to be intimidated by places or people unknown to him. So how to explain this sudden unsteadiness?

He forced himself to stand still and upright and he sniffed the air like the coyotes in the hills, seeking his bearings. He scanned the four directions and saw houses and flowers and trees and breathed in the scents emanating from them, including the jacaranda, which was the name of this place. Most of the houses glowed golden from light within and once or twice he caught the swift shadows of people passing before the windows. Again, he sniffed the air, allowing the odor of food to override the scent of the foliage. He was hungry. He should return to his friends. He should never have left; the *jefe* would be angry. But so what? The *jefe* always seemed angry about something. Angry enough to leave him hungry? Yes. The *jefe* was the kind of man who would punish so cruelly.

Unconsciously and instinctively his knees bent slightly and his head drooped. He cursed to himself as every sense and emotion intensified: hunger, thirst, and anger at the thought of being deprived of sustenance. Then he cocked his head. Footsteps. He moved toward them. Perhaps the *jefe* had been angry enough to come for him. And if not, perhaps the person could direct him to his friends.

He could tell that she was an old woman, though she was different from the old women of his home village: she was thin and walked straight and strong, if slowly. The old women at home were *gordo* and shuffled as they walked. He scrutinized the two bags she carried, one in each hand, then he stepped forward.

*"Buenos noches, señora. ¿Donde esta la casa seguro?"*

"I'm sorry, señor, I don't understand," she said with a slight smile of apology. "My Spanish is not at all good and I am sorry." She shook her head apologetically. She had understood only that he'd said, "good evening," and that he was asking where something was. That was all she understood and she was sorry that she could not help. After more than forty years in America, her English was excellent; but it was only after moving to Jacaranda Estates that she began to learn Spanish.

He did not understand any of her words and he misunderstood the message of her shaking head. His anger rose and he reached out to her. *"¿Digame, señora, donde esta la casa seguro?"*

She backed several steps away from him, confused by his anger, stepped off the walkway and into the grass, and began walking rapidly. But not rapidly enough. She was old and frightened and he was young and angry. He had her in his grasp in a single lunge. It had been his intention to demand a response from her until he saw her eyes. He couldn't name what exactly he saw reflected there, but he knew it was ugly and directed at him. His fists became their own agents, pummeling her face and head. Briefly and quickly. Not much more was required. She was old and frail and he was young and strong. She dropped into the grass and he looked down at her and the rage drained from him.

Because he had never before experienced terror he didn't know what to call this feeling he had. But he did understand the basics of survival, so he retrieved the bags that the woman had dropped and, turning in a tight circle like a dog seeking just the right location, he chose a direction and began to run.

# ❧ *two* ❧

Her feet pounded out the rhythm of her frustration on the asphalt path angling down through Rock Creek Park toward the Potomac. She literally was trying to outrun weeks of sleepless nights and anger and sadness and solitude. But as she ran her mind picked up and played an old refrain: *You can run but you can't hide.* So, if she couldn't run away from her misery, she would happily accept running herself into a state of fatigue that would guarantee a full night's uninterrupted sleep.

Her body and her mind were equally fatigued and her behavior was the result made manifest. She could not live the rest of her life apologizing for her bad behavior—behavior over which she had no control.

The more she thought about Jake Graham the angrier she became and the harder she ran. It was his own fault that she'd snarled at him.

When he'd appeared unannounced and uninvited at her door the night before, politeness forced her to open the door and let him in. Then he'd accused her of drinking too much and wallowing in her misery, as if he had a right to say these things. Damn him! She had every right to drink as much as she wanted and to wallow with all her might.

"I don't want to feel better, Jake, I want to feel what I'm feeling. Go away and leave me alone!"

"I can't leave you alone, C.A., I care about you."

"I don't want you to care about me, I want you to leave me alone."

Then he'd looked at her in a new way. Sort of quizzically, but with a heavy layer of pain, and, walking toward the door, he'd told her that she was the only person outside his immediate family that he'd ever truly cared about.

"It takes me all my life to learn how to care and you tell me not to do it." And he'd walked out, gently slamming the door.

She ran harder and faster with anger, frustration, pain, and guilt hard on her heels. Her own Four Horsemen. She worked at laying the blame on Jake. He deserved it. *HE-DE-SERVED-IT.* Her feet echoed the rhythm and the message. She had other friends and none of them did the things Jake did. They didn't smother her with unwanted advice and concern. They didn't have food from her favorite restaurant delivered twice a week to make sure she'd eat. They didn't appear like some kind of divine visitation at her door when she refused to answer the phone for days at a time. They didn't count the empty wine and beer bottles in the recycling bin by the kitchen door. They didn't chastise her announced intention to come completely unhinged over the course of the coming week. So what if Jake had saved her life? She'd saved his—figuratively if not literally—which evened their score card in her estimation. So why couldn't he just love her from a distance, like the others? Why couldn't he be a real friend and leave her alone!

Carole Ann Gibson was a criminal defense attorney who no longer was associated with a law firm and who hadn't set foot in a courtroom in a year. Jacob Graham was a homicide detective who no longer worked for the police department and who hadn't investigated a murder for almost exactly the same length of time. The two of them were inextricably bound.

The Watergate complex and the Kennedy Center came into view as she rounded the bend where Virginia Avenue bisected Rock Creek Parkway, sterile and pristine and sturdy like the monuments they emulated. The lazy Potomac meandered toward National Airport and Virginia. She should, she knew, make the left turn, cross the parkway, and head home. She'd run her four miles and she was tired. But she was not exhausted, and without exhaustion, she would not sleep. And she needed to sleep. Wanted desperately to sleep.

So, she continued to run, past the oval Watergate and the alabaster KenCen, beside the Potomac, toward the real monuments—Washington, Jefferson, Lincoln—that, for many, defined Washington, wanting desperately to experience joy in the golden union of river and sky and earth that was taking place in the west; to acknowledge in a more than intellectual way the return of spring.

But when she thought of spring she remembered that one year ago she still had a husband, still had a life; and for some reason, that thought, at that moment, produced an overwhelming sense of fatigue. Without slowing her pace, she changed direction and headed home, not caring why the one thought that had not left her for a single second during the last year had finally exhausted her. Perhaps it was the fact of carrying it for a year. Maybe that was it. Maybe after a year all things changed shape and form and became something else. That thought made her weak in the knees, forced her to slow her pace to keep from falling.

# ∾ *three* ∾

She faced him across the desk and they took their time, each taking the measure of the other. Carole Ann sat erect in the cushioned armchair because that's how she sat—not because she was tense or nervous. She was more relaxed than she'd been in months. The beige linen suit and the white silk and linen skinny tee shirt she wore exhibited barely a hint of a wrinkle. She rested her arms on the chair's arms and crossed her long legs. She'd said what she'd come to say and was comfortable waiting, still and silent, for his response.

Jake leaned back in the swivel chair that enveloped him like a schoolkid who'd sneaked into the principal's chair and which would have made many men look ridiculous. His hands were folded on the top of the darkly gleaming rosewood. Only someone who knew her well—and Jake Graham knew her better than most—could have seen past the surface elegance to note that the exquisite suit, tailor made for her, hung too loosely on the too-lean frame.

She was a striking woman—only three inches shy of six feet tall and so sure of herself that many who encountered her thought her arrogant. Jake knew better. He hadn't known her very long—just a year—and didn't presume to think that he knew all there was to know about her; but he did know that she'd earned the right to be called the best damn trial lawyer in town. And in a town like Washington, DC, where the criminals sometimes were the people who wrote the laws, that was no mean feat.

"I've been begging you for the last month to help me out on this case," he said, tapping the maroon file folder in the center of his desk. "And for a month you've been telling me to shove it up my ass."

"I have never, ever said those words to you, Jacob Graham, and you know it." She leaned forward, her eyes flashing as she fixed him with a stare that unnerved every human who'd experienced it—except him.

"Intent, Counselor," he said with a small smile, the one that if it grew would transform his compact, dark brown face into a thing of miraculous beauty. "I understand what you mean no matter what you say." He pushed the chair back, stood up, and began to pace the room slowly, deliberately, nothing in his movement giving clue to the fact that four months ago he needed two crutches to walk; that not quite a year ago he was confined to a wheelchair, unable to move his legs, the result of a bullet he'd taken in the back while investigating the murder of Carole Ann's husband.

"You're what made me change my mind, Jake. The fact that you're so often correct about my life. You've been insisting for weeks now that I should help you with this case, and I agree with you. So I come here ready to help, but instead of the welcome mat I get questions and suspicions. So. What am I supposed to do with that?" She shrugged, raised her hands palms up, beseechingly, and looked past him, as if she could see through the charcoal mesh curtain that covered the wall of extra-thick security glass behind his desk.

He strolled back to the desk and lowered himself into the chair and resumed his *tap-tap-tapping* of the folder. Then he looked directly at her. "You wanna tell me what's chewing on your ass so you can stop chewing on mine?" he growled at her.

So she told him about the article she'd read in Sunday's *Washington Post* about a young man arrested for assaulting and robbing a female jogger the previous Friday evening and tossing her into the Tidal Basin, where she'd drowned in just a few feet of water because she couldn't swim. He watched her face as she explained how, five years ago, when she'd been that young man's attorney, she'd pushed and prodded and pleaded and cajoled until the system finally blinked and she was able to get that young man tried and sentenced as a juvenile instead of as an adult, as the prosecutor had intended. And because of her efforts, instead of still being in jail as he would have been had he been tried as an adult, he had served his time and had been released to commit another murder. A woman was dead and it was her fault.

"You're here because you're feeling guilty?" Jake asked.

She nodded. "In part."

"What's the other part?" Unease crept in as he recalled an old adage: Be careful what you ask for because you just might get it. He'd asked for her help and now that she was here, it could prove to be a major mistake.

She sensed his shift. "I felt badly about not helping you," she said, eyeing him warily. "You came to me as a friend. I should have responded as such." She sat back in her chair and folded her hands in her lap. She began turning the heavy gold wedding ring on her finger—a recent habit that she vowed to end.

"Timing is either everything or it ain't shit," he muttered, running his hands through hair he didn't have.

"What does that mean?" His unease had spread to her and she sat even more upright.

He tapped the folder that was almost the same color as the desk with his index finger, then picked it up, studied it as if deciding what he should do with it, and tossed it across the glossy surface of the desk to her. "Does the name Gloria Jenkins ring a bell?" And when she shrugged he added, "How about Ricky "Ricardo" Ball?"

*19*

Carole Ann stared at the folder in her hands, then dropped it into her lap, still staring at it as if she could read the words through the cover. Eyes still down, she nodded slowly as the recollection of Gloria Jenkins and Ricky Ball rushed back. *It's not his fault,* she told herself as she recalled another case, a much earlier one, in which she'd defended a young man whom she later came to believe should have been incarcerated.

"He's in prison and she's in the witness protection program, probably thousands of miles from here. So what's the case, Jake?" She struggled to maintain her normal voice.

"He escaped from a halfway house and she's behind that glass," he said, gesturing with a nod of his head over his right shoulder to the security room behind the wall behind his desk.

"Ricky Ball in a halfway house? How is that possible?" He'd been convicted of three counts of premeditated, first-degree murder, as well as rape, aggravated assault, kidnapping, malicious wounding, and a few things she couldn't remember. What she did remember was that he remained one of the most vicious people she'd ever encountered and that she'd had no regrets when her defense of him failed.

She'd been his court-appointed attorney, back in the days when there existed a pool of private defense attorneys from which judges would choose defenders of the indigent. Back in the days when she was just building her reputation as one of the best criminal defense attorneys in town. On the entire East Coast. She'd lost the case but had won considerable attention for her handling of it. That case had put her on the map.

"He served a third of his sentence. He behaved himself in the joint, where he also found Jesus. Or Mohammed. Or some damn kind of savior. He got his high school diploma. And he convinced the parole board that he was a worthy risk. It's all right there in the file," he drawled, pointing to the closed folder in her lap, and she knew that his jaws were clenched so tightly to prevent him from expressing the disdain that most, if not all, cops who've worked homicide have for most, if not all, lawyers who've defended murderers. She also could discern his regret at confronting her with exactly the brand of guilt she'd been battling when she walked in the door.

"What's Gloria Jenkins doing in the next room?"

"First thing Ricky did was go after her mother."

"Jesus Christ." Carole Ann flipped open the folder in her lap and read the details that would define Gloria Jenkins, the only witness brave enough—or foolish enough or angry enough—to testify against Ricky Ball. Even after two other scheduled witnesses were fished out of the Anacostia River, she'd testified. Carole Ann had tried—without much force, as she recalled—to shake Gloria Jenkins's testimony. But the woman was steadfast in her identification of Ricky Ball as the man who stood on the corner of East Capitol Street and Kentucky Avenue, illuminated by the streetlight and the full moon, within spitting distance of RFK Stadium, and sprayed a backyard barbecue party with machine-gun fire.

Gloria Jenkins had been sitting in her own backyard, on the screened porch, with her mother, her two children, her female lover, and a gay male friend, talking among themselves, drinking lemonade, and enjoying the music and noise from the party across the alley. They knew the party-givers but had not been invited because Gloria's newly proclaimed sexual freedom made her neighbors uncomfortable. Anyway, it was the middle of July and too hot to be inside. She'd seen the black BMW convertible screech to a halt, had seen Ricky Ball get out of the backseat, stand on the trunk, raise the weapon, and begin firing. For several seconds screams and machine-gun fire vied with each other for control of the summer night air. Then the odors of blood and fear overwhelmed the scent of chicken and burgers.

Gloria Jenkins had hustled her mother and children into the house, and she and her lover and their friend had run to the end of her backyard, toward the alley and closer to the yard that had become the scene of a massacre, and looked through the fence. They'd seen Ricky Ball drag a bleeding, screaming girl from the yard, drag her to the end of the alley, and force her into the waiting BMW. At the trial this girl would not testify against Ricky Ball, but the driver of the BMW testified that he got on the freeway and drove south, into Virginia, where Ricky raped the girl and tossed her out of the car and into a ditch along the George Washington Parkway, where a jogger had discovered her early the next morning. He also testified that the girl was Ricky's former lover, who'd left him for the man who was giving the party that night. Gloria Jenkins testified about everything else, including the fact that the two murdered witnesses were her female lover and their best friend. Those murdered witnesses, coupled with the fact of the kidnapping, the trip across the state line, the rape during the course of a kidnapping, turned Ricky Ball's case into a federal offense, and Gloria Jenkins into a candidate for protection in exchange for her testimony. Her lover was dead, but she had two young children to consider.

Carole Ann closed the folder. She didn't want to read any more or remember any more. Or be responsible for any more evil. "What do you want from me, Jake?" she asked wearily, a little afraid of what the answer could be.

"Miss Jenkins wants her mother in protective custody. The government is balking."

"Why didn't her mother seek cover thirteen years ago?" she asked with ill-concealed and misplaced irritation, thinking that Jake knew as well as she did how slim were the chances of gaining some kind of retroactive protective custody, especially for someone who was neither witness nor victim.

"The mother is blind. She never saw a thing that night. But she's had a stroke now, and is terrified. Only reason she's alive today is because Ricky Ball's informant is dyslexic."

Carole Ann shot him a withering look till he continued. "Ricky bought an address from some dipshit who inverted the numbers of her address. So, Ball shot up a house on the same street but several blocks away. An elderly, blind woman who resembled Mrs. Jenkins lived there."

Carole Ann knew by the way that he closed his mouth around those last few words that she didn't want to know more, but she needed to ask.

"And the old woman, Jake. How is she?"

"Not dead, unfortunately."

"Dear God . . ."

"If I still enjoyed the protection of a badge, I'd personally rid the planet of Ricky Ball." He spat the man's name as if it were deadly venom.

"You're not capable of a thing like that, Jake."

"You don't know what I'm capable of."

This time, Carole Ann blinked first, breaking eye contact with Jake. She placed the maroon-colored folder in her briefcase, stood up, and walked toward the door. "I'll call you when I have something to tell you."

"This is a freebie, C.A. You know that, don't you?" He was standing now, facing her, his face rid of the venomous residue of discussing Ricky Ball.

She offered a small smile of acceptance. Of acquiescence. Of friendship. Then asked, "How'd Gloria Jenkins get to you after all this time? Was this your case in the beginning?"

Now it was Jake's turn to smile. He nodded, the smile lifting the left corner of his mouth. "It was. Until the Feds took it from us. Story of my life, huh? Feds taking my cases and me with nothing to show for it."

"You have me to show for it, Jake, so count your blessings." She walked out, closing the door and thereby missing the smile that transformed his face and made him beautiful.

# ❧ *four* ❧

Late-morning sun shone directly down on the purple and lilac and pink and white bougainvillea; shone easily through the tops of towering royal palms that lined the streets of Jacaranda Estates; shone down like a spotlight on the dense, wild-growing jade and birds of paradise and uncounted species of desert succulents. Shone without shadow, though high noon was still more than an hour in the future, in a perfect and smog-free sky, down on the incongruous corpse of Sadie Osterheim. Incongruous because Sadie Osterheim was the only nonliving thing upon which the perfect Los Angeles morning sun shone.

Five women created a loose circle around the corpse. From a distance they could have been mistaken for participants in some kind of children's game where a circle is formed and hands are joined and a little song is sung as a little dance is done. Up close, the lack of mirth was pervasive: the five bodies were tense and tight; five heads bent low as if in prayer; five pairs of lips held firm—not praying. There was no light in the five pairs of eyes as they stared down at the corpse. Four pairs of the eyes were more than three score years old and were seeing memories; the fifth pair youthful, still surprised by death. And it was that pair of eyes, the youthful ones, that first sought other sights—the four other faces in the circle. It was that pair of lips that parted first.

"I'm Jennifer Johnson from radio station BLAK. Can any of you tell me who she is? Do any of you know anything about her?"

"We know everything about her. She's the same as us. We could be her, lying there like that." The words came fast and angry from a mouth still held tight, and the eyes in the face of Grayce Gibson flashed, but they did not shift focus; they held to the inert form of Sadie Osterheim like a grip.

"It probably will be one of us one day, the way things are going." These words came softly and sadly from lips that quivered and then tightened as Angelique Arroyo won the struggle to regain control.

"This is the third woman attacked. The second to die. Both of them from right here in this complex. And nobody's done a thing about it." Roberta Lawson pushed the words through taut lips. Her hands, clenched into fists, hung at her sides. She breathed as if she'd just completed strenuous exercise.

"They don't care what happens to us." Luisa Nunez's eyes opened and closed rapidly, allowing the tears to spill out and fall. "Madre de Dios, help us," she whispered. "Nobody else will."

"I will," Jennifer Johnson said quickly. "If I can," she added more slowly. "I want to try," she said, making those last words an appeal for permission.

For the first time the four pairs of world-weary eyes looked directly at the stranger among them. Looked directly into the eyes of the young woman who bravely kept eye contact. The young woman held their collective gaze until they broke contact to survey their surroundings.

Grayce Gibson glanced over her shoulder, across the wide expanse of green grass, to the white-with-green-trim duplex that had been her home for more than thirty years, and mourned the loss of safety. Angelique Arroyo raised her eyes and looked directly ahead

of her, at the crazy-quilt colored wall of crisp, paper-thin bougainvillea that resisted all attempts at pruning and trimming and taming,
and mourned the loss of beauty. Luisa Nunez scanned the strange
faces in the gathering crowd drawn and fascinated by the presence
of death, and mourned the loss of familiarity. Roberta Lawson
looked at all of those things—at her pale-gray-trimmed-in-black
triplex, at the royal palms, at the flower beds, at the gathering vul-
tures—and then returned her eyes to the ground and mourned the
loss of Sadie Osterheim, who had been her neighbor in the pale-
gray-trimmed-in-black triplex for a dozen years. Then she looked at
Jennifer Johnson.

"What do you think you can do? The police said there's nothing
they can do. Our city council lady said there's nothing she can do.
Our liaison in the mayor's office said there's nothing he can do. And
the preacher told us to pray. So you think you can do what?"
Roberta's words were quick and clipped and angry, but they were
not unkind.

"I'm a reporter and I think I can make the police and the council-
woman and the mayor and maybe even your minister regret their
lack of response to your needs." Jennifer had spoken softly. Slowly.
And had in no way attempted to disguise the threat inherent in her
words.

Grayce Gibson looked at her for a long moment and a tiny smile
lifted the corners of her mouth. "Who does she remind you of?" she
asked, and her smile broadened as recognition dawned on Roberta
and she picked up the chuckle, as Angelique's brow wrinkled in concentrated wonderment, as Luisa crossed herself and whispered a
prayer and shook her head as if warding off trouble.

The reporter looked from one to the other, waiting to learn who
she reminded them of, but the woman who posed the question had
returned her attention to the body on the ground. So had the others.
So, too, did Jennifer Johnson, asking one of the questions that had

chewed at her since her arrival: "How could something like this happen in broad daylight? First thing in the morning?"

"Go ask them," snapped the one Jennifer had come to think of as "the angry one."

Jennifer looked where Roberta pointed, toward the edge of Jacaranda Estates, at a playground inhabited by half a dozen young men. Jennifer had noticed them when she drove up, noticed that they looked like gang members, and then had chastised herself for jumping to stereotypical conclusions. She knew better. She was a twenty-six-year-old black woman with three younger brothers—two of them college students, the third still in high school—and she knew what she felt when she saw them stereotyped. But she'd also been a reporter for three years and she'd covered gang activity enough to recognize gang members when she saw them. A second look at the young men completing the destruction of the Jacaranda Estates playground equipment was enough to convince her that these men were gang members.

"Why is it taking so long for the police to get here?" Jennifer asked instead. She'd been on the scene for at least ten minutes, having heard the call on the police scanner at the radio station, and it had taken her less than twenty minutes to drive here.

"Ask them yourself," replied the one Jennifer had dubbed "the tough one," with a slight shake of her head, "and let us know what they say," she added dryly as the sound of wailing sirens grew ever closer.

Then the energy shifted. The police and the paramedics hopped the curbs then sped their vehicles toward the gathered crowd. Bodies repositioned. Doors slammed. Voices queried. The reporter reached into a black canvas shoulder bag and extracted a microphone. One hand held the microphone while another did something inside the bag and when the first policeman reached the circle of women, she spoke a question into the apparatus and thrust it toward the uniform, a question not heard by the women who had other, more pressing business, and who did not need to observe again the ritual surrounding the removal of the body of a neighbor and friend.

"Who's going to call her son?" asked Grayce—the tough one—briskly leading the group away from the death scene, silver head held high and sparkling in the sun. And silver it was, not gray or white; and wearing it closely shorn as she did, her hair seemed a glittering, skull-hugging cap that offset the pecan-brown smoothness of her skin. She was a small woman. Those given to cliché would have described her as birdlike. Those paying closer attention, the Jennifer Johnsons of the world, would not, however, confuse her smallness with frailty. Her hurry to leave the scene merely reflected her decision not to be a ready witness for the police. Not again. Not until she'd had the benefit of counsel.

"Not me! I called Peggy's people after she got killed. It's somebody else's turn." Angelique was adamant as the memory of being the bearer of bad tidings surfaced, and she wrapped her nutmeg-colored arms around as much of her self as they would encompass as she shivered in the noon heat. Sudden tears made her eyes glisten like black diamonds. There was not a single strand of gray in the wild, burnished mane that blanketed her shoulders, nor a single line to suggest the passing of time in the smooth face. Only the downward pull of her shoulders and the depth of the sigh she released gave hint to the fact that she was old enough to have borne a massive burden for a good many years.

Angelique and Luisa walked in front, Grayce and Roberta followed, letting Jacaranda Estates' distinctive cobbled pathways lead them home. At its inception forty years earlier, Jacaranda Estates was an island, an oasis. An anomaly. It was a planned community of duplex and triplex clusters, in a culture accustomed to ranch single family homes or stucco-and-tile apartment complexes constructed around kidney-shaped swimming pools. Jacaranda Estates was experimental, developed by a Black man and a Mexican man who believed that Black and Mexican Angelenos should and could learn to share the similarities in their rich heritages instead of continuing to mistrust because of the differences between them. After all, reasoned the pioneers, whether you were Black or Brown didn't matter; both spelled Colored for the Anglos.

The four women walking slowly away from the death scene were the last of the original Jacaranda Estates residents. Observing them, a stranger would believe the old experiment a failure, for the two Mexican women walked and talked together and the two Black women walked and talked together. What no external observation could discern were the ties that bound them to one another, ties that were powerful and permanent. For them, that small experiment had not only worked, it had defined their lives. Now they lived in fear, each of them, that something awful would happen to one of them. Not that one of them would have a heart attack or a stroke or develop breast cancer—that kind of thing happened as part of the natural order. After all, they were closer to seventy than any of them cared to admit. No. It was the unnatural that unnerved them.

Grayce and Roberta followed Luisa and Angelique up the walkway and into the duplex where Grayce lived upstairs and Angie lived downstairs, then the three stood aside while Grayce inserted and turned the three keys required for entry. They always came to Grayce's around noontime if they weren't otherwise occupied, for tea and talk and to plan the numerous activities that filled their days and evenings.

It was dark and cool within, the draperies having been drawn against the heat of the day. Grayce swung them open, brightening the room if not their spirits. Luisa put on water for tea and laid out the big mugs they liked and plates for the fresh fruit that Grayce, their self-appointed health and fitness guru, insisted they eat at least once a day. Roberta stood in the window. She wanted to watch the removal of Sadie Osterheim's body. Angelique settled into the sofa, punching the television remote control. Grayce studied them, struggling to push from her imagination the sight of one of them sprawled lifeless in the grass. Struggling, as they all were, to push ugliness from their minds and to restore the calm and peaceful order of their lives.

"There's nothing worth watching on TV this time of day," Roberta said to Angie, still looking out the window. "One dumb talk show after the other."

"It's almost twelve o'clock. We should see if they say anything about what's happening to us on the noon news."

"Dammit, Angie!" Roberta exploded but still did not turn her attention from the window. "When are you going to understand that they don't care about us? Just another old Black woman . . . just another old Mexican woman . . ."

"She was an old white woman!" Luisa interjected with an uncharacteristic raised voice.

"She's just as dead," Roberta intoned in a lifeless voice. "And nobody cares. Just look at 'em. And look at her, still lying there. And those little bastards. Those hoodlums. Standing there watching her death."

Grayce trotted from the kitchen through the dining room and into the living room. "They're still out there? The police didn't run 'em off?" She squinted into the distance, able to discern blurry shapes in the vicinity of the playground but needing Roberta's verification that those shapes were indeed the hoodlums they believed responsible for the reign of terror in Jacaranda Estates.

"Oh! And look!" Both Angelique and Luisa joined the other two at the window, drawn by the edgy excitement in Roberta's voice. "That Jennifer what's-her-name is having a set-to with that police detective. Look at her! She's all up in his face!"

"Johnson. And she looks madder than a litter of wet cats." Angelique, clearly impressed with Jennifer's display, pulled Grayce in closer. "Can you see, Grayce?"

"No," she sighed, turning from the window and returning to the kitchen. "And I suppose I shouldn't complain about what I can't do and focus on all the things I can do." Grayce's introspection was cut short by a simultaneous whoop from Roberta, a gasp from Angelique, and a whispered prayer from Luisa.

"I like this girl! Will you look at her?" Roberta was doing a little dance at the window, wiggling her butt and punching the air with her fists as if she were at her aerobics class.

"Will you look at *them,*" screeched Angelique, punching Roberta's shoulders. "They're running away!" She jumped up and down and punched Roberta some more.

Grayce hurried back to the window, wiping her hands on a dish towel and demanding information, which rushed at her from three fronts.

"You could tell she said something really ugly to that cop 'cause I think he would have hit her if that other cop hadn't pulled him back."

"Then she headed for the playground, holding that microphone like it was a weapon."

"It *is* a weapon. People hang themselves with their own words every day."

"Then they started running, cowardly little bastards!"

"And she started running after them! Chasing them!"

"But she couldn't run as fast as them—"

"So now she's walking back this way. . . ."

"Where are you going, Grayce?"

"To invite Miss Johnson to lunch," she replied with grim determination, rushing out and slamming the door, being grateful as they all were that they had something to focus on other than the ugly horror of murder; hopeful that perhaps, finally, somebody cared enough to help them understand what had gone so terribly wrong.

"This is Jennifer Johnson reporting from the Jacaranda Estates community in West L.A., where it appears that after almost forty years, the naysayers can finally say, 'I told you so.' In the late 1950s, a Black man and a Mexican man had a dream, that Blacks and Mexicans could live together in peace and harmony. In 1959, fifty Black and Mexican families—twenty-five of each—moved into Jacaranda Estates. The first Anglo moved in in the mid-1980s. The first reported crime occurred six months ago and escalated into a pattern of vandalism that has included burglary and automobile theft. And there's been a crime committed within the boundaries of Jacaranda Estates practically every week since, including, in the last two months, the murder of two longtime residents—an elderly Black woman and an elderly white woman. A third victim, another elderly Black woman, a native of Ethiopia, lies helpless in a coma. First terror gripped the community, and then anger. Why? Because the police so far have identified no suspects, have made no arrests despite the belief by several longterm residents, including four original members of the Jacaranda experiment, that the perpetrators are a group of young men who have taken over what once was a children's playground within the community boundaries. The police and several of those young men have confirmed that the young men have not been questioned about the crimes, nor are they considered suspects. This report is the beginning of an ongoing investigation. We will keep you informed about events in what is still, forty years later, a unique living environment."

# ᦙ *five* ᦙ

*Weary.* It was one of those words that carried the weight of the struggle of peoples and cultures. It was one of those words that conjured up images of invincible people standing firm in the face of unthinkable obstacles: Sojourner Truth and John Brown and Nat Turner and Harriet Tubman and Gandhi and Martin King and Mother Teresa. People who served as examples to others how not to get weary but to stand firm and persevere. People whose weariness should have killed them but for whom weariness became armor against evil.

Carole Ann knew she was neither saint nor savior, but she was weary and she had reached the point of being willing to succumb to it. She didn't know how the Harriet Tubmans and Mother Teresas kept going. Didn't know why they kept going. Didn't understand the motivation.

That she had succeeded in securing federal-witness-protection-program status for Gloria Jenkins's elderly, blind, sick mother was of little consequence to Carole Ann; she should have succeeded at that task. There was no good reason or possible excuse for failure. And yet she almost had failed. It had taken more than two weeks of asking, and then of begging; cajoling and wheedling; and when those tactics had not produced the desired results, she had resorted to bullying and threatening and demanding the return of past favors. And then she'd gotten nasty: had threatened to open doors and let skeletons fall where they may. And only then did she get what she was after. But meanness shouldn't have been necessary, wouldn't have been necessary had the whole damn town not been blaming her for what happened.

Goddammit! She was being treated like a pariah and she was the one whose husband had been murdered, the one who almost had lost her own life in pursuit of her husband's killers. She wasn't the bad guy, but that was difficult to believe. People she'd known for more than fifteen years, people whose respect she'd earned had refused to see her or to receive her telephone calls. They treated her as if she were something deadly and contagious. So she stalked them and threatened to rub up against them. She knew where they ate their power breakfasts and lunches and dinners; she knew which racquet and health clubs they belonged to; and she knew where many of them lived—they'd entertained her in their homes. When she threatened to infect them with whatever they thought she had, they gave her what she wanted. But the victory had cost more than she had to give, and when finally she reported to Jake and presented the signed, sealed document that meant anonymous freedom for the woman whose name never again would be Anna Mae Jenkins, his hasty thanks and change of subject wounded her.

Not that Jake hadn't been properly supportive and properly angered by her travail: he'd called her tormentors some names she'd never even heard and had vowed to get even on her behalf the very moment the opportunity presented itself to him. And Carole Ann had no doubt that opportunity *would* arrive, but she didn't want vengeance. She wanted her life back. She wanted to eat, to play, to sleep, to dream. To be who and how she was before she was a pariah.

Before Al was murdered. And here was Jake with another case for her, with yet another opportunity for her to see how far down the heap she'd fallen.

"I don't want to do another job for you, Jake."

"This one pays big time, C.A. This is no freebie."

"I don't care. I don't want to do it. I'm not going to do it. In fact, I'm going to see my mother. I leave Thursday."

Jake's lips compressed into a tight line and his eyes became narrow slits through which anger still managed to flash. "You can run but you can't hide," he intoned, and sat back in the huge chair that enveloped him, watching her through the half-open lids.

"My mother needs me," she said wearily. "She's having some kind of difficulty with the police."

Jake snapped fully to attention. "Your mother is in trouble with the cops? Out in L.A.?"

Carole Ann sighed heavily. "She may or may not be a material witness to a crime, but instead of sharing her information with the police, she chose to tell a reporter." Carole Ann spit out the last six words with a distaste that curled her lips. "Why she would choose to talk to a reporter is beyond me."

"Oh, get over it, C.A.," Jake said, but he chuckled as he said it, his anger and irritation riding in the backseat for the moment. "It was reporters who took the heat off your ass in the first place, and then made you a hero in the second place. In case you don't remember," he added dryly.

She remembered. She'd always remember. How could she forget? For the better part of a month, every aspect and detail of her life— and of her husband's death—had been picked apart and fed to a ravenous public ready and willing to make a heroine of her, a cultural icon, if she had permitted it. Newspapers, radio, television—local, national, and international—told everybody who cared to know, and a few who didn't, how she had discovered who killed her husband.

And it was the media who snatched the blindfold off a justice system hesitant to bring down a wealthy, powerful man. A member of the United States House of Representatives. A man who just happened to be a murderer.

"OK. So there's such a thing as a decent reporter."

"Yeah," he snarled at her, nasty back on the front seat, hands on the steering wheel. "Just like there's such a thing as a decent lawyer or a decent cop."

Carole Ann stood up and began to pace. Jake's office was perfect for it. It was smaller than the one she'd occupied in her days as a senior partner in a megabucks law firm, but just right for pacing. "I'm sorry, Jake. You don't deserve this ugly stuff I'm tossing at you. You deserve my best, but I don't have it to give. That's why I'm leaving. I've got to get away. Please understand that. I can't find or feel or see anything good inside me, Jake."

"But we see it, C.A. Your friends see who and what you really are."

She paced over to him and hugged him—hugged his head because he was still seated—then paced back to the other side of the desk, not seeing his reaction to the spontaneous and extremely uncharacteristic gesture.

"You like me, Jake. I like you. That's why we're friends. But in that place where 'like' carries no weight, Jake, we also respect each other. I spent more than two weeks trying to talk to people I knew and respected and liked before I knew you existed, and those people treated me like dogshit, and I don't have the words to tell you what that feels like."

He swung his chair around, stood, and crossed to her. He did not hug her but took her hands in his and looked into her eyes, reminding her that the power of his presence belied his physical size, for he had to look up at her to make eye contact. He squeezed her hands so tightly that she winced, and he immediately relaxed his grip; relaxed but did not release.

"You frighten them, Carole Ann," he said in a voice she'd never before heard from him. "You are their worst nightmare and their dream come true in one package."

She freed her hands and turned away. "You're not making sense."

"You've got real power, C.A., because you're free. They're still chained to their damn silly little jobs pretending to be powerful. And not only do you have power, but you're really, really rich. No matter how much money they earn, most of 'em still need to work those sixty-hour weeks to keep the bills paid. That's what's killin' 'em. That's what they hate. Not you. Not who you are, but what you represent."

"That doesn't make it hurt any less, Jake."

"So you're gonna walk away and let 'em win?"

"I don't give a damn about them! It's me I care about and I'm trying not to lose anything else because if I lose another thing I won't have anything left." Carole Ann failed to control the hopelessness she felt.

"You have everything, C.A.! You're a wealthy woman—"

"Aw, shit, Jake! If I give you all my money, can you bring back my husband? Can you restore my reputation? Can you buy me a definition of myself?"

He grinned. "The last part I can do for free. You're my friend and my wife's friend. You're still Al Crandall's wife. And you're still the best damn trial lawyer in this town. But if you insist on running home to your mama, at least tell me what it's all about so I can help."

They both relaxed after that and she told him what she knew about her mother's predicament, which wasn't very much. In fact, that's why she was flying home to Los Angeles. Her mother steadfastly and stubbornly had refused to provide more than the sketchiest of details about what she glibly referred to as "the hoodlum murders." She wrote down for him her mother's address and telephone number. "I'll be with her until we start to drive each other crazy." And she good-naturedly accepted his instructions—he called them suggestions—regarding her cellular telephone, her rental car, her credit cards, and her choice of accommodations should she and her mother come to a parting of the ways. Then she gave him a quick hug, a real one this time, and headed toward the door.

"Give Grace my love," she said, one hand on the doorknob. Carole Ann had met Jake's wife exactly twice but liked her enough to consider her a friend. "Tell her when I get back I'll call the Southerners, invite them up, and we'll have a seafood feast. At your house." And she closed the door and was gone.

Jake looked at the empty space just vacated by Carole Ann for a long moment, then picked up the phone, but the Grayce on his mind was not his Grace. "I need to run a check," he growled into the receiver. "Grayce with a *y* Gibson," and he read off the address Carole Ann had just written.

**Valerie** and Tommy Griffin and Carole Ann sniffed appreciatively as they transferred aromatic and steaming food from shiny white carry-out cartons into heavy, multicolored serving bowls. Carole Ann was all but drooling. She'd desperately wanted food from Yangtze River, her favorite Chinese restaurant, for her last night in town; she just hadn't wanted to put on clothes, to ride the elevator downstairs, to walk through the building lobby, to get into a car, to ride down to Chinatown to sit in a restaurant with several dozen other people in order to have this food. In short, she hadn't wanted to disturb the progress of her descent into melancholia, so Tommy and Valerie generously and graciously had made the journey. Though not without sotto voce commentary from Tommy that made him sound too much like Jake for comfort.

"You're gonna have to snap out of this, C.A.," he'd muttered to her as he closed the door to her apartment on his way out, guaranteeing that he wouldn't hear her response. She'd had time to improve her disposition while they were gone, and now they all were focused intently and totally on the food.

"This one is especially for you," Valerie said, lifting a carton with Chinese characters written in red on its top. "Mrs. Chang says it is 'food for safe journey.' " Valerie laughed at her failed attempt to imitate the gentle cadence of the voice of the restaurant's proprietress. Or head chef. Or whatever she was. Carole Ann wasn't certain, though she *was* certain that the woman's name was not Chang. She suspected that was a name acquired for the convenience of Americans, who, in defiance of the cultural mores of others, insist upon knowing the names of strangers. Mrs. Chang had prepared a special meal for her when Al was killed—food for hope, she'd called it—and it had been a culinary masterpiece.

"Sorry. I can't wait," she said, opening the top of the carton and reaching in with a pair of chopsticks to retrieve and sample Mrs. Chang's culinary bon voyage. It was chicken and it was hot. It ignited her taste buds and opened her sinus passages and then deposited a faint sweetness in the open places. "The woman is a genius," she breathed, still chewing. "A pure genius. And so are you!" she exclaimed happily as Tommy withdrew a six-pack of Tsing Tao beer from the final bag.

By the time they got everything to the table, nobody was talking, and nobody spoke except to praise the food or to request a serving bowl, until they were on second helpings.

"You sure you don't want me to take you to the airport?" Tommy asked, slowing down to catch his breath. Tommy ate like what he was: a young, healthy male. Valerie called him a growing boy; and though he was twenty-six and six-foot-three and almost two hundred pounds, he was boylike in that he was sweet and gentle and playful and loving.

"Positive, thanks. It's a five-minute taxi ride."

"Yeah, but the taxi driver don't love you like I do." He crooned it to the tune of a thirty-year-old Motown hit by one of the guy groups and Valerie scrunched up her face like she'd caught the scent of something long dead. He took on a wounded look and she made to soothe him, the two of them giggling all the while like three-year-olds.

Carole Ann enjoyed their banter through an overwhelming sadness. They were young and newly married and believed they had ages to love each other. Carole Ann knew differently, knew the joy could be ended in a moment and what would remain would be the memories of moments like this one; knew that having the memories was better than having nothing.

Then she stopped that train of thought in its tracks. True, she no longer had Al, but she did have more than nothing. She had these wonderful and loving young people, and she had Jake and Grace Graham, and she had Cleo, formerly her secretary-cum-assistant at the law firm for ten years, and her husband, Billy, who now were friends; and her father-in-law, Dave Crandall, in Atlanta; and Lil Gailliard and her brother, Warren Forchette, in New Orleans. And she had her brother, Mitch, in Denver, and her mother and Roberta and Angelique and Luisa in Los Angeles. She had love all around her. And with the exception of her family, all of it from people who either were strangers or, at best, peripheral to her life before Al was murdered.

She had defended Tommy against charges that he was a drug-dealing cop and he had repaid her by saving her life when she'd been in pursuit of Al's murderers. Jake, still confined to a wheelchair in those days, had sent Tommy to Louisiana to save her even though he should have been on patrol in southeast Washington. The D.C. police department fired him for dereliction of duty and he now worked for Jake.

"Jake said to remind you—"

"Tell Jake to leave me alone," she growled in a weak imitation of the man himself, and Tommy and Valerie laughed. Then Tommy repeated, no doubt verbatim, everything Jake told him to tell her, and she nodded dutifully, confirming that she already had done the things he'd instructed her to do here, and promising that she would follow orders once she arrived in Los Angeles. And she dropped her charade of feigned annoyance and asked Tommy to thank Jake for his concern.

They cleaned up the aftermath of their feast, Tommy and Valerie agreeing to take home with them what little remained, home being a one-bedroom apartment six floors below Carole Ann's penthouse in a high-rise building in the Foggy Bottom section of Washington, D.C. Carole Ann owned both apartments—and two others in the building—thanks to Al's wise investment planning. A junior associate in Al's firm—funny how she still thought of it as Al's firm, even though Al was gone and so was the firm—had been renting the unit until he screamed at Carole Ann across the marble lobby of the building that she was responsible for the collapse of a venerable legal institution and the ruination of two men's lives and careers. He'd actually called her "a castrating bitch," and still managed to look surprised when she told him to pack his belongings and vacate her apartment. She now rented it to Tommy and Valerie, who happily would check on her place and drive her car and water her plants in her absence.

"I'll send you a postcard from Muscle Beach," she teased Tommy, an incorrigible gym rat, "and to you I'll send photographs of the best stores on Rodeo Drive," she said to Valerie, a shameless shopaholic. They hugged each other warmly, tightly, and Carole Ann closed the door wondering whether Jake was correct in his assessment—in his accusation—that she was running away from herself and her life in Washington, rather than merely making a return visit to her hometown to assist her mother.

# ☙ *s i x* ☙

Carole Ann liked cars and she liked driving. Perhaps that was the one aspect of personality and self she could claim as her California birthright, for she certainly didn't recognize or claim any of the other characteristics or traits generally—and often negatively—attributed to native Angelenos. In fact, only recently had she come to understand and acknowledge the power of place on outlook and attitude and behavior.

In the year since Al's murder, she'd come to define her husband in ways that both amazed and amused her; and by any one of those definitions, he definitely was a New Yorker. The way he walked, the way he talked, the way he viewed the world, the way he hated cars and driving.

In Al's view, a car was a unit of a subway train that, when linked to a dozen or so other cars, transported many people to many different destinations simultaneously. One or two individuals alone in an automobile—which is what Al called cars—made as much sense as a Dr. Seuss rhyme, he'd once told her, while in the process of insisting that they ride the Metro, D.C.'s humble version of a subway, from their Foggy Bottom neighborhood to Chinatown for dinner, instead of driving their automobile.

She'd been only too willing to accept Jake Graham's advice on the matter of a rental car: "Go L.A. all the way," he'd recommended. So she'd arranged to have a Mercedes Benz 300 CE convertible waiting at the airport, sterling silver with gunmetal-gray interior. The car was a dream, and she was grateful that she hadn't given her mother an arrival time because she'd just accelerated past the exit, in the far left lane, and was now going away from her mother's home.

She was still shaky from having survived the first year of Al's murder and from the treatment she'd lately received from former associates and colleagues in the legal establishment. She knew that she was not required or expected to put on a happy face for her mother's benefit; she also knew that she did not wish to give her mother cause for worry or concern. Not that she would't worry anyway. Mothers did. But Carole Ann knew that she looked, in the words of Tommy Griffin, "like warmed-over death on a rusty plate," and she did not want to exacerbate that impression by being wired and jumpy as well.

She aimed the car toward the beach and, as if it were an animate, organic thing, it surged forward, hurrying toward its mission and its destination. The vast expanse of the Pacific Ocean glimmered blue-gray and cold on one side of her; rough, scrabble-covered hills rose above her on the other side. She knew this ocean, knew these hills, knew this winding stretch of road. Yet it was so strange to her, so unfamiliar.

The evidence of out-of-control fires that had scoured the canyons three of the last four years obliterated proof that rain had, indeed, come to the desert. Funny, she mused, that outsiders never thought of Southern California as the desert. At least never thought of Los Angeles as the part of Southern California that was the desert; and it was, indeed, a difficult concept to reconcile: on one side of the road a million miles of ocean. On the other side, rising above and beyond all that water, hard, burnt, rocky earth.

And between the two, herself. A stranger in and to her homeland. She recognized these vistas yet did not know them. Because she did not know herself. This much truth she could know and claim: the problem was not with the ocean and the desert. The problem was with herself. With her unknown self. She was as strange and misplaced here as in Washington. Her fleeting moment of certainty had been buried with Al.

She pulled the car onto the graveled road shoulder, turned off the ignition, leaned her head into the steering wheel, and wept. For one day, thirteen months ago, she had known with absolute certainty who she was: a criminal defense attorney no longer willing to sacrifice her personal principles on the altar of legal theory and practice. She'd quit her job. Al had quit his job. They were planning the creation of a new life for themselves. And then Al had been murdered. So far, Carole Ann had been unable to find enough pieces of herself to fashion something resembling a whole person. She gazed upon the ocean, mutable yet constant; and upon the mountains, shaken but not moved by eons of earthquakes. And as she pondered the strangeness of herself, she knew who held the answer to the question of who she was. Or at least who she had been, once upon a time.

She'd mellowed considerably by the time she exited the freeway, and she was borderline lethargic by the time she sailed the Benz into Pancho Villa Drive, the main street leading into Jacaranda Estates, a lethargy inspired by familiarity and the expectations familiarity brings. For though her mother did not know the time of her arrival, she knew the day and date, and she would have prepared.

Carole Ann's room would embrace her like her mother's hug— sheets crisp and fragrant, the pillows plumped, a wide array of books and magazines in the wicker basket next to the bed, sprigs of bougainvillea in little vases on the bedside table and on the dresser and on top of the television and in the bathroom, along with aromatic bath salts and oils. And there would be so much food, all of Carole Ann's favorite childhood foods. Tastes and scents mingled in her memory as she let the car coast around the corner onto Harriet Tubman Drive and ease to a stop before the house she had called home all of her life.

She suddenly was overcome by the relief of familiarity and was surprised to find her face again wet with tears. Carole Ann forced a wry chuckle from her constricted throat. "You're gonna have to snap out of this, C.A.," she muttered to herself, imitating Tommy imitating Jake, and gathering her purse and small carryall and deciding to leave her large luggage in the trunk until after dinner.

She got out of the car and looked around. So different and yet so very familiar. The beauty of the foliage almost, though not quite, disguised the creeping shabbiness evident everywhere, even in the grass, which needed clipping and watering. And the shrubbery needed trimming. And the houses needed painting, her mother's included. But everything was the same. Except smaller. The streets seemed narrower and the houses smaller and closer together than she recalled.

The distance between the different clusters of buildings where her mother, Roberta, Angelique, and Luisa lived had once seemed great, the expanse of lawn between them green and unending. Now, one glance encompassed all four. This was not merely a function of having grown up and away. Carole Ann had visited her mother twice a year every year since graduating from college, the two years spent in the Peace Corps in West Africa being the exceptions. No. Al's death—Al's murder—had compressed her view of the world, had narrowed its scope.

She walked briskly up the path to her mother's duplex and was certain that Mrs. Terrell peeked at her from behind the drapery in the side window of her triplex next door. Mrs. Terrell had begun the practice of peeking at the world when her husband was invalided by a construction accident. He would not permit her absence, even for a moment, so when he slept, she peeked. It had taken him almost twenty years to die, and by that time, Mrs. Terrell's peeking had become habit, one that she continued. Carole Ann was tempted to wave, but thought better of it.

She fingered the key to the door, extended it to insert, then stopped, frowning. Three new keyholes stared brassily at her, none of which was a receptacle for the key she held in her hand. But she attempted to insert it anyway, then turned the doorknob.

"Who is that? Who's there?" Her mother's voice called out with an unfamiliar sharpness and an underlying fear that chilled Carole Ann.

"It's me, Ma!" she called out, too quickly, too loudly, and felt all the tension that she'd left on the freeway inch back into her body as she listened to the three locks click open.

"My baby!" Grayce Gibson called out, swinging open the door and sweeping Carole Ann into her embrace in one fluid motion. "Oh, I'm so glad you're here." They stood holding each other for a long moment.

Carole Ann was her mother's daughter. Taller by several inches— her father had been tall—but delicately constructed like the older woman, lithe and supple and comfortable in her own skin. And, like her mother, a woman who would grow more beautiful with time. "Ma, you look smashing! How do you manage to look younger every time I see you?"

"Clean living," Grayce replied slyly, holding her daughter at arm's length and scrutinizing, her gaze squinty because she'd left her glasses on the dining room table. "You should try it some time," she added pointedly, taking in her daughter's too-thin frame and tear-reddened eyes, seeing her daughter with a mother's practice-perfected scrutiny.

Carole Ann laughed. "From this day forth, Ma. My word of honor," she said, raising her right hand like a witness being sworn. Then she stopped and stiffened as she felt her mother's energy shift.

"That car, C.A.!" her mother exclaimed.

"What about it?" Carole Ann, startled, puzzled, turned and looked at the car and then at her mother's stricken face.

"Let's put it in the garage right now!" her mother snapped. "Where are my keys? And my glasses?"

"What garage, Ma?"

"The one I had built after my car was stolen for the third time. With the lock bar on the steering wheel, thank you."

Carole Ann trudged after her mother, down the walkway to the street, noticing for the first time that hers was one of only three cars parked at the curb. Noticing the absence of people despite the fact that it was a beautifully sunny, warm, late-spring afternoon. Noticing the absence of the evidence of people: no bicycles or wading pools or sliding boards; no lawn chairs and tables and colored umbrellas; no barbecue grills with cans of fluid and bags of charcoal on the shelf beneath.

What now was her mother's garage once had been called the carport, a six-inch thick, poured-concrete block at the end of the yard behind the house, facing the houses on the next street, large enough comfortably to park two cars, topped by a protective awning suspended by metal poles. The block was still there, now surrounded on three sides by cinder-block walls, a roof above, and a metal door that took commands from an electronic remote control. Carole Ann sat silently as her mother pressed the button. The garage door lifted and rolled up into the ceiling and a million-watt spotlight shone from within. She parked the Benz next to her mother's white Chrysler New Yorker and lost the argument over whether the older woman should carry one of the suitcases into the house.

"You know I need to let Bert and Angie and Luisa know you're here," Grayce said, leaving quite a bit unsaid.

"I can't wait to see them," Carole Ann said truthfully, then added, "We have all the time in the world, Ma. We'll talk." But not now, not yet. She was not ready to confront the reality that necessitated three locks on her mother's front door and the construction of a garage and the barricading of neighbors behind their own locked doors. Or of her own lack of awareness and understanding. What had she imagined her mother meant when she'd expressed concern about a series of attacks? After all, her mother had told her, one woman had been shot to death and two others brutally beaten, one of whom remained hospitalized, comatose, unlikely to recover; and she had specifically and directly requested Carole Ann's assistance.

Grayce Gibson was not an alarmist, did not frighten easily or often. Did not ask for help, ever. And yet her only daughter had completely misread and misunderstood because, Carole Ann recognized with shame and embarrassment, she'd been completely focused on herself. She'd assumed Grayce's call for help was like Jake's projects for her: designed to keep her from going off the deep end.

She should have known better, should have known her mother better. Should have known Jake was right again. She hadn't come home to Los Angeles to help her mother. She'd run away from D.C. hoping to help herself. Now, she was going to have to face her mother's problems if not her own demons.

**Carole Ann** couldn't stop yawning, so it wasn't until the third attempt that she succeeded in reading her mother's note in its entirety, and several moments more were required for the words to convert themselves into facts and concepts. Almost as much as emotional trauma and mental exhaustion, Carole Ann detested jet lag. She'd forced herself to remain awake until after midnight, with able assistance from Angelique, Roberta, and Luisa, hoping to adjust her body clock more quickly to West coast time. She'd succeeded only in making herself feel like she had a cheap-wine hangover.

She walked with the lilac-colored and scented note that her mother had left propped against the vase of flowers on the dresser, down the hallway and into the kitchen. There, as described in the note, were coffee beans, a grinder, filters, and a coffeepot. A basket of fresh, homemade bran muffins. A crock of strawberry preserves, complements of Roberta. The newspaper. Keys to the house. The garage door opener. Grayce was at her yoga class, after which she had an appointment with her ophthalmologist. Carole Ann was to do whatever she wished, as long as she didn't go near the playground. STAY AWAY FROM THE PLAYGROUND! She frowned at bold, underlined words that ended the note, and dropped it into the trash.

Carole Ann drank three cups of coffee, ate four bran muffins, read the *L.A. Times* from front page to back, donned jeans, tee shirt, and sneakers, and strolled over to the playground. It was located in what always was called "the corner" of the development, facing one of the streets that surrounded and enclosed and provided entry to Jacaranda Estates. The side of the playground frontzing the street was protected by an eight-foot chain-link fence, which climbing vines had all but covered. Two sides and half the front of the playground were hugged by a lower fence—perhaps four feet in height—made of wood and wrought iron and designed to be more decorative than protective, though it would serve to keep smaller children corralled. The front of the playground was open and invited entry. Only there was nothing inviting about what once had been the playground.

She stared in dismay at the destruction before her. The stench of urine was overpowering, even from a distance. The broken beer and wine bottles not withstanding, no child could ever again play in this sand that held an odor worse than a thousand baby diapers and probably concealed drug needles like land mines.

Both sliding boards had been beaten and hacked and twisted around on themselves so that they resembled tornado detritus—or perhaps a truly skewed notion of abstract sculpture. There were no swings on the heavy triangular frame though a thick rope with a noose at one end hung from the top. The chain-link fence had been attacked—no other term applied—so that it sagged and leaned and perhaps would have succumbed were it not supported by the vines firmly rooted in the ground. This was deliberate, vicious destruction that was frightening in its intensity. This was hatred made manifest.

"Whatchou lookin' at, bitch?"

Carole Ann looked up and into the hatred. Into two pairs of eyes that burned with the brand of intense hatred reflected in the twisted play toys. She hadn't heard their approach and wondered where they came from. She could not imagine that they lived in Jacaranda Estates. Then her imagination shifted gears, into reality. They faced her across the stinking sand. She looked into the distance behind and beyond them and tried to recall the adjacent neighborhoods, tried to place them in some reasonable and rational context. Tried and failed.

"I'm talkin' to you, bitch. You crazy or somethin'?" They started across the sand toward her, obviously not caring that their two-hundred-dollar sneakers would smell like piss.

"Do not come another step closer to me." Carole Ann didn't move and the two of them stopped walking. Frozen, they seemed, as if they'd been playing that kids' game . . . Carole Ann didn't remember was it was called, only that participants were required to engage in frantic, frenetic activity for several seconds and then freeze on command.

Their facial expressions, too, were frozen in place. Then their surprise was replaced by anger, which, in turn, was replaced by the snarling hatred. Carole Ann thought it a pity, the ugliness of their expressions, since they could have been—should have been—such handsome young men. Both reminded her of actors. One resembled the gorgeous Jimmy Smits, and the other could have been the offspring of the elegant Edward James Olmos. She wanted to tell them that if they resembled such lovely, creative men, they could behave creatively instead of destructively. She also wanted to kill them.

"Carole Ann! Carole Ann! Carole Ann!" She heard her name screeched over and over again, followed by the *flap-flap* sound of feet running. "Leave her alone, you bastards!" More screeching, more running, and the two boys Carole Ann was strategically killing in her imagination turned and sauntered away.

She turned to face Angelique and Roberta, irate and out of breath. "What are you doing here?" Angie hissed.

"Didn't Grayce tell you not to come over here?" Roberta's hands were on her hips and her glasses were riding low on her nose and she was peering at Carole Ann over their top rims.

"Who in God's name are they?"

"Murderers."

"Terrorists."

"And God has nothing to do with it," Roberta snapped with rapid shakes of her head and a flash of her eyes at Carole Ann.

"We were coming to have breakfast with you," Angie said, gently now, taking her arm and holding it much tighter, Carole Ann thought, than she probably was aware. And that's when she realized that they were afraid. All of them. Her mother and Roberta and Angelique and Luisa and Mrs. Terrell and all the people who were not outside in their yards playing with their children and grandchildren and watering their lawns and gossiping with their neighbors and entertaining their friends. They all were afraid. Afraid and confused, it seemed, for nobody could explain the sudden outbreak of violence in Jacaranda Estates.

Of course things had changed in the neighborhood; things had changed in the world. Bert and Angie readily accepted that. But never, ever had there been violence among them in their special enclave. Never, ever had homes been burglarized or cars stolen. And certainly never had anyone been attacked. Or murdered.

Like the symptoms of some malignant disease, it had begun six months ago, they told Carole Ann, with petty incidents: bicycles stolen from yards; garden hoses slashed; graffiti spray-painted on a fence. Then the damage had become increasingly sinister: barbecue grills turned over and charcoal spread in a yard and ignited. Car tires slashed and windshields smashed. Cars stolen. A pattern was discerned. Each cluster of houses was victimized in some way.

First, people talked. Then, people worried. Finally, people got angry and began to plan some kind of neighborhood watch program. Then, six weeks ago, the violence began. And again a pattern was discerned: every two weeks an attack, each time on a woman alone. And then people became frightened and retreated to the safety of their homes, behind double- and triple-locked doors. And abandoned talk of a neighborhood watch.

Carole Ann, wedged between Roberta and Angie, listened as they walked her home, and saw her home with new eyes; felt it with new feelings. But, when they reached her home, remembered it in a very old way.

⤜⤚ ⤛⤝

*"¡Hector! ¡Hector! ¡Ven aca! ¡Ahora!" Luisa Nunez's exhortations go unheeded because chubby, four-year-old Hector is busy exercising the glorious option of chasing both squirrels and pigeons, first one and then the other, screeching and squealing in delight, churning the grass underfoot and waving a twig about like a sword. Carole Ann bounds after him, like always, but stops before needing to be summoned by her mother. She watches as Hector, running too fast, stumbles and falls and then, howling, hauls himself to his feet and runs to his mother for comfort.*

*The four young women and the youngest of their children stroll together in the early evening sun, as they do every day that is warm enough. They are new friends but already close and bonded. Luisa soothes the injured Hector, whispering words of comfort as well as admonition.*

*"In English, Luisa. How many times must I remind you?" Angelique Arroyo's smooth, beautiful face wrinkles itself into a small frown of frustration as she touches her friend's shoulder. "You will never learn if you don't practice."*

*"Sí. Yes. You are correct. I know I must practice, but I forget. The words and what they mean." Luisa Nunez smiles softly and shyly and returns*

*Hector to the ground. "I think I will say English and the words come out Spanish."*

*"It takes time, Angie." Roberta Lawson adjusts her hands on the stroller she pushes to allow little Carole Ann to help. "After all, she hasn't been here that long."*

*"I was born here," Angie hisses, "and speak better English than most Anglos. But they look at me and see a wetback and—"*

*"Angie, don't you say such a thing!" So sharply does Grayce Gibson speak that her young daughter looks at her mother in alarm, releasing the baby carriage and grabbing her mother's hand.*

*"It's true, Grayce. Just as it's true what they call you. Do you want me to say it?" Angie stares levelly into her friend's eyes.*

*"No," Grayce answers. "I know what they call me."*

*"What, Mommy? What does somebody call you?" Carole Ann pulls on her mother's hand, little girl voice high and shrill and on the verge of panic.*

*"Now look what you've done." Roberta is deliberately calm so as not to further incite the children.*

*"Truth is truth, Bert. You know that," Angie says.*

*"She is right." Luisa sighs. "I will practice more and learn quick. I want a job like all of you, in a real place, not in a house, cleaning." She shakes her head quickly back and forth, dismissing the possibility of such a thing.*

*"Look, Mommy! It's Daddy!" Carole Ann, fear forgotten, shrieks and runs forward, leaving four startled women staring ahead, seeing finally the ugly green car and the four men standing at attention beside it. Grayce draws breath and whispers words that have no meaning. Roberta and Angelique each put an arm around her, each search for words that do not come.*

*"Madre de Dios," Luisa whispers and crosses herself again and again, completing the silent tableau.*

*"That's not Daddy," Carole Ann yells, scampering back to the four women clustered together. "That's not Daddy," she says very quietly. Even Hector is quiet.*

*One of the soldiers walks slowly toward them, reaches them, stops, salutes. "Mrs. Grayce Gibson?" He, too, speaks very quietly. "May I speak with you, please?" It is not really a question and he follows Grayce up the walkway to the house. The hands that had held the widow now hold Carole Ann. Too tightly. She begins to cry. "I want my mommy. I want my daddy."*

෪ ෫

**Carole Ann** shook off the resurrected memory and focused her eyes on the present. She and Angie and Roberta stood alone on the cobbled walkway, not far from the spot where her mother had learned of her father's fate those many years ago. With understanding that was more than memory, she knew that the entire community knew that afternoon of her father's death in Vietnam because some member of practically every household had been outside and witnessed the soldier salute her mother. Her memory told her that before the sun set that day, their home had been filled with people and food and support and comfort. And she much preferred that memory to the current reality.

She shivered and Angie and Roberta moved in closer, each putting an arm around her. Roberta asked what was wrong and C.A. told her.

"You remember that?" Angie was astounded.

Roberta almost smiled. "My children remember things I swear they've invented. It's amazing the stuff that's trapped inside the preschool brain."

"Do you all remember that day?" Carole Ann asked.

Instead of answering, both women tightened their grip on her and she leaned into the comfort and allowed them to lead the way into the house.

It was easy for her to sit quietly, listening, as they talked and talked. One of the first and best lessons she'd learned as a young attorney was the value of allowing others to do most of the talking. It was easy to listen to these women because she had grown up listening to them, as she listened to her own mother. But it was not easy to hear the fear that crept into the spaces between the anger and the outrage. It was not easy to witness the apprehension and uncertainty in their eyes, to notice how tightly they held their bodies, and she was relieved to hear her mother's key turn the three locks and open the door. She was grateful for the relief her mother's presence brought. She stood to greet her, to welcome the hug. And Luisa.

"Good afternoon, sleeping beauty," Grayce said with a laugh, holding her daughter in the embrace. "Been awake long?" she asked with a lift of voice and eyebrow.

"It's all your fault," Carole Ann replied, struggling to sound accusatory. "All of you." She waved her arm to encompass Angie, Bert, and Luisa. "Keeping me up until the wee hours. You know I need my rest."

"It's your own fault, for trying to keep up with the big girls," Roberta shot back dryly. "How long have we been telling you that you can't do what we do?"

Carole Ann felt the warm glow of memory and familiarity spread through her being. She recalled those precise words, first as true direction to go to bed, and later as a joking welcome to the ranks of the real women, with the unspoken reminder that to them she'd always be the daughter. Here was a definition of who she was and she clung to it.

"How was yoga, Ma?"

"Wonderful. As always. I wish you'd give it a try. It's much better for your body than all that running. Better than that karate, too, all that chopping and hacking," she said, chopping at the air.

Carole Ann grinned and dropped down onto the sofa next to Angie, who grabbed and held her hand, fingers intertwined. "You no doubt are correct. Like Jake, you usually are. And one of these days, I'll try it, Ma. I promise."

"Humph," Grayce snorted. "Don't do me any favors. You're the one who'll need joint-replacement surgery when you're my age."

"Oh, thanks a lot," Carole Ann said with a hint of real irritation.

"Grayce doesn't like it when you don't take her advice right away," Roberta sniffed. "She harrassed me until I quit smoking and now she wants me to give up my coffee, which I will not do, Grayce Gibson!"

"I already substitute turkey and chicken in my tacos and burritos," Luisa added. "And that no-fat cheese stuff. That's enough."

"Tell that to your doctor the next time she checks your blood pressure and cholesterol level," Grayce snorted.

Angie laughed and Roberta joined in before Luisa could open her mouth to defend herself, and Carole Ann once again experienced the rush of belonging in a place. This casual bickering had been a staple of her childhood, usually two against two, the composition of the duos shifting with the issue. She waited with amusement to see who would side with Luisa and who would take her mother's side, when Angie surprised her.

"We caught Carole Ann on the playground," she said, a four-year-old reporting on the behavior of a sibling.

Carole Ann sighed in exasperation and silently accepted the four-way tongue-lashing that rained down upon her. And she heard more than words. She heard, again, their fear. This time, for her. And, recalling the hatred that had oozed from the boys on the playground, she knew that the fear was justified.

"Who are these boys?" Carole Ann asked.

"We don't know!" Angie wailed.

"Nobody knows who they are," Roberta snapped.

"Or where they come from," Luisa added.

"Which makes the whole thing so confusing," Grayce said, slapping the palm of her hand against the table with enough force to rattle the vase. "Why pick on us? Why come from wherever they come from to Jacaranda Estates and destroy our community? It just doesn't make sense!"

Criminal behavior rarely made sense, Carole Ann mused, but often a reason could be found, if one knew where to look. "Do you know if the gang task force is in charge of the investigation?"

Snorts of derision were expelled from the four women simultaneously. "C.A., we're not even sure there *is* an investigation," her mother spat through her teeth.

"There were two murders here, and an assault, and a definable pattern of vandalism. Of course there's an investigation." Carole Ann looked from one to the other of them, expecting confirmation and receiving instead four blank, almost hostile gazes. Then she realized that the looks they were giving her were old and familiar, the look that warned against repeating unacceptable speech or behavior. She raised a hand to request forbearance as she made a request: "Please tell me how you know for certain there's no task force investigation."

And she listened with a growing apprehension as Grayce, with surprisingly few interruptions from the other three, recalled in precise detail their encounters with the police, beginning with Grayce's discovery of the first victim early one morning as she was leaving home for her tai chi class: Mrs. Asmara, a native of Ethiopia, beaten about the head and face and lying in the dew-covered grass. Mrs. Asmara who remained in the hospital in a coma.

"Since that first morning, nobody from the police has called or visited. Nobody has asked what, if anything, we've seen or heard or know. And the last time *I* went to *them*, the bastards got surly with *me!* Wanted to know how it happened that I found the body! And that's why I wouldn't talk to them about Sadie. That's why we told that reporter everything. And now they've got the nerve to threaten us with some obstruction charge! Like we haven't been begging them to listen to what we have to say."

Carole Ann sat up straight. "What reporter, Ma?"

"Jennifer Johnson from BLAK," Roberta answered.

"I told you about her, C.A."

"You've talked to her again?" Carole Ann didn't try to hide her disapproval.

"She's going to help us," Angie offered.

"She's the only one who will," Grayce added. And then, "I certainly hope she can. At least she's trying."

**So was** Carole Ann, and it took her the better part of a week to ascertain that her mother's version of events was correct, down to and including her final snort of derision. Not that she had doubted any of them; not really. She just understood that the ordinary citizen's view of the workings of the criminal justice system had been formulated by television network programming and therefore was often faulty. It was no more true that the police and the courts were on top of every situation every minute of every day than it was that mistakes and errors in the system were either aberrations or manifestations of evil. C.A. knew that cops and judges and lawyers were like human beings everywhere, and that they made mistakes.

But even allowing for the enormous challenge of policing a city larger than some states, with more than nine million inhabitants, and for the possibility of mistakes, there was no excusing the Los Angeles Police Department's handling of the crimes at the Jacaranda Estates. And Carole Ann had made excuses—for herself and for the LAPD.

For herself, she reasoned that it had been many years since she'd personally performed the footwork of the criminal defense attorney—walking the hallways and checking the filed documents at the police department and the corrections department and the courthouse. But she knew that paperwork was required, whether in D.C. or L.A., and she knew where to find that paperwork. She checked every possible and available public record, including the calls for police response on the dates of the Jacaranda Estates incidents and the calls for an ambulance. She found and talked to the paramedics who rushed Fatima Asmara to the hospital, and she visited the woman at the Charles Drew Medical Center and looked down on her tiny, close-to-dead body. She talked to the harried resident in charge of Mrs. Asmara's case, who, when he understood that Carole Ann was an attorney (she'd been quick to say that she wasn't Mrs. Asmara's attorney), shrugged and readily offered the information that no police officer had wondered in person or via phone whether the victim had regained consciousness . . . or would.

Carole Ann looked for ways to excuse the LAPD, for there had to exist some credible reason for the absence of an investigation into the crimes committed at Jacaranda Estates. She talked to the desk sergeant, the watch commander, even the lieutenant over the patrol division, and not one of them even claimed knowledge of a months-long pattern of criminal activity at Jacaranda Estates, to say nothing of knowledge of a task force investigation. And she'd left four messages for the officer who'd first responded to Grayce's call when she'd found Mrs. Asmara. Left the four messages when she could never locate the officer—Howard MacDougall was his name—in person, on or off shift. And Officer MacDougall had not returned a single one of her calls. Just as he had never returned Grayce's calls.

**She spent** an entire day reintroducing herself to her old neighborhood. She walked every inch of Jacaranda Estates, up and down every street, surprising herself along the way by how much she remembered about who had lived in which house, which of the kids in a family she had played with and which had been the friends of her four-years-older brother. She was even more surprised to discover that the world beyond Jacaranda's borders had become, in the terminology of the cultural demographers, "upscale."

The north end of Jacaranda always had been called "the business end" because the adjacent streets were home to the small businesses that had catered to Jacaranda residents: a shoe repair shop and a dry cleaners; a barber shop and beauty parlor; vegetable, fruit, and meat markets; a sweet shop cum soda fountain; a diner where the short order cook could rustle up an order of burritos as easily as a burger and fries.

Similar services still were offered on the business end, but in markedly different environments. There now was a bagel shop and a French market and a Starbucks, a Ben & Jerry's ice cream store, a Barnes & Noble book emporium, and two chain grocery stores. There were boutiques, bazaars, and salons. There were Italian, French, and vegetarian restaurants—and not a single place that served a burger or a burrito. And the reason for such an extraordinary transformation existed on the south or "home end" of Jacaranda. What once had been modestly priced California and Mediterranean-style homes on double-wide lots now were mid-to-high six-figure "exclusives" for the upwardly mobile. Carole Ann had to work to keep from gaping open-mouthed at the architecturally altered and landscaped vista before her. Most of the houses now were concealed by privacy walls in front, and she imagined that most of them also now had pools and guest houses in back.

**She walked** back to the business end and stopped at the first coffee shop she encountered, not the stylized chain store but a warm, snuggly, bistro-looking place called the Espresso Express. She really wanted a drink, but coffee would be more conducive to rational thought. And she needed clarity to reconcile disparate realities: Jacaranda Estates was an island of mid-Americana melting pot surrounded by creeping affluence. So. Where did the creeps on the playground come from?

She swallowed her pride along with a hot sip of latte, reached for her cell phone, and dialed information for the number of radio station BLAK. She had, she realized with a nod to Jake, drastically changed her attitude toward the media.

# seven

Carole Ann lay flat on her back, eyes closed, limbs spread and motionless. Her breath came deeply and rapidly, the steady rise and fall of her chest the only sign of life.

"Damn, you're good, C.A. Really and truly good. I mean that. And I claim full responsibility for your prowess."

Carole Ann opened her eyes, tried to sit up, groaned, and fell back into a prone position. "If I'm so good, Robbie, why am I lying here dying?" She opened her eyes again, focused them, and fixed Robert Cho Lee with her infamous stare. He laughed at her and his image multiplied and reflected off the mirrored walls of the studio, and many Robert Cho Lees laughed at her.

"You're dying because you were trying to kill me, that's why!" He continued to laugh as he retied his waist-length ponytail on top of his head and adjusted his jacket and belt. "You threw me so hard that last time my teeth rattled. I responded with a perfectly acceptable defensive maneuver."

"You tried to kill me, Robbie, damn you," Carole Ann muttered, accepting the hand extended to her and rising slowly to her feet. She adjusted her jacket and belt and bowed humbly to her most worthy opponent, then grinned and hugged him tightly. "You gotta teach me that move, Robbie. I swear I never saw it coming."

"Thank you, oh most worthy opponent," Robbie said with a return bow and a grin of his own. "And you weren't supposed to see it coming. That is the sole purpose of that maneuver. Surprise."

"But how do you defend against it?" Carole Ann asked, catching multiple reflections of herself in the mirrors that lined two facing walls of the studio.

"You don't," he answered, the smile gone. "You're not supposed to get up after that one. And you didn't even receive the full treatment."

Carole Ann looked steadily at him. Playtime obviously was over for the day. "So you really were trying to kill me." It was not a question and he did not respond. "If you'd really felt threatened, I'd really be dead," she said, and again he did not respond. "So, is that your only killer move, or do you have a full arsenal?"

An hour and a half later, Carole Ann could barely move. They sat facing each other on the gray carpeted floor, reflecting themselves and each other in the mirrors. She was as sore as when she had taken her first karate lesson—taught by Robbie—more than twenty years earlier. She was sore in spirit as well, for Robbie had explained, between lethal kicks, punches, and throws, that he'd devised the moves to protect himself from the gang thugs that proliferated in his neighborhood, including those who were paying customers in his studio. She had heaved a big sigh of relief when Robbie, before she could ask, explained that he did not teach his custom creations to his gang customers, but used them solely to protect himself in class. The gang-bangers, it seemed, didn't understand or embrace the concept of respect for one's worthy opponent on the mat. They understood power and pain only, and Robbie had needed to devise moves to protect himself in class. The gang-banger students tried to inflict damage.

"But why teach them at all, Robbie?"

"They're the bulk of my business, C.A. Not too many people from Westwood and Hollywood and Silverlake drive to east L.A. for karate and tai chi and yoga these days. I had to open a second studio on Sepulveda, near the 405, just to accommodate my long-term clients, who're scared to death to come here." He shook his head ruefully at the truth beneath the truth of his words.

"Here" was a warehouse owned by his maternal grandfather in which Robbie Lee had opened his Eastern Arts Studio while still a student at Southern Cal. Those were the days before there was a yoga studio on every corner in L.A., before karate and tai chi had spread so far from their roots in the Asian community.

Carole Ann looked slowly around the room, rubbing her hands gently across the carpet. The studio was a beautiful and functional room. The two walls of mirrors were bracketed on both ends by sections of fold-away bleachers, and Carole Ann imagined that Robbie held martial arts tournaments and demonstrations here. The ceiling had been lowered, and stylish light fixtures with wide chrome shades, perhaps two dozen of them, hung down like stalagmites. There was a water cooler near the door, above which glowed a red exit sign. The place looked not only stylish but prosperous. A far cry from the old days and her first karate lesson, on rubber mats on a hardwood floor.

In those days, Carole Ann Gibson and Robbie Lee were a couple. They'd begun dating as high school juniors and had continued into college, Robbie at Southern Cal, Carole Ann across the city at UCLA. Not only were they lovers, they were best friends. Soul and spirit mates. It made perfect sense to Carole Ann that Robbie, a business major, thought that opening his own business—a karate and self-defense school—was a perfect means of learning the textbook lessons of B school. She'd signed up and brought along enough sorority sisters, dormmates, and classmates to fill Robbie's first class.

She had never minded, indeed, had barely noticed that she was two inches taller than he, and certainly she'd never understood the issue made of Robbie's ethnicity. Like his height, it was not something she noticed until others called attention to it. But Robbie had noticed it. Every day of his life somebody somewhere reminded him that he looked "different" or "funny." What Carole Ann found exceedingly handsome, the outside world found odd or strange or different: Robbie's father was Black, his mother Chinese. To Carole Ann that meant dinner at Robbie's was her opportunity to eat real Chinese food. It meant a true and firsthand understanding of Chinese New Year, which in L.A. was reduced to a few colorful seconds on the evening news. It meant learning enough words in Chinese—words she learned from Robbie's father—to make a proper greeting to Robbie's mother's mother. It meant an extension of the life at Jacaranda Estates, and it served as living confirmation of the belief that people, especially Colored people, could only benefit by sharing and understanding each other's differences. To Robbie it had meant constantly proving or defending himself.

It had helped, of course, that the spirit of sharing and understanding had pervaded the larger culture for a few bright and shining moments in the 1960s and 1970s, and had lasted long enough to make such a success of Robbie's karate school that he quit business school to run his ever-expanding business. And now the pendulum was swinging—where?

"So, does this mark a return to the good old days when hoodlums engaged in hand-to-hand combat instead of mowing down entire blocks with machine-gun fire?"

Humor returned to Robbie's face briefly, then his eyes clouded again. "I'm not sure what's up with those clowns, C.A. I hear bits and pieces. Something about the Mexicans and Indians reclaiming their land from the Anglos. And from the Chinese and the Blacks and anybody else who ain't Mexican or Indian." Robbie shrugged and shook his head again. "And it's not like you can disagree with the concept. After all, the land *was* stolen from them. My problems begin with what happens to all the people they want to send packing. My mother may be first generation, but there are thousands of other Chinese who were in L.A. when the first Anglo murdered the first Mexican and the first Indian. What are they supposed to do? And what about people like your mom and her pals over at Jacaranda—"

Carole Ann snapped to attention so hard and fast she gave herself whiplash. "My mom? What's my mother got to do with it?"

"Jacaranda Estates is one of the places the brothers in the barrio claim belongs to them. Something about some Mexican dude owning the land and being swindled by some Black dude."

"That's a lie!" Carole Ann jumped to her feet, and to the defense of Arthur Jennings, the cofounder of Jacaranda Estates. "You know that, Robbie! You know how Jacaranda Estates came to be!"

"I know, I know, I know," he said swiftly, attempting to calm her. "I remember the entire story. I'm just telling you what these dudes are saying, C.A. You know how common it is these days for people to rewrite history to suit themselves. Like, Black folks loved slavery, like the Holocaust didn't happen, like Nixon was a patriot and a saint."

"OK, Robbie. I hear you. But what are they saying about Jacaranda Estates? Tell me that."

"The boys from the barrio say they're taking it back."

Carole Ann recalled the faces of the young men she had encountered on the playground: young Mexican men. Mean and angry and violent. She recalled her mother's accounts of the vandalism and the violence and the suddenness of the onset and the apparent lack of a reason for any of it. And she realized suddenly and awfully that all of the victims, of property damage or of personal attack, were either Black or white. Or, more significantly, that none of the victims was Mexican. A shudder coursed through her body.

This was insanity. Madness. Impossibility. A group of young Mexican-American men waging a war of attrition against every non-

Mexican in Los Angeles? And her home turf was going to be a battle site? She wondered for the first time ever whether the stories she'd heard about the establishment of Jacaranda Estates were true, and knew she'd have to find out. Soon.

"How exactly are they planning to reclaim their lost land, Robbie? Have you heard any details?"

"You're not taking this seriously, C.A.? These are a bunch of loud-mouthed punks looking for somebody to blame 'cause they can't find a job. What could they possibly do . . ." He stopped himself mid-sentence, mouth still hanging open, words half out. His eyes widened in surprise, which turned to concern. "Is your mom OK, C.A.? And the others? What were their names?"

"They're not OK at all, Robbie. They're terrified. They're under siege." And she outlined in broad strokes the occurrences at Jacaranda Estates, the lawyer in her preventing her from sharing all the details. Other people told all to lawyers; lawyers did not tell all to other people. But she did mention her puzzlement about the origin of the playground thugs and wondered whether Robbie could offer any possible rationale for their presence. He could not.

He stood shaking his head, his ponytail flipping back and forth in wide arcs like the real thing and multiplied in the wall of mirrors. "What you're telling me is too bizarre to believe. And why hasn't there been a word of this on TV or in the paper?"

Carole Ann responded with a snarl. "Seems the only reporter in town who thinks it's a story is Jennifer Johnson from BLAK."

"And I almost never listen to the radio," Robbie said.

"I don't think anybody in this town listens to the radio! She keeps doing these stories and nothing happens. It's like the information justs falls into a black hole somewhere in space."

Robbie shook his head again. "I can't believe your mom never said a word about all that," he muttered, almost to himself, and it was Carole Ann's turn to experience jaw drop.

"You've talked to my mother, Robbie?"

"Of course I've talked to your mother, C.A.," he replied, speaking slowly and deliberately as if to a subhuman species. "Every Tuesday, Thursday, and Saturday morning."

"My mother takes tai chi from *you?*"

Robbie's hackles rose. "And yoga from my wife. At our Sepulveda studio. You got a problem with that, C.A.?"

She grabbed his arm and held on until he relaxed. "Of course I don't, Robbie. Don't be ridiculous. I just didn't know. She never said. I wonder why."

**Because** I thought you were still angry at him," Grayce said with such wide-eyed, innocent conviction that Carole Ann had to work to stifle a giggle. They were clearing away the dinner dishes and wrapping leftovers and bumping into each other in the never-was-large-enough kitchen, the only negative to the house.

"Ma, why on earth would I be angry with Robbie Lee?"

"Because he dumped you," Grayce said calmly, matter-of-factly, and Carole Ann winced at the memory.

They were sophomores in college and not seeing much of each other. Carole Ann was living on campus that year and the trek between Cal and UCLA was a pain; Robbie had all he could manage between school and his new business. And then Robbie met Millie Wolf and fell instantly and completely in love. He'd come to Carole Ann immediately, contrite and remorseful, more surprised than she at his change of heart.

"She's like me, C.A. She's a mutt like me."

"What do you mean, 'mutt,' Robbie? A mutt's a dog."

"Yeah. A mongrel. She's a mongrel just like me. She knows how it feels to be a little of this, a little of that, and never fully anything. She knows how it feels to have people look at you and frown, wondering what you are."

"And is that feeling strong enough to be a love bond?"

"Yes, it is. Because when we met, we already knew each other."

"So who is she, Robbie? And what makes her a mutt?"

"She's Millie Wolf and she's part Chiricahua Apache, part Hopi, and part Mexican."

So on the days that Robbie Lee didn't instruct Grayce Gibson in the ancient art of tai chi, Millie Wolf instructed her in the equally ancient practice of yoga. So many years and so much life later, so many things remained constant and familiar. Carole Ann smiled a silent gratitude and felt something warm flow within. She was still angry at the treatment of Jacaranda Estates, both by the hoodlums and by the system, and she was still fearful for the safety of those she loved. But for the first time in more than a year, she had a clear sense of self and of place. She no longer felt like some strange thing out of place, marching a half step behind the crowd. She no longer felt people looking at her, frowning, wondering what she was; no longer felt *herself* frown and wonder what she was.

**"You're** smiling."

"Yeah, Ma. I'm smiling."

"I'm glad."

"Me, too. It feels good."

"Good enough that you feel like helping me prepare for my bridge club?"

Carole Ann laughed out loud and hugged her mother and kissed the top of her head. "Nice try, Ma. And not a chance. When is bridge club?"

"Saturday night."

"Then I leave Saturday morning for San Francisco. I told you I'd be spending a few days with Marge."

Grayce took a swat at her daughter with the dish towel, intentionally missing but delivering her message with full clarity. "It wouldn't kill you to help us. You're such a terrific cook. And Mable and Alice and the girls would love to see you. You know they love you like a daughter, C.A. I don't know why you have to be such a brat."

Carole Ann giggled and the memories returned in a flood. The bridge club that rotated every month among the twelve members so that each member hosted one meeting a year. And Carole Ann always pressed into service, under extreme duress, her mother always berating her "recalcitrance."

"Just to keep you on your toes, Ma."

"Don't do me any favors," Grayce harrumphed. "And be sure to give Marge my regards. I'm glad you kept in touch with her. I always liked her."

Marge Hammond was Carole Ann's roommate the two years she lived on campus and they had kept in touch, had remained friends. In fact, Marge and Robbie and Millie were the only ones of her hometown contemporaries from whom she heard when Al was killed, the only ones who called more than once, who wrote often, who made it clear that their concern was real, their grief deep. And she'd promised Marge a visit, though she hadn't intended to journey up north so soon after her arrival. After all, she'd been in L.A. less than two weeks. But the conversation with Robbie was aching and throbbing in her brain like a diseased tooth and she needed to get to Sacramento, to the state archives.

She'd visited the Los Angeles County archives and the L.A. Historical Society the day after her killer karate lesson with Robbie to check on the history of the land upon which Jacaranda Estates had been constructed and to satisfy her belief that the land had not been stolen from Enrique Jamilla by Arthur Jennings, and she'd found the information lacking. She'd visited the office of the recorder of deeds and the surveyor's office and found the details of the land ownership inconclusive. Her best bet, said the administrator in the recorder of deeds office, was the state archives in Sacramento. And Sacramento, the state capital, was but a short jaunt from San Francisco. Three days with Marge, a day in Sacramento, back in L.A. by Wednesday night or Thursday morning.

"Suppose I cook before I leave, Ma? I'll make a seafood gumbo and a big salad and bread pudding with hard sauce for dessert. I'll call Tante Sadie for recipes. The girls'll think they're dining in the French Quarter."

"Can you make it low cholesterol?"

Carole Ann gave her mother "the look," and the older woman dissolved into giggles.

**Carole Ann's** meeting with Jennifer Johnson was reminiscent of her session with Robbie Lee in that the young radio reporter was a no-holds-barred kind of woman. She asked tough questions, expected honest answers, and flat out refused to divulge any of her own information. When Carole Ann refused to answer any of Jennifer's questions until Jennifer had answered hers, the reporter actually stood up and began walking away. Carole Ann prevailed only because she'd had more practice at getting her own way.

"Oh, sit down and stop behaving like a child," the lawyer snapped at the young reporter, annoyed with herself for having to orchestrate the other woman's return to the meeting.

Jennifer Johnson halted midstep and turned to stare in openmouthed wonderment at the woman who'd issued the command. Carole Ann was all the way in the corner of the booth, her back against the wall and her legs stretched out in front of her on the black leather of the seat. Her right arm rested high on the back of the banquette; her left arm was propped on the table, forming a holder for her chin. A study in casual disdain.

"Who the hell are you calling a child? I don't have to take this crap from you! You called me, remember?"

"You need me a lot more than I need you, Miss Johnson, and if you don't believe it, ask your research librarian to do a search on me."

"There is no research librarian at my station, Miss Gibson; you've got me confused with a network reporter. But I will do my own search on you. And if you don't need me, why did you call?" Jennifer Johnson was controlling her anger, but just barely.

Carole Ann swung her legs down to the floor and sat up straight, folding her hands on the table. "I didn't say I didn't need you. I said you needed me more than I need you. But need you I do, Miss Johnson. So, please have a seat, have another cup of coffee, have a pastry, and let's talk."

After a three-second ponder, Jennifer Johnson resumed her seat across the booth from Carole Ann, angry still, and very wary, but sensing something that made it necessary to bury all the personal feelings and deal only with the issues of instinct. And before she could decide whether she even wanted a pastry, the waitress had arrived and she ordered it, kiwi tart, along with the coffee that she definitely did want.

"The only way this is going to work, Miss Gibson, is if we share information. No matter how much you may think I need you, I'm not going to just feed you information and get nothing in return. It's quid pro quo or nothing."

Carole Ann grinned in spite of herself with the realization that she was beginning to like this young woman. And after an hour of playing by Jennifer Johnson's rules—that is, sharing information—C.A. knew why she liked the young reporter with the Alfre Woodard eyes: Jennifer Johnson was aggressive and smart and she possessed a well-honed and razor-sharp instinct. The only thing she didn't have was clout. She was a cub reporter working for a small, independent station. No incentive for the LAPD to respond or react to her queries or her reports. Not yet.

Carole Ann had walked through Jacaranda Estates to the business end of the complex for her meeting with Jennifer Johnson at the Expresso Express, and she gladly accepted a ride home so that Jennifer could demonstrate to Carole Ann "something that just doesn't make sense."

Slowly they cruised past what once had been the children's playground at Jacaranda Estates, Jennifer downshifting the boxy Bavaria 2002 to an almost stop as they turned the corner, catching an unobstructed view of six gang-bangers hanging from the denuded swing frame.

"See what I mean?" she asked, as much puzzlement as excitement in her voice.

Carole Ann did see.

**"You tell** that daughter of yours she redeemed herself, but just barely." Alice trumped Roberta's jack of diamonds, smirked, and collected the trick. "That was the best gumbo I've ever eaten."

"Well, she's totally redeemed in my book," added Mable from the next table. "I haven't had bread pudding like that since I was a child. And you know I'm not much for reminiscing."

"Don't blame you. Reaching so far back could give you a headache," Roberta tossed over her shoulder, feigning distance from the snickers the remark produced.

"Who did you say she got the recipes from?" asked Eloise.

"Never mind the who. Will she share them?" demanded Mable. "I want the recipe for that bread pudding!"

Grayce, taking advantage of her position as dummy at her table, was refilling water glasses and coffee cups and generally surveying her turf, satisfying herself that all was in perfect order. Grayce liked festive occasions, giving them and attending them, and never minded the effort involved in hosting her club members. Fresh-cut flowers colored and scented the combination living-and-dining room, and candles of all shapes and sizes glimmered and shimmered and glowed throughout, creating a holiday effect. She was delighted that the food was a success, and that her daughter was responsible.

The only damper on the evening was the empty place at the third table, the place normally occupied by Helen Smith, who hadn't come because she was frightened by the outbreak of violence at Jacaranda Estates. Grayce shook off the feeling of dismay, refusing to allow any intrusion on her mood, and she put her mind to work formulating an appropriate response to the requests for the recipes that Carole Ann certainly would not divulge, when Luisa, standing at the front windows, let out a shriek.

"Oh, Mother of God! Somebody stop them! *Stop them!*"

Roberta threw her cards across the table and knocked over her chair in her haste to hurry to the windows and to Luisa. Eloise spilled her water, Mable spilled her coffee, and Angie tripped and fell across the ottoman, landing on her face. Grayce gathered her up and the twelve of them gathered in the front windows, looking toward the playground, and held collective breath as they watched two thugs beat an old man and try to wrest from his grip what appeared to be a grocery bag.

"That's Mr. Asmara," Angie whispered.

"What the hell is he doing out there this time of night!" Roberta hissed. "Dammit, man, are you crazy!" she yelled at him, her anger at the old man's attackers a huge, living thing, her anger working against her struggle to open the window.

"Somebody call the police!" shrilled Mable.

"*Mira! Mira!* Look what's happening!" Luisa was out of breath, as if she'd been running.

They looked, the twelve of them as one eye, to see a man rushing toward the attack brandishing a bat and wearing nothing but jockey shorts that gleamed bright white against his chocolate body in the moonlit darkness. Running hard and fast as only a strong young man can run, and waving the bat with a fury evident even from so great a distance.

The window, finally open, admitted a rush of chilly night air that carried a hoarse yell: *"You slimy bastards! Get away from him! Leave him alone!"*

They hesitated, the two attackers, then dropped the old man's bag and quickly evaporated into the night. Twelve hearts, beating too fast for good health, finally slowed, releasing a reluctant hold on shallow breath. But they retained their grips on one another's arms and shoulders and hands, and watched as the young man finally reached the old man and grabbed him, held him up as the old man sagged, then, ultimately, sank to the ground with him, holding and rocking him as if he were the child he'd left when he ran out into the chilly night in his underwear.

They watched, still barely breathing, as the old man opened the brown grocery bag that he refused to relinquish to his attackers, and withdrew from it small, thin, filmy things. Grayce's breath caught in her heart and hurt sharply as she tried to speak. "It's her night-gowns. Mrs. Asmara's. He must have just come from the hospital. He brought her nightgowns home to wash."

Drained and exhausted and weak in spirit they watched until the young man walked the old man to his house, unlocked the door, and put him inside. They watched the young man return to his own home, walking slowly, head down, shoulders drooped and heaving, trailing the bat behind him. They watched him wipe tears and snot on his arm. They watched him until he reached his wife standing in the open doorway of his home with outstretched arms. They watched until there was nothing more to see except the moonlight that was bathing the yards and trees and shrubs in a falsely peaceful glow. They watched until they were able to think and move and speak.

"What the hell is happening here! I can't stand this! Suppose it's one of you next time?" Mable's hysteria was catching. Alice and Eloise began weeping and damning thugs and hoodlums to everlast-ing hell. The terror and anger that a moment ago had hung sus-pended in time was released and the eight women who did not live in Jacaranda Estates attacked the four who did with the same inten-sity as of the recently witnessed attack, the principal difference be-ing their weapons were expressions of love and fear and pain and sorrow.

"You all will have to move!" exclaimed Mable, looking frantically from Grayce to Roberta to Angie with a look that managed to be both tearful and fiery. "You, too, Luisa!" she added, for though she was not an official member of the bridge club, Luisa was and had been a presence at the meetings hosted by her three friends for so many years that she routinely was invited to the other members' meetings.

"Nobody's moving," Grayce replied with a calm that was made a lie by the tremble in her hands as she poured a glass of water for herself.

Eight voices lifted simultaneously in a cacophony of disbelief, anger, reproach, none of the babble of words capable of masking the fear that enveloped the room, extinguishing the festive joy so recently pervasive. Fear converted loving words to angry ones; pleading words to dismissive ones; caring words to selfish ones. Fear blurred the ability to make the distinctions, and the willingness.

"Then don't come here anymore." The words from Roberta's mouth were calm and quiet and they cut through the raised voices with the efficiency of a power tool. "I officially cancel my meeting next month. Mable, you can have two meetings this year. Or you, Eloise. Or Helen. And perhaps by the end of the year, everything will have returned to normal. Or perhaps we'll all be dead and it won't matter."

The weight of those words was too heavy to bear, even for the twelve of them together, and they crumpled under the weight. Sagged. Onto the sofa, onto the abandoned chairs at the bridge tables, onto the floor. Empty and emptied.

"It's all so different now. Too different. Everything is different. And wrong." Eloise allowed the tears to flow unchecked down her smooth, brown face, and the mucus from her nose. "The things we allow these days. So different and so wrong."

"What do we allow, Eloise?" Grayce asked.

"Murder," she responded, her voice dead.

"You think we allow this?" Angie spoke for the four.

"If Grayce's husband or Roberta's husband were alive, these

things wouldn't be happening. The men of our generation wouldn't allow this kind of carrying on. Look at how Mr. . . . what'd you say his name was? . . . fought against those thugs. Old as he is, he wasn't allowing their sickness to rule him. And suppose five men had come running in their drawers, ten men, all the men . . . but there was only one." Eloise slumped deeper into the pillows of the sofa, oblivious to her own tears. Reflexively she received the bundle of tissues offered by Grayce and sat holding them, staring nowhere.

Roberta knelt before her, took one of the tissues, and wiped her friend's nose with the expert hand of the mother and grandmother. "We're not going to be dead, Eloise. And I'm having the club next month. And I want you to come. All of you. Helen, too. I'll call her myself with the promise of fried chicken and biscuits."

"Too much cholesterol, Bertie!" Luisa exclaimed, puncturing the atmosphere and releasing everything painful and ugly that had been held there since they had borne witness to the worst thing they'd ever seen. They sighed and heaved their breasts like the grandmothers they were, and giggled behind their hands like schoolgirls they remembered being. They rocked and hugged one another, confident once again of their ability to provide succor and comfort in the face of danger. And the eight prepared to take their leave, aglow in the necessary belief that the four would be safe.

They embraced the ritual of packing up leftovers: each hostess understood her responsibility to prepare extra food and each club member brought a container for that purpose. Grayce ladled out gumbo, pointedly ignoring Angie's "I told you so" look, while Roberta doled out bread pudding, mumbling unintelligible things under her breath, unaware that Angie had insisted that Grayce withhold a pot of gumbo and a dish of pudding just for the four of them, overriding Grayce's assertion that hiding food was unnecessary.

When every known morsel of food was packed and they were ready to depart, the women helped one another into their coats, retrieved their purses and parcels, and agreed on their method of departure: Grayce, Roberta, Angie, and Luisa would walk their guests to their cars; Grayce and Angie would walk Roberta and Luisa to their respective homes; Grayce and Angie would run like hell across the grass, back to their duplex.

"The moonlight makes everything look so peaceful and pretty," Grayce whispered with a sigh. "Romantic."

Bert and Angie simultaneously performed a somewhat less than professional version of the moon-as-pizza-pie song from the film *Moonstruck*, leaving Grayce with a case of the giggles and Luisa feeling left out, since she hadn't seen the movie.

"There's nothing wrong with love and romance and the moon," she said and stuck her chin out, thinking they were mocking the subject.

"We love romance and the moon, Luisa, but the sad truth is, tonight, up close, the moonlight makes the grass look like it needs cutting and the shrubbery like it needs pruning," Angie responded sadly.

"And it makes us look like we're the only people in the world," Grayce added, shivering.

"Which is not a warm and fuzzy feeling in this moment," Roberta offered, with her own shiver. "And speaking of warm, I'm not, so could we pick up the pace, girls?"

They were walking arm-in-arm diagonally across the grass, walking rapidly and angling for Roberta's, where, they'd agreed after a change of plan, Luisa would spend the night—a faster and safer alternative than walking the extra block to her place. Besides, from Roberta's upstairs window, the two of them could watch Grayce and Angie, could see them all the way across the lawn and home. They walked faster, concentrating on closing the distance to the pale-gray-trimmed-in-black triplex in which Roberta occupied the largest unit.

"Why didn't you leave your yard and porch lights on, Bert?" Angie asked with real agitation and felt herself jerked to a halt, as her left arm was linked tightly in Roberta's right.

"I did leave my lights on," Roberta said quietly. And she withdrew her arm from Angie's and thrust her hands into her pockets. "Who the hell is that on my front porch?"

They all saw the shadow's movement a fraction of a second later, and screams erupted from their throats in bad harmony, as if ordered by a drunken choir master. The shadow moved swiftly, but not away from them, not around the side of the house to the rear and to escape on the next street. It ran toward them, dark and amorphous, something in its hand, pointing. They flinched and cowered at the sound of deafening noises. Three of them. And the running shadow was falling, first to its knees, then to its face. And the shadow—they could see it was a man—was still.

They obeyed the instinct to run, individually and together, to Roberta's door, the door that already was opened but not with a key. As if following taped *x*'s on a stage floor, they tumbled inside, one after the other, without pushing or shoving or contesting primacy. And once inside, they waited in the dark silently, patiently for light. Light and sight convinced them that they each and all were safe and unharmed. That Roberta's living room was the victim. That Roberta was the avenger.

"Where on earth did you get a gun?"

"*Bang! Bang! Bang!* You shot him just like that and you didn't miss, not once!"

"I didn't know you could use a gun. How do you know how to use a gun?"

"Bert, say something!"

"Roberta Lawson, if you don't tell me right now where you got that gun . . ."

Roberta raised her right hand and looked at what was in it. "It's Charlie's Army pistol. He kept it after the war. Lots of men did. Then, when he started long-distance trucking, he was worried about me at home alone with four girls. So he taught me how to use it. I buried this gun in the back of the closet when I buried Charlie." She raised her hand closer to her face and turned the gun from side to side, studying it. "I dug it out and oiled it last week. Just in case . . ."

"What are we going to do now?" Angie was speaking to the group but her eyes were on Roberta's hand. "Shouldn't we call the police?"

"Those same police who can't find anybody to arrest for killing Sadie and Peggy and for bashing in Mrs. Asmara's head? You want me to call them and confess? Never."

"Suppose . . ." Angie began, and then stopped to wait for her brain and her mouth to synchronize. "He's laying out there . . . suppose he's not dead?"

Roberta shrugged and tightened her lips into a fierce grimace. She seemed to push the words out through them. "They left Mrs. Asmara laying there and she wasn't dead."

"Suppose . . ."

"Suppose what, Angie?"

"Suppose somebody saw us? Heard the shots and saw us?"

"I don't care."

"Give me the gun, Bert." Grayce's voice was quietly authoritative.

"We need this gun for our protection, Grayce! Which of us do you think would be out there in the grass right now if I didn't have this gun?"

"That's not the point, Bert—"

"The hell it's not! It's the only point. We're alive and I intend to keep us alive. Me and my friends Mr. Smith and Mr. Wesson and their six cousins." Roberta blew on the gun and thrust it into her pocket and looked around at her living room, as if noticing the damage for the first time. "The bastard!" she hissed.

"Mother of God," Luisa whispered and crossed herself.

"Roberta, please stop talking like John Wayne. It is not becoming to a gentlewoman of color."

"That's the second time tonight you've said 'Mother of God,' Luisa."

"She says 'Mother of God' a thousand times a day."

"She says *'Madre de Dios'* a thousand times a day. Tonight she said it in English. Twice. I think that must mean something."

# ❧ *eight* ❧

"This is Jennifer Johnson with an update on events at Jacaranda Estates. The violence continues, but with a twist. Two nights ago, there were two attacks. One victim was a seventy-two-year-old Black man, the husband of an earlier victim who remains hospitalized in a coma. The second victim was a young Mexican man, identity unknown as of this report, who was shot three times at close range. A loaded but unfired automatic weapon was in the man's hand. Police are investigating, and the residents of Jacaranda Estates are angry. They are angry that the police have launched a full-scale investigation into his death, while ignoring the murders of two of their friends and neighbors, the beating of a third, and a six-month reign of terror that has left them all fearful for their own lives. Police officials would not confirm or deny the existence of an ongoing investigation into crimes at Jacaranda Estates."

**Smog,** dense and heavy, prevented the sun from warming a significant portion of the Los Angeles basin, including the portion that was Jacaranda Estates; and though not a cool afternoon, not by Southern California standards, more sun would have been appreciated. But its absence did not dampen the excitement and spirit of the dozen people clustered together in the grass, behaving, for a change, like neighbors; standing and talking together in a way that they almost had forgotten once was the norm. Over and over again they reminded one another that this was the first time in months that they had stood in their yards, relaxed and comfortable, and communicated. Though the topic of conversation may not, in some quarters, have been considered neighborly.

"I don't care who shot him! I hope whoever did it will shoot the rest of 'em! He deserved just what he got!"

"That's exactly what I told those police officers who came asking about it."

"And the nerve of *them!* Kept me up half the night asking me over and over and over again if I was sure I didn't see anything. And acted like they didn't believe me when I told them no!"

"Me too! Like it's my job to do their job. I told 'em I don't go out at night, don't look out at night, and it's their fault."

"Didn't they question you, too, Roberta? I heard 'em knocking in your door, beating on it like they were trying to tear it down."

"I told 'em she wasn't home. That it was her bridge club night and that she was probably still at Grayce Gibson's."

"Thank God you didn't come home to find a dead bum in your front yard."

Roberta inhaled deeply, tried to speak, and failed. For her efforts, she received two pats on the the shoulder and a wise and understanding nod of the head.

Angelique and Roberta were part of the group but so far had remained silent, Angie because listening was more natural for her than speaking, and Roberta because she was still too numb to speak: from the shock of having taken a life, and from the ordeal of restoring order to her home following the destruction wrought by him whose life she had taken.

"That's what we all need to do. Get a bat or a stick or a brick, and use it to fight back."

"Or a gun."

Roberta shivered and Angie grabbed her arm and pulled her in close, and whispered that they should go home. Roberta nodded but didn't move. Seemed not to be able to move.

"Notice anything different about the playground today?"

Bodies, heads, eyes, swiveled in the direction of the playground and once again the group reacted as a unit, as if rehearsed and directed. Nods, smiles, gratified murmurs.

"That's why we can't ignore them or show them fear. The cowards are gone. If we keep fighting back, they'll stay gone."

"But I don't have a gun."

"I don't want one!"

"I do!"

"Who's that in the fancy car?"

Their energy and attention shifted and, as a unit, they watched Carole Ann drive slowly up John Brown Drive, turn into Pancho Villa Drive, turn again into Harriet Tubman Drive and cruise to a stop before her mother's house. There were several more murmured queries about the occupant of the "fancy car." Roberta waited for Angie to respond, and Angie waited for Roberta to respond. Finally the answer came, half authoritative and half speculative.

"That's Mrs. Gibson's daughter. I don't know her name, but she's a doctor or a lawyer or something like that. She lives on the East Coast. New York, maybe?"

"Washington, D.C.," Roberta finally said, thinking it better to have the facts, rather than more gossip, circulating about the complex, and realizing with a tinge of sudden sadness that most of the people in the circle didn't know Grayce's daughter. Wouldn't know her own four daughters. "And she's a lawyer."

"I wish my daughter was a rich lawyer. I'd get her to move me out of here in a hurry!"

Humor circulated among them, good-natured and relaxed and easy again, as they watched Carole Ann push the button on the key chain that locked the car and set the alarm, and walk toward them.

"Is that little Carole Ann? I haven't seen her since her college days," one of the few remaining old-timers murmured in a reminiscing tone.

"Good-lookin' girl, whoever she is," one of the men said, and one of the women punched him on the arm. "Well, she is!" he replied defensively, rubbing his arm. "She married?" And the giggle was still roaming the circle when Carole Ann approached.

She was dressed casually in beige linen slacks and a gold silk tee shirt that somehow seemed not to have gotten wrinkled on the six-hour drive down from Sacramento, and she walked loosely and easily, her long legs covering the distance swiftly. Two weeks of being overfed by her mother and a long weekend of collegiatelike pigging-out with Marge had filled out her frame, and her skin was burnished deep bronze by the sun and the sea air. She smiled as she reached the group, encircling Bert and Angie, one under each arm, and offered a general greeting to the crowd. The older woman, Mrs. Philpot, whom she greeted by name and with a wide smile, blushed in gratitude to be remembered by a woman who'd remained a child in her memory.

Despite the warm greeting and the wave of small talk, Carole Ann felt an underlying uneasiness. She was not unaware that it was unusual for so many people to be gathered outside, no matter that it was the middle of the day. She made a casual but careful scrutiny of the people now surrounding her—for the circle had opened to receive her and had closed again around her—and then surveyed her surroundings. Her glance held for a long moment on the empty playground.

"Is anything special happening?" she asked quietly.

"She's a lawyer, all right!"

Carole Ann joined the laughter at her own expense and waited for an answer.

"Somebody killed one of the bums."

"Shot him dead, the bastard."

"Right over there."

"And the police got the nerve to be asking us if we saw or heard anything."

"I heard they couldn't identify him."

"Yeah, I heard that, too. He didn't have any ID."

"Nothin' in his pockets. Not even dust."

"But he had a gun in his hand!"

"Praise God he didn't get the chance to kill one of us."

"My husband chased two of 'em with a baseball bat that same night. They were beating up on an old man—"

"That was Mr. Asmara."

"That's the one! I called the cops when Bobby ran outside in his underpants, and do you know they haven't come yet? But they can come here to see about that thug."

Carole Ann looked from Roberta to Angie, waiting for a contribution from them to the discussion; expecting one from Bert, who had an opinion about everything. And she grew immediately uneasy when she closely scrutinized the expressions on their faces.

"Why do they treat us like that? We've always been law-abiding citizens in Jacaranda Estates. Police never had a bit of trouble from us. But they act like they don't care what happens to us."

"That's why we have to take care of ourselves! Can't wait for the police. Like Malcolm X said: By any means necessary!"

A heavy silence prevailed for a long moment, then it rapidly was filled with murmurs of assent. Heads nodded and lips smiled tightly and at least two pairs of hands applauded as if affirming the Sunday sermon. So there was a stunned reaction when a young Mexican woman, a stranger to both Roberta and Angelique, spoke up, loudly and with an edge.

"No. The best thing is to ignore them. If you try to fight them, it will only be worse."

The young woman withstood the hostile stares and suddenly angry murmurings for several seconds before she turned and hurried away.

"Worse! How can it be worse?"

"Who is she? She must be a newcomer."

"I don't care who she is, she's wrong! We've got our homes back today, our peace and quiet. No hoodlums on the playground."

"We should all buy baseball bats."

"A bat won't stop a bullet. That fool that got shot the other night had a gun. And it was a gun that stopped him."

That comment stopped all others. They regarded one another, these participants in what still was an experiment, for each of them, old-timers and newcomers alike, shared the belief that people could and should put aside their differences and live together in peace, despite daily confirmation to the contrary. And because they held such a belief, it was against their most basic and natural instincts to commit a violent act. And yet . . . and yet . . .

"Who was that girl?" Carole Ann asked into the silence. "The one who said we shouldn't fight back. Does anyone know her?"

As a reply, she received a circle of shrugged shoulders, shaken heads, puzzled glances, furrowed brows.

"I've never seen her before."

"Me either."

"Does she live here?" C.A. asked. "Does anyone know for certain if she lives here?"

As a reply this time, she received nothing.

Carole Ann didn't hear much more of what was said; the alarm going off in her brain was making too much noise. Someone had killed a man who couldn't be identified. The police were taking that killing seriously. Roberta was eerily quiet, almost as if she were afraid. Peaceful people were contemplating vigilantism. Against the unwelcome advice of a stranger. No way all those jagged pieces ever could fit together in a picture that made sense.

But Carole Ann tried. Much as she regretted having to do it, she rejected Roberta's invitation for dinner: "Just the two of us." Instead, she went shopping. She bought what must have been the most expensive pair of binoculars on the planet—the highest power with night-vision capability. And she bought black spandex tights, black sneakers, and several black tee shirts. She spent the remainder of the afternoon selecting a suitable place to spy on the playground from outside the Jacaranda complex.

She had an early but subdued dinner with her mother and, without having to be dishonest about it, claimed fatigue and went to bed. She slept deeply for five hours, waking before the travel alarm she'd placed under her pillow had an opportunity to sound off. It was eleven-thirty. She lay in the darkness listening, certain that her mother was asleep—Grayce went to bed at eleven every night—but allowing a few extra minutes of insurance. At midnight she rose, dressed, and, shoes in hand, crept out of the house and into the night. She slid around the side of the house, keeping close to it, angled toward the garage, and ducked into the dense shrubbery beside it, where she sat beneath a spreading jacaranda and amid dense bougainvillea and put on her sneakers.

She sat for a few moments longer, fiddling with the binoculars, adjusting them to her and herself to them. They were worth every penny. She could see Roberta's house across the expanse of lawn as clearly as if she were standing next to it. She surveyed the entire complex in every direction, making certain that she was alone in the darkness. And with the binoculars, she could be certain.

Walking briskly, confidently, though with care and awareness, Carole Ann left the confines of Jacaranda Estates with as much dignity as she could after skirting garbage bins and climbing over backyard fences. She was on the far south end of the property, the quiet and upscale residential area that she realized was slightly frightening so late at night. Frightening because, behind the protective and private walls of foliage-covered stucco and wrought iron, Carole Ann could discern no signs of the lives she knew were being lived there.

She slowed her pace to a stroll and got control of the anxiety that was making her jittery. The very circumstance that was unnerving her—the absence of life—also was her guarantee of safety and protection. Because there was no visible sign of life, there was nobody to notice her or to be suspicious of her presence or her actions. That's why she'd chosen this route and this location, she reminded herself. So she could sit in the enormous bough of an ancient eucalyptus tree and watch the Jacaranda Estates playground. To be certain that what Jennifer Johnson suspected, that what she and Jennifer had seen—or hadn't seen—several nights ago was not an aberration.

Carole Ann, with the aid of the powerful binoculars, watched the playground for two hours and saw it and its inhabitants as clearly as if it were noon and she were standing next to it. During that time, the six young men in the ugly gang-banger clothes sat quietly talking with one another. Twice, as if on a scheduled patrol, four of them left, two walking east and two walking west. Both times they were gone for half an hour. But not once during the period of Carole Ann's surveillance did anyone approach them, nor did they approach anyone.

**Choosy beggars** were a tacky breed in anybody's lexicon but Carole Ann was on the verge of complaining about the air-conditioned chill in the empty office in his warehouse/studio that Robbie had loaned her to work in. Her fingertips were numb, her teeth were chattering, and her shoulders were hunched so tightly her neck and back ached. She had to work to remind herself that things could be worse: she could be attempting to organize the unruly mass of papers and documents—and her equally unruly thoughts—at home with her mother and Angie and Bert and Luisa hovering, questioning, wondering, prodding, probing. And that thought sent a real chill through her.

She cupped her hands around her mouth and blew on them, achieving momentary warmth, and continued the task of entering almost forty years of information she'd collected into the laptop computer that was as much her companion these days as her tiny cellular phone.

She had been gratified to confirm that Arthur Jennings had not in any way defrauded Enrique Jamilla. Half a dozen sources of information were required for that confirmation, but Carole Ann eventually was able to piece together the facts that supported her knowledge of the history of Jacaranda Estates.

Jennings and Jamilla had met in the early 1950s while working on the same construction site, and had become friends. Both also had been isolated and ostracized by the other workers—the Blacks berated Jennings, a carpenter and painter, for hanging around with a wetback; the Mexicans berated Jamilla, a bricklayer and paperhanger, for fraternizing with a nigger.

Both bore the ridicule in stoic silence until, one day while eating lunch together, Jamilla demanded of his friend, Jennings, to state the difference between a wetback and a nigger. According to the newspaper clipping in the archives, Jennings looked from the contents of his lunch box to the contents of Jamilla's lunch box, and replied, "It is the difference, my friend, between red beans and rice and tortillas for lunch and black-eyed peas and rice and cornbread for lunch."

The friendship between the two men solidified in that moment, and grew into a partnership. They formed their own construction company—J and J Contracting—and, riding the tide of wild growth and development that characterized Los Angeles during that time, became wealthy. They pooled their savings and, over the objections of both their wives, bought eleven acres of land in an undeveloped section of the western part of Los Angeles. That was in 1955. They began building houses a year later—houses with a mission, houses with a purpose. They built only duplexes and triplexes, which necessarily required an unavoidable physical proximity between and among neighbors. All of the units had two, three, or four bedrooms, two or two and a half bathrooms, and a den or family room, both to accommodate the large families preferred by Blacks and Mexicans, and to offer their own people the basic luxuries usually denied them by other home builders.

Cobblestone walkways linked the clusters of houses and led to covered carports. There were no fences at Jacaranda Estates in those early years, and the wide and welcoming expanses of grass were natural playgrounds for children and gathering places for adults. Jamilla and Jennings would sell the units only to Blacks and Mexicans, at a reasonable and affordable rate. But with a caveat: Blacks and Mexicans would be required to live next door to each other and to learn about each other. And only those persons agreeing, in writing, to those terms were allowed to buy into Jacaranda Estates.

Carole Ann had succeeded in locating the original bill of sale for the eleven acres of land to J and J Contracting, the original landscape and architectural plans, photostatic copies of the transfer of many of the original titles and deeds, including those of her parents, Mitchell and Grayce Asher Gibson; of Charles and Roberta Williams Lawson; of Angelique Arroyo de la Cruz; and all of the signed agreements by the original inhabitants to adhere, in spirit and action, to the principles of friendship and understanding, and the codicil requiring that all subsequent residents adhere to those principles. She found no documentation of any kind relating to Hector and Luisa Nunez.

J and J Contracting grew and thrived until 1986, when, at the age of sixty, Enrique Jamilla suffered a massive stroke and died. Arthur Jennings sold J and J Contracting to a construction conglomerate for several million dollars and retired. And that is when the controversy commenced. The altruism of Jennings and Jamilla did not cloud their business sense; they sold the individual housing units in Jacaranda Estates, but they retained ownership of the land itself. Upon his death, it was discovered that Jamilla had bequeathed his interest in the Jacaranda Estates land and in J and J Contracting to his partner, Arthur Jennings. His family received other investments and funds worth several million dollars, but they wanted Jacaranda and they wanted J and J Contracting. They sued for it. They lost. And that is how it happened that a Black man owned the land upon which Jacaranda Estates existed, on the current market worth tens of millions of dollars. And the bad feeling had existed within the Mexican community ever since.

What Carole Ann could not do was isolate the source of this feeling. It seemed not to emanate from the Jamilla family; indeed, she'd found no mention of the man's widow or of his two sons and two daughters since they failed in their court action. They appeared to have accepted the judgment and moved on with their lives. There were several brief clippings from community newspapers about a group called *Dame Que Es Mío*—"Give Me What's Mine"—that seemed to have formed in the wake of the Jamilla lawsuit, and then fizzled when its organizers failed to garner support either from the Jamilla family or from the Mexican power structure in L.A. Statements from the spokespersons of a couple of Hispanic pride groups alluded to an unwillingness to coalesce with other racial groups, but Carole Ann could find no indication that any of those groups had embarked on a mission to reclaim land belonging to the original natives of California.

She also could find no trace of Arthur Jennings and his family since the settlement of the lawsuit. The last mention of him was a quote from *The Los Angeles Times* in which he expressed sadness and regret that his friendship with Enrique Jamilla should have resulted in litigation, and his belief that Enrique would be as hurt by the situation as he was himself, followed by a statement issued through his attorney that Jennings was relieved that the proceeding had ended, and that he would have been satisfied with the judge's ruling, no matter what. And not another mention of the man.

Carole Ann did locate information that in early 1990, management of Jacaranda Estates had been assigned to a professional property-management company, but she could find no current listing for that company. She made notes to herself to track it down; to check birth, death, and marriage records for the Jamilla and the Jennings names; to check property-transfer lists; to check the tax assessor's records; to check the various agencies of the criminal justice system. And she made a note to determine why there existed no record of Hector and Luisa Nunez's residency at Jacaranda Estates.

Then, as had become her habit, she compiled a detailed report of her activities for Jake Graham. She included every fact and every detail, and her every thought and reaction to those facts and details. She also made a copy of every document, and sent Jake the originals. The entire process had consumed a week since her return from Sacramento, and she was relieved when it was completed. She enjoyed a feeling of lightness as she exited the Federal Express office, knowing that tomorrow Jake would know as much as she knew— and didn't know—about why three murders could have occurred within a tiny oasis of civility in a violent city.

She had developed a dependence on the gnarly detective. She trusted him. She felt safe knowing that she had a support system, and was instantly surprised and gratified by that understanding: she no longer was a lawyer without the safety net of a high-powered law firm to support her; she was a lawyer backed by an international investigation and security company. Muscle. She had muscle and she liked the feeling.

Imagining Jake's and Tommy's reaction to being considered her "muscle" sustained Carole Ann on the stress-producing diagonal drive across Los Angeles. Tommy would grin and flex his pectorals and instantly claim the sobriquet. Jake would frown, growl, mumble something about it being undignified, and be as secretly pleased as Tommy was outwardly pleased. She unbegrudgingly shared the good feeling with the unease that came with not having solutions to what should not be problems: the whereabouts of Arthur Jennings and his family, the name of the entity that paid taxes for the land beneath Jacaranda Estates, the proof that Luisa and her family always had lived there—dammit! Carole Ann chastised herself. She need only check Luisa's address against the tax roles to ascertain that she paid annual taxes on the place. A first-year law student possessed such basic common sense.

Carol Ann still was marveling at her own stupidity when she turned into Harriet Tubman Drive and punched the automatic garage door opener, and she spent a long three or four seconds wondering why the million-watt spotlight her mother had installed on the garage roof didn't illuminate the entire yard when the garage door lifted. Then she saw the figures in her headlights as they frantically sought the cover of darkness, and messages and signals jumbled in her brain and she drove the car over the curb and across the grass, directly toward them. It was still in motion when she jumped out.

She kicked the first one on the run, with the side of her foot, perfectly placed at the end of a perfectly executed turn. The blow landed on the right side of his face and he went down hard and fast. She didn't have to change direction for the second one. She grabbed his arm with her right hand, twisted, turned, and dropped him to his knees. She stood over him and in some part of her consciousness was wondering what to do when he punched her in the stomach. All reason fled and, propelled totally by instinct, she hit him three times: twice in the neck and once in the chest and when he dropped, she

knew he was dead. That's what Robbie had said was the sole purpose of the maneuver. To kill. She stood quickly and looked around,
looking for another one. There had been three of them, she thought.
Three forms captured in the glare of her headlights. Unless the
third figure had been her mother. . . .

And then she heard the sound that threatened to destroy her
spirit: the moan and cry that was her mother in pain.

She ran to the garage, and knelt beside Grayce and gathered her
in her arms and wept when her mother cried out in agony. Carole
Ann was lifting her when Angie careened around the side of the
building waving a bat in one hand and a wide-beam flashlight in the
other. She dropped both when she spied the tableau, and rushed to
help Carole Ann carry Grayce into the house and to the living room
sofa. Then Angie placed a hurried call to Roberta providing sketchy
but pertinent details, and returned to assist Carole Ann in caring
for Grayce.

What she found was mother caring for daughter. Angie was momentarily confused by the sight of Carole Ann out of control—a crying, screaming, shaking, cursing Carole Ann. Angie had known and
observed this woman since her infancy and had never, even when
Carole Ann was badly injured as a child, seen her on the verge of
hysteria. She was further confused by the sight of Grayce badly
damaged, and struggled against losing control herself.

Roberta's almost immediate arrival served to restore rationality.
Carole Ann obeyed Roberta's order to get a grip on herself, and to
get the first aid supplies from the bathroom. Angie obeyed Roberta's order to boil water and to make ice packs. Grayce obeyed
Roberta's order to let it all out and wept tears of fear and anger and
pain and gratitude.

Roberta supervised the cleansing of Grayce's wounds and the
placement of ice packs where bruises and swelling were manifest-
ing, cursing under her breath all the while. She cursed every social,
cultural, and technological novelty of the past generation, and the

role it played in leading to the attack on Grayce. And as she was making a pot of herbal tea, she finally cursed Luisa, which halted all other activity and momentarily even superseded Grayce's pain.

"I am sick and tired of her foolishness! She's been acting like a pure jackass for the last two weeks and I am sick of it! Where the hell is she! I called her as I was walking out and told her to get over here now, because something bad had happened to Grayce. How long could it take, even for Luisa!" Roberta ran out of words and breath at the same time, and slammed the cup on the counter so hard it shattered. "Goddammit!" Ceramic splinters and shards flew up and then quickly down to the floor, as if in a hurry to be out of the way of such fury.

Grayce struggled to her feet. "Bert! Bert . . ."

Roberta looked up in time to see Grayce sway and slump. By the time they revived her, Roberta had calmed down and regained control of herself and of the situation, and Luisa had arrived, breathless and frightened.

"Luisa, help Carole Ann with the ice packs and the bandages—Grayce, you might need a stitch or two over your left eye—and Angie, you come with me." She was down the hall and out the door before Angie registered the command and caught up.

"Bert, wait! Roberta Lawson, do you hear me!" Ire and a raised voice from Angie was an attention getter and Roberta stepped off the cobbled path into the grass and waited for her to catch up.

"Where are you going?" Angie hissed.

"To see if she killed 'em," Roberta hissed back, and swung around the side of the house. Angie quick-stepped behind her, caught up, and grabbed her arm.

"What are you talking about? And stand still and make sense."

"Carole Ann kept screaming that they were dead, that she'd killed them. Didn't you hear her? And they sure as hell were laying out there when I first got here. And C.A.'s car was open and the motor was running and the garage door is standing wide open. Now, will you come on?"

Angie followed Roberta around the side of the house to find her flashlight and bat lying where she'd dropped them. The silver Benz was still open and running, the interior light casting a mellow glow on the surrounding area, exposing the gaping garage and Grayce's Chrysler, the contents of the two bags of groceries she had been carrying, and an inert form. Angie picked up her flashlight and shone it on the body, then she swept the area with the light. There was only one body. And it was not alive. They stood looking at it, one of them filled with sorrow, the other filled with rage, and both emotions springing from the same well: the realization that Grayce might well be the corpse had Carole Ann not arrived when she did.

Roberta slid behind the wheel of the Benz, shut the door, engaged the gear, and the luxurious beast eased itself forward into the garage. She pushed a button on the wall and hurried out as the door began its slow, rattling descent. Then she helped Angie finish gathering the scattered groceries, hurriedly stuffing everything into plastic bags.

"You know we have to move him," Roberta said quietly, no emotion in her voice.

"No, I don't know that!" Angie snapped back, equally quietly but oozing emotion. "Move him where? And why? And *how?* Dead people are heavy."

"Out there, behind the garage, so it'll look like he came from Pancho Villa Drive and not from Grayce's. And we'll have to carry him, Angie, you and me."

"I'm not carrying a dead person anywhere! And why should we, Bert? We haven't done anything wrong! Carole Ann saved her mother's life! She doesn't have anything to hide from and we don't either."

Roberta moved in closer to Angie and put her face inches from her friend's face. Eyes locked in the darkness. "You're trying to make sense, Angie, in a place where there is no sense. Nothing that's happened here in the last six months makes any sense and you know that! Don't you, Angie?"

"We should call the police, Bert."

"And tell 'em that Carole Ann killed the bastard that was killing her mother? And oh, by the way, Officer, I killed another one of 'em a couple of weeks ago? Think they'll let me and C.A. be cellmates? Think they'll let my grandchildren visit me in the slammer? Think it's better for my grandchildren to visit me in the slammer than out at the cemetery?"

Roberta inhaled deeply, filled her depleted lungs, leaned over, and lifted the feet of the dead man. She raised her eyes to Angie's face and was surprised to see tears flowing, fast and heavy. Angie heaved a heavy sigh that lifted and dropped her shoulders. She sobbed once, then leaned over, grabbed the dead man under the shoulders, and began backing up, around the garage, toward the expanse of grass that led to the adjacent street.

Angie gestured with her head over her left shoulder. "See that rise there? There's a culvert beneath it. We can put him there." She was breathing heavily, and still crying.

Roberta nodded, opened her mouth to speak, then closed it again. The gentle downward sloping of the land propelled them forward and they scurried the last few feet to the place where, as Angie had said, the land then rose gently before dropping off into a drainage ditch. When they reached the place, Angie immediately released the dead man and walked away, leaving Roberta to roll him down the embankment. She hurried to catch Angie, who now was running. Each of them grabbed a grocery bag and Angie picked up her flashlight, pointing to the bat, which Roberta retrieved. They both were running by the time they charged into Grayce's front door.

"Where have you two been?"

"We've been terrified!"

"Angie! Why are you crying?"

"And you're both out of breath. . . ."

Angie and Roberta refused comment until they satisfied themselves that Grayce was alive and that she would, in time, be well.
She was stretched out on the sofa, her head in Carole Ann's lap, and
she struggled to sit upright. Carole Ann lifted her shoulder and
Grayce cried out in pain. Roberta and Angie each took a hand and
pulled her up to a sitting position. Once again she swayed, but
maintained consciousness. Bruises and contusions had totally dis-
colored her face, and her left jaw was swollen like she had the
mumps. Blood still oozed from the laceration above her left eye, and
her top lip was split. An ice pack hid the lump on top of her head.
She tried to speak and could not.

Roberta sat on the other side of her and Angie sat on the floor at
her feet. They touched her gently and whispered soothing words, as
if to a child. They wept together quietly and then, as if cued, simultaneously looked up and across the room toward Luisa, who sat
rigidly in one of the dining room chairs, staring at them, her lips
moving silently.

"Luisa. What in the world . . ." Roberta began.

"Are you sick, Luisa?" Angie struggled to her feet and rushed
across the room. She reached out to touch Luisa's forehead but,
without speaking, Luisa pushed the hand away. Too stunned to give
meaning to the gesture, Angie reached down and wrapped Luisa in
a tight embrace and could just as well have been holding a corpse.
She shuddered at the thought, wiped her hands on her pants legs,
and backed away.

"She's been like that since you all left. And where did you go, by
the way? Why did you rush off like that?" Carole Ann pushed herself
upright and stood staring down at Roberta.

"We went to see if they were dead. One of 'em was, and one was
gone, so we dumped the dead one in a ditch and cleaned up the mess
and put your car in the garage."

None of them was prepared for the explosion that followed. Even
Luisa roused herself. Carole Ann screamed and cursed and pound-

ed walls and tables with her fists. They'd disturbed a crime scene. They'd tampered with evidence. They'd obstructed justice. They'd committed any number of felonies, compounding the felony that Carole Ann herself had committed. All of which could result in immediate disbarment for Carole Ann, who just happened to be an officer of the court. "I'm sitting in here like an asshole waiting for you two to return so I could call the police, and you're out there turning the key to my cell door! How could you do something so incredibly stupid! I'm going to jail! Maybe forever! I'll certainly never practice law again. Not in California. What in the hell were you thinking! What have you done to me?"

They watched her in silent amazement, awed by the power of her fury and uncertain how to accept such behavior from their child. Her own mother was mesmerized by the transformation. This incarnation of her daughter she'd never seen: cold, brutal, violent. This daughter, so different even from the one who just moments ago had readily killed in defense of her. This mother now didn't recognize her own daughter. What was the difference between the two? Grayce looked up at the raving, stalking Carole Ann and saw an absence of love. Saw a Carole Ann who was a stranger.

Then, as suddenly as it manifested, the apparition crumbled and disappeared. Whatever had been supporting the Carole Ann that was a stranger drained away and she collapsed onto the sofa, limp and weak and vulnerable.

"I don't understand what's happening here. I don't understand how any of this could be happening. What have I done? What am I going to do? I don't know what I'm going to do." She leaned forward, her head so far between her knees that it almost touched the floor. She hung there, barely breathing, not moving.

Roberta took a step toward Carole Ann, and stopped. She reached toward her, then quickly withdrew her hand as if she expected to be burned. She opened her mouth three times before words were formed. And then, when they came, the words made no sense. They were just words, not thoughts or sentences or feelings.

Grayce reached out to her. "Ssshhh, Bert," she said in a caressing tone, as if she were soothing an upset child. "Be quiet now, Bert."

Roberta stopped babbling and there was an instant of pure silence before sirens split the air and pounding rattled the doorframe. Simultaneous assaults on the senses and emotions froze them. They sat motionless, the five of them, unable and unwilling to respond. The pounding intensified, accompanied this time by angry shouts.

"This is the police! Open the door!"

Carole Ann responded at the cellular, molecular level. She stood quickly and by the time she reached the door, her mind and emotions were clear. She released the two top locks and began to turn the bottom handle when the door swung in against her with such force that she was propelled backward into the hallway wall. Two uniformed officers rode the wave of force into the small space, momentarily confining Carole Ann behind the door. The two officers strode into the living room. Carole Ann slammed the front door and followed them.

"What do you want?" The unconcealed, quiet fury in her tone caused the larger of the two uniforms to turn on her, and she saw that he was accustomed to using his size to control people and circumstances. He was tall, three or four inches over six feet, and broad. He'd be called fat in a couple of years. He took a menacing step toward her.

"You shut your mouth, lady, and keep it shut until I tell you to open it."

"I am an officer of the court, California Bar Number 000 123, and I am putting you on notice right now that your conduct violates—"

He cut her off with a snarl that almost succeeded in its intent. "I said shut up!"

Carole Ann's eyes narrowed to nasty slits and she leaned forward, toward him. "I don't take orders from thugs. Whether they're wearing gang colors or blue uniforms."

He blinked, swallowed, and backed up a step and his partner stepped into the breech. He was not as tall as his partner, and much thinner.

"We're investigating a murder and we'd appreciate any help you people can give us." His eyes held Carole Ann's and she swallowed her fury.

"What murder?" she asked.

"There's a body in the ditch out behind this house . . ." he began, but stopped at the sound of moans and gasps and weeping. They turned their attention from Carole Ann to four women huddled on the sofa. They focused their attention on Grayce.

"What happened to her?" the big, surly one growled and moved toward the sofa. Grayce winced and cowered and that sight rekindled the burning anger within Carole Ann.

"What do you care?" she snapped at him, and watched with some small degree of satisfaction as he fought to control himself.

"I got a newly dead body down the hill from this house, and I got her in here with her face bashed in and still bleeding, and I wonder if the two things are connected."

No one moved or spoke or otherwise acknowledged having heard his words, and both officers shifted uneasily in the dense but strangely calm silence.

"Did you report this assault?"

"What would be the point of that, Officer MacDougall?" Carole Ann took a step toward him, hands clenched into fists at her sides. "I left four messages for you concerning an earlier homicide here. My mother found the body. That's my mother over there with the bashed-in face, by the way. You never returned her calls or mine. Concerning a homicide. Why would we call you concerning a simple assault?"

Recognition registered all over his broad face, and the red flush followed the recognition. He was breathing quickly and beginning to sweat. His body strained the fabric of his uniform. He still was more muscle than fat, but the fat was gaining ground and would take control in a couple of years. The drink showed in his face and in the slowness of his mental processes. Carole Ann studied him, assessed him, measured him, and concluded that he wasn't motivated enough to make his suspicions of them a sticking point tonight; and for that she was grateful. She needed time.

She'd already decided that she wasn't confessing to murder tonight, and certainly not to Howard MacDougall and his partner, ever. The queasiness roiling in her intestines now had less to do with the attack on her mother and her own commission of a violent crime and more to do with the fact that the police were investigating a homicide Carole Ann was certain no resident of Jacaranda Estates had reported. Not only did they know of the homicide, they knew the location of the body. And only Roberta and Angie knew where he lay.

MacDougall's partner, P. Schindler, confirmed Carole Ann's worst suspicions and validated her decision when he said, "It now seems that three people were assaulted here tonight, if we count your mother. Any assistance you people can—"

MacDougall cut him off with a look that would have frozen spit and removed all traces of lingering doubt and guilt from Carole Ann's conscience. She had taken a life and she certainly would claim ownership of her crime and accept the consequences. But she would not do so behind a veil of possible criminality constructed by the Los Angeles Police Department itself. She'd surrender to the FBI if necessary, and when necessary. But before she sacrificed her effectiveness, she intended to uncover whatever secrets Jacaranda Estates was hiding. And once again she felt the chill of isolation, the loneliness of being without a place. For how could this place be her home, her safe haven, and have secrets from her?

Her decision made, she escorted Officers MacDougall and Schindler to the door, triple-locked it behind them, and went into the kitchen and activated the sprinkler system for the backyard.

# ∽ *nine* ∾

She listened to Jake Graham breathe into the receiver. Listened for what seemed like hours. She tried to picture him and found that she could not conjure up an image of him, of how he looked at this moment. She'd expected him to explode, to curse, to berate her, to chastise her, and she'd prepared herself for that; had been awake all night reliving the horror and preparing herself to receive his anger. She'd even prepared herself for his refusal to help and had prepared herself to beg for that help. But she was not prepared for his silence and did not understand how to accept it. So she held the telephone and listened to him breathe.

"I'm speechless," he said finally.

"I noticed," she replied, and waited again.

"I don't know what to say to you, C.A."

So she listened to him breathe for a while longer, until her own breath constricted and caused pain. "I didn't know what else to do, Jake. I was so frightened."

"Frightened? You were frightened?"

Something in his tone lifted Carole Ann a few notches out of her slump. "Yes, I was frightened," she replied, a shade shy of defensively. "My mother was beaten. I heard her moan in pain. I've never experienced such fear. Then the police seemed to know everything when logically there's no way they could know. And to contemplate the implications of that created a new kind of fear. And I just didn't know what to do."

"You just made me speechless all over again. I was sitting here picturing you the worst kind of mad. Mad enough to kill and cover it up. Now you tell me you're scared, and that I can't picture." And he got quiet again, recalling the night he'd told her her husband was dead, the victim of what at the time appeared to be a random street mugging. He recalled her strength that night; and he recalled the anger that grew inside her and fueled her hunt for her husband's killers to the point that she risked her own life in the process. He re-called her year in mourning, her grief and loneliness so deep he prayed for relief for her. He'd seen this woman who'd come to be his friend display a variety of powerful emotions. He'd never seen her frightened. But he embraced her right to be, if for no other reason than he, too, shuddered to think what the behavior of the L.A. police as so far described could portend.

"Will you help me, Jake?"

"I'm already on it," he growled, sounding like himself. "I got the stuff you sent by FedEx and've got somebody looking for that Jennings character, and for any of the other guy's . . . what's his name? . . . Jamilla, for any of his survivors. Until something breaks, I want you to sit tight."

"Jake . . ." She tried to slow him down, to deflect him, because she knew that he was primed and ready to roll over her and flatten her like ten miles of rural highway.

"You listen to me, C.A. I want you to stay in the house. Don't go *anywhere*. And don't let that wrecking crew out of your sight, espe-cially that Roberta. And keep an eye on that Luisa. She sounds like she's about to crack. Don't let the cops near your mother and don't you go near the cops. Don't let anybody in and don't you go out. Not until I tell you. In fact, don't even answer the telephone—"

"We have to answer the phone, Jake!"

"Then screen the calls first. I don't want you talking to the press or to the cops. Did you download your computer, or is what you sent me still in the hard drive?"

"Yeah, it is."

"Then clean it out! And send me the disc."

"You told me not to go anywhere," she muttered through clenched teeth then stopped short, her breath caught in her throat.

Jake heard. "What? What is it!"

She cradled her head in her hands, then squeezed her eyes shut. "It's in the car. In the trunk. The computer and the file. The copies of everything I sent you."

Jake cursed for a while. "Well, we'll have to take our chances. Leave it there for now. And stay put until I call you. You got that, C.A.?"

"I liked you better when you were quiet," Carole Ann snapped at him.

"So does my wife," he snapped back.

"She's stuck with you," Carole Ann retorted, not kindly.

"So are you," Jake replied with similar unkindness, and ended their conversation.

**The staying-put** part was easy. Carole Ann was emotionally, physically, and spiritually depleted; and even had she not been, Grayce was too sick and in too much pain for Carole Ann to contemplate leaving her mother alone even for a moment. Keeping Roberta and Angelique tethered proved quite a bit more difficult once they'd all passed a night and were into the next day. They kept wanting to go get things for Grayce: herbs and teas and fresh juices and a fruit tart from her favorite bakery and videos and magazines and books.

They finally accepted that Grayce didn't want to do anything but sleep, so they took turns sitting by her bed watching her, providing Carole Ann with the opportunity to pump them individually for information about the history of Jacaranda Estates in general, and about Luisa in particular, Luisa being of particular concern since she had yet to make an appearance—odd behavior on a normal day, and inconceivable on this day when Grayce was lying wounded in body and spirit. And what she learned was disturbing, as much because Luisa had an abusive grandson as because that fact had been kept from her.

"No need for you to know," Roberta told her in the tone of voice she reserved for Carole Ann the child. "Besides," she added, peering at Carole Ann over the tops of her glasses—an interesting feat since they were full-sized trifocal lenses and not half-frame reading glasses—"something like that doesn't just come up in casual conversation." And the flatness of her tone warned against pursuit of the topic.

Roberta was much more forthcoming in discussing the history of Jacaranda Estates and its two founding partners, having had a warm and mutually respectful relationship with Enrique Jamilla, and a long-term friendship with Arthur Jennings and his wife: she'd been invited to the weddings of the Jennings children, and all the Jennings had attended her husband, Charlie's, funeral. "But that was years ago," she said with the kind of sigh that yearns for the return of some long-ago time and place. "Before they started spending more and more time out of the country."

"Where?"

"One of the islands," Roberta responded absently. "Not one of the more familiar ones . . . A-something. Starts with an *A*."

"Antigua?" asked Carole Ann hopefully. "Aruba?"

"No. Leave me alone about it and it'll come to me. My brain doesn't like being pushed. You know that." Roberta bristled and assumed the hunched-shoulder posture that signaled her readiness to defend herself.

Carole Ann grinned and the older woman relaxed and they talked easily and wistfully about the old days, Roberta doing most of the talking, until, like a preschooler, she could sit still no longer and bounced up to "go check on Grayce."

Carole Ann watched her go, then went into the kitchen and, after a moment's indecision, opted to brew tea instead of coffee, wishing while the water boiled that she'd been more receptive to Al's suggestions that she learn meditation techniques. She desperately needed for her mind to slow down and quiet, so that she could order her thoughts, and so that she could sleep; she'd been awake the entire night. She gave up on the tea, returned to the sofa, and stretched out, wanting to give in to the fatigue. But her frantic brain kept replaying the jerky images of the attack of her mother and of her attack on the attackers. And her conscience reminded her over and over that she'd killed a man. Killed him and participated in a cover-up of the crime.

And, she realized, she'd been steeling herself for Roberta's rehashing of the event. But Roberta had said not a word, had behaved as if last night never happened. And that gave her something else to worry about: in addition to what was wrong with Luisa, what was wrong with Roberta? The woman never passed up an opportunity to worry a subject to death.

And speaking of Luisa, Goddammit, where the hell was she! Suddenly Carole Ann jumped to her feet and in an almost single motion she grabbed keys off the table, lunged to the front door, and swung it open. Nothing seemed as important just then as talking to Luisa and finding out why she wasn't there. She was outside in a surprisingly gray and cool day before she remembered Jake's admonition to "stay put." Well, it was too late now. She was running, not flat out and hard, but at a good clip, and she looked around her as her feet slapped against the cobblestones. No sign of cops. Or of anyone else. The entire complex seemed deserted. The pallor of the day added to the sense of isolation and desolation she felt inside.

She reached Luisa's and began to frown even before she knocked on the door; and the lack of response to her hard raps, which had become pounding, confirmed that the abandoned-looking house was, indeed, empty. And not just gone-to-the-store empty but the cold, hollow emptiness of long-term absence. Carole Ann was furious. How could Luisa leave Grayce at a time like this? And without telling anyone? She kicked the door hard enough to leave an indentation in too-weathered wood.

"What the hell is wrong with her?" Carole Ann muttered curses to herself as she headed back home, running slower but keeping a steady pace and a careful eye out for cops. "Where could she be? What could make her stay away in the middle of a crisis?" She was still asking herself out-loud questions when she inserted the key into Grayce's lock. Before she could turn it, the door jerked open and Angie snatched her inside.

"Where have you been, C.A.? I was worried sick!"

"I'm sorry, Angie. I went to find Luisa. She's not home!" Carole Ann said, almost whining. "And why didn't anybody ever tell me about her grandson?"

She followed Angie to the dining room table, where a pot of tea was steeping, and as the older woman sank with a deep sigh into a chair, C.A. lifted the pot and poured tea into two cups.

"I didn't know you didn't know," Angie said with a shrug and a noisy sip of peppermint tea. "Anyway, Ricky only comes around when he's in trouble, and he only stays long enough for whoever is looking for him to stop looking for him." And she shrugged again, dismissing Ricky with a heavy sigh and a look of sadness that alarmed Carole Ann, especially since her hands shook when she placed her cup on the table.

"Does he hurt Luisa?" Carole Ann asked, her own hands forming themselves into involuntary fists; and when Angie ducked her head and didn't reply, she jumped to her feet and began pacing. "The little bastard! I can't wait to have a little talk with him—"

"No!" Angie grabbed Carole Ann's arm and pulled her back into her seat, the sadness in her face transformed into real fear. "Don't say anything, promise me. You'll only make it worse."

"Make it worse how, Angie? What does he do to her?"

"Nothing, Carole Ann. Please believe me. She just doesn't like him being there because he drinks and smokes and listens to that loud, stupid music and . . . and . . . he talks crazy."

Angelique sighed deeply and her shoulders lifted and fell and she sank back onto the chair and crossed her arms over her bosom, and her legs at the ankles. Her eyes locked with Carole Ann's for a brief moment before they began roaming. It was not, Carole Ann mused, an evasive or secretive action; rather, it seemed a true assessment of her surroundings. Angie's eyes roamed over the furnishings in Grayce's living room and Carole Ann could almost see her memory working, recalling when and where and why Grayce had obtained a table or a chair or a painting or a vase. Carole Ann could almost feel the older woman's heart imagining a life without her old and dear friend, could feel it feeling how close tragedy had come to being a disaster.

"Angie . . ."

The older woman shook her head and the mane of burnished, thick hair swished. She met Carole Ann's eyes. "I don't want to talk about Ricky. Not now, Carole Ann. Not when there are truly important things to say and do."

There were only two years of Carole Ann's life, the first two, when Angelique Arroyo was not a presence; Carole Ann thought of Angie as always having been there. Angie was a known quantity, familiar and comfortable. Yet, in this moment, she realized that there was something about Angie that was unknown. Unknown because it was unavailable. Some place deep within, Angie was sad, and Carole

Ann just recognized that truth for the first time. Perhaps because now she had her own sad place. *It takes one to know one.* . . .

"Then what about Luisa? Don't you find it odd that she's not here, today of all days? And where would she go?"

"It's typical Luisa behavior, C.A. She's always been a doormat for the lousy men in her life. Wherever she is, it probably has something to do with Ricky."

"And that's more important to her than Grayce?"

"He's her grandson, Carole Ann. He's family."

"And we're not?" Carole Ann's anger at Luisa returned full force.

"Not to Luisa. Not like you mean," Angie said, her lack of further interest in the subject proven by her pronouncement that it was her turn to watch Grayce and that Carole Ann could make herself useful by making some soup. Grayce needed nourishment, she said, and because her face and mouth were so swollen and sore, soup would be all that she could manage. And, like Roberta had done earlier, Angie left the room, left Carole Ann sitting at the table staring at the teapot, without, by word or gesture, acknowledging the events of the night before.

She sat there thinking, elbows propped on the table, her chin supported by her hands, until she realized she was nodding off. Gratefully she staggered to the sofa, stretched out, and drifted off into a deep, dreamless sleep. When she awoke, Roberta was sitting in the armchair, nodding, and she stirred when Carole Ann awoke, stretched and rotated her neck to release the kinks.

"I went to check on Luisa," she said to Roberta, keeping her tone of voice neutral. "She's not at home."

Roberta looked at her for a long moment, but, Carole Ann thought, didn't really see her. Her next words proved the point. "Hector never really fit in around here," Roberta said, going to the window and parting the draperies and staring out at the desolate playground. When she turned around, Carole Ann saw that she'd retreated to some distant and past place. Not the past that she, Carole Ann, shared with the four old friends, but a past of conflict and confusion that they'd deliberately kept a secret among themselves. The past that included Luisa's husband, Hector, who, Roberta said, emerging from her thoughtful place, drank and gambled and fought and more than once spent a long weekend in jail. Unlike the other men of Jacaranda Estates, Hector Nunez did not mow his lawn or paint his house or build go-carts for his sons or playhouses for his daughters. Nor did he work hard or even often.

Luisa's response to her husband's behavior was to light candles and pray for him, and to envelop her children—two girls and three boys—in a protective and smothering love. The girls, both older than Carole Ann by several years and therefore not close friends, married right out of high school and moved away. They kept in touch with Luisa, Roberta said, and sent for her to visit on a fairly regular basis. But the girls had little or nothing to do with the boys, not one of whom "amounted to a hill of beans," Bert said with a snort. Little Hector, Enrique, and Carlos.

"And Hector is the worst. You remember Little Hector, don't you, Carole Ann?"

Of course she remembered Hector. Bright-eyed, happy, frisky, chubby Hector, six months older than herself. She followed him around, climbing where he climbed, running where he ran, jumping where he jumped, until her big brother Mitch called a halt. She surprised herself with the memory, and its clarity: Mitch calling the then twelve-year-old Hector a punk and sending him home, daring him to return. Hector, now serving a life sentence at Lompoc Penitentiary for rape and murder.

"Ricky is Hector's son," Roberta said. "A chip off the old block," she added dryly.

"Angie said Luisa was a doormat."

Roberta's snort became a chuckle. "You must've really caught Angie in a melancholy mood for her to have said that. But she's right. Big Hector treated Luisa like dirt and all she did was pray, even after he abandoned her and the kids. Little Hector and his brothers learned from their father and treated her worse than dirt and she kept on praying. And now Ricky, that little shit! I wish one of my grandkids would talk to me like he talks to her! I'd send 'em to meet their Maker in a big hurry!"

Carole Ann disguised a giggle with throat clearing and quickly crossed to Roberta and gave her a hug before she could launch fully into her well-rehearsed discourse on how she would, if provided the opportunity, single-handedly transform the behavior of contemporary youth, and asked her what happened to Luisa's other sons, Enrique and Carlos.

"Enrique is a professional gambler. Horses, dogs, roosters, cards, sports, the weather. If there's odds, he'll bet on it," the older woman replied in a flat tone. "And Carlos is a drug addict. The harmless kind. Funny," she said with a sad shake of her head, "how you change your perception of things. Imagine calling heroin 'harmless.' But compared to that crack and cocaine stuff, a heroin addict is harmless. At least to other people."

Carole Ann could not fathom a response and Roberta didn't seem to expect one, so they sat quietly for a while.

"Anguilla," Roberta said into the silence, and, to Carole Ann's blank stare, she added, "That's where Arthur Jennings lives now."

Carole Ann nodded thanks but kept the discussion on track. "Angie also said Ricky 'talks crazy.' What does that mean, Bert?"

"Silly little bastard!" Roberta, already poised on the precipice, leapt into the breach, landing with catlike poise in the middle of her theory connecting discipline and respect. And with uncharacteristic restraint, she quickly returned herself to the matter at hand and revealed that Ricky Nunez belonged to a Mexican-American group that wanted to return California and Texas to the Mexicans.

Carole Ann stood abruptly and shoved her hands deep into her jeans pockets, as if hiding her hands could conceal the rage that suddenly had resurfaced and threatened to erupt. "Isn't that some heavy-duty politics for a 'silly little bastard,' Bert? It takes *muchos co-jones* to carry a belief like that, to say nothing of acting on it. And Ricky sounds like a midget dick if ever there was one."

Roberta snickered and nodded. "He is. And I don't know any more than what Luisa told me, which, knowing her, is just talk." She paused for a moment, then shook her head. "If she even got it right what he was talking about."

"But you know Ricky, Bert. Is it possible that he could be part of a political movement?"

"Hell, no!" the older woman snorted. "What you said about people having strong beliefs is the truth. Ricky Nunez doesn't believe in anything stronger than tequila and marijuana." She shook her head back and forth. "Don't pay any attention to that kinda stuff, C.A. It's just talk."

But Carole Ann now had heard enough to believe that talk of a Mexican reclamation of California had a basis in substance somewhere, if not with Ricky Nunez. But where? And were its advocates capable of action? Robbie Lee had called them loud-mouthed punks, and Roberta just called them silly little bastards—and both categories of people had the potential to be dangerous and lethal. But who were they? Students of martial arts, students of history, or juvenile delinquents who made sport of intimidating their grand-mothers? And were her mother's attackers last night part of that clique?

Memories of last night rushed back suddenly and forcefully. Every one of them had behaved the entire day as if the attack on Grayce was the only significant occurrence of the previous night. Perhaps for them, Carole Ann thought, that was true. And immediately after having that thought she annulled it; she knew better than to believe even for an instant that her mother or Bert or Angie or Luisa would ever minimize the severity of what had happened to Carole Ann as a result of what had happened to Grayce. And to prove the point, Roberta leaned over and took her hand.

"I'm really sorry about last night, baby. I wasn't thinking that what we did—that what I made Angie help me do—could get you in trouble."

Carole Ann was grateful for the strength and comfort of the older woman's hand. "I know, Bert. I'm sorry I yelled at you."

"What are you going to do?"

"I don't know. I—"

"Don't you think it's strange," Roberta asked, her nose crinkling as if suddenly a bad smell permeated the room, "that big cop, whatever his name was, knew where the body was? We'd barely had time to get back in the house and he's at the door."

"I think it's more than strange, Bert," Carole Ann replied, wanting to add that what she was thinking that it was chilling and terrifying and demoralizing. "And that's why I'm not sure what to do. At some point I'll have to turn myself in."

"No!" Roberta grabbed Carole Ann's arm, nails digging in and wounding flesh. "You can't do that, C.A.!"

Carole Ann felt the force of Roberta's fear but did not understand its source. "I have to, Bert, I'm an officer of the court. But I'll be OK. The worse that can happen isn't really so bad since I don't practice law in California anyway."

"But that's just it, C.A.!" Roberta wailed, now shaking the arm she'd been maiming. "I need you to practice law here! I need you to help me."

Roberta's strange plea was interrupted by a shuffling motion and an intake of breath and Grayce entered, leaning heavily on Angie's arm. Carole Ann jumped to her feet, followed closely by Roberta, and the three of them led Grayce to the sofa and spent the next few minutes arranging her amid pillows and quilts until some degree of comfort had been achieved.

"I know it's a dumb question, Ma, but how do you feel?" Carole Ann said, still bending low over her mother, searching the battered face for signs of familiarity.

"I remember a saying my father had," Grayce began, then grimaced and shifted around until she found a more comfortable position. "Whenever he got over feeling really bad, he'd always say, 'First I was afraid I was gonna die, then I was afraid I wasn't.' That's how I feel. That and hungry, which I suppose is a positive sign. If the fact that I'm not dying, therefore ending this misery, is positive."

"It is, Ma. Trust me," Carole Ann said dryly. Then, in a different, more hesitant tone, she said, "I've got to call Mitch, Ma, and tell him what happened."

"No!" The word exploded from Grayce's cracked and swollen lips and she winced in pain, but continued talking with more force than she should have been able to muster. "They're on a vacation, C.A. You know that. They're in Paris."

Carole Ann sighed. "I know that, Ma. I also know my big brother and he'll be furious when he finds out you were hurt and nobody told him."

"Leave your brother to me. I'll tell him when I'm ready," Grayce said, indicating that the discussion was over.

"Fine," Carole Ann said, barely concealing her irritation with her mother. "What kind of soup do you want?"

"Don't want soup at all," Grayce replied, demonstrating the health and well-being of her cantankerous streak. "I want rice."

"You can't chew rice," Carole Ann, Angie, and Roberta replied in unison, and they all jumped in unison at the sound of a knock on the front door.

They looked at one another, communally dreading the possibility of a return visit by the police, but each aware in some level of her consciousness that the knock on the door was too polite for the police. Carole Ann draped herself protectively over the back of the couch, an arm across her mother's shoulders. Angie stood in front of them. Roberta trudged to the front door as if to the gallows.

"Who is it?" she asked, all but snarling, and a wary surprise flooded her face at the response that none but she could hear. "From where?" she asked the door, suspicion heavy in her voice. And the reply brought a grin to her face as she released the three locks and swung open the door.

Carole Ann leapt to her feet and ran to the door. Tommy Griffin caught her up and swung her around before she recovered her composure. "Put me down, Fish," she growled at him, after she kissed him on the cheek. Then she stepped away from him and into Warren Forchette's embrace. They held each other for a long moment before she stepped away from him, too. "What are you two doing here?" she asked.

"Jake sent us," they answered together, and both shrugged as if to indicate the implied sufficiency of the response. Then Warren moved quickly toward Grayce and knelt before her.

"Aunt Grayce," he said, and took her hands.

"Warren," she said to him, and smiled. "You don't know how good this is for my spirit. I just might live after all."

"No doubt about it," Warren replied with a big grin. "Just wait 'til you see what all Tante Sadie sent to cure you!"

Then everybody began to speak at once. And to laugh. It felt and sounded like a party. Joy was in the room. Or perhaps it was only the absence of fear. Or perhaps the one was the definition of the other. Carole Ann introduced Tommy and Warren to Grayce and Angie and Roberta, even though they all knew of one another from Carole Ann's stories; and because they knew of one another, they thought they knew one another, and behaved accordingly. They hugged and kissed like long-lost cousins. Roberta, mother to four daughters and mother-in-law to their husbands, hung on to Tommy's arm as if he were the son she somehow misplaced years ago and just found. Angie looked from Tommy to Warren—looked up at them, for both towered over her—as if they were rare and ancient treasures.

They filled all the spaces in the house that, prior to their arrival, had seemed quite spacious. They both were large men, though different in their largeness. Twenty-six-year-old Tommy Griffin was six-foot-three and two hundred pounds of muscle. He was a happy man—exuberant and effusive and spilling over with good humor and goodwill. Warren Forchette was fifteen years older, two inches shorter, and twenty pounds lighter than his comrade. He was an introspective man, quiet and dignified, but not without humor and his own brand of quiet joy. He listened more than he talked. His clean-shaven head and silver-rimmed eyeglasses gave him the look of a peaceful—though powerful—Gandhi.

Carole Ann was so relieved and grateful to see them that she almost forgot to feign irritation at Jake for sending them. She allowed herself to be fully embraced by the swirl of delight circulating about her, aware that her mother seemed to be feeling no pain; that Angie seemed to be relieved of her mantle of sadness; that Bert seemed relaxed and at ease.

Carole Ann busied herself in the kitchen, aided at one time or another by everyone present except her mother. When finally they ate, the feast was a wonderfully palatable sampling of the refrigerator, freezer, and pantry: pasta and rice, chicken and tofu, carrot soup and spinach soufflé and collard greens and salad, sourdough bread and cornbread, and fresh fruit and yogurt and cheese. They drank red wine and white, and iced tea and lemonade. Carole Ann equated her feeling at this gathering with her feelings at the party last year in Louisiana that Warren and his family had for her, the party at which it was discovered that Carole Ann's grandfather—Grayce's father—was Warren's father's uncle. And understanding dawned: her place was with people she loved and who loved her. Wherever those people were—D.C., L.A., New Orleans, Atlanta. Place didn't matter. People did. Love did.

The rightness of her feeling was confirmed when, just as they had during the preparation of the meal, everyone shared in the preparation of the healing potions and tonics Tante Sadie sent from Louisiana to cure Grayce. Sadie Cord was Warren Forchette's great-aunt and somewhere between seventy and ninety years old; Carole

Ann didn't know and knew better than to ask. Not that it mattered. What did matter was that the old woman knew about healing body, mind, and spirit.

Carole Ann recalled in vivid detail the two weeks she spent in bed healing from the aftermath of having solved Al's murder: from the physical beating she'd taken from Leland Devereaux; from the mental and emotional anguish of losing her husband; from the spiritual devastation wrought by the entire experience. It was Tante Sadie who had made her body whole again, and offered as yet underutilized tools for healing her battered spirit.

Finally, when it was well past midnight, Grayce, who'd been bathed in a Tante Sadie potion, was drowsy enough to fall asleep, and the rest of them, Carole Ann included, were relaxed enough to think sleep possible. Roberta, who had the largest house, offered lodging to both Tommy and Warren, and only Carole Ann witnessed and read the look the two men exchanged before Tommy accepted the offer and Warren gracefully declined it.

"I'll bunk here on the couch. Tante Sadie made me promise to give Aunt Grayce a cup of this tea every two hours, and she'll have my head if I fail." He grinned when he said it, and Carole Ann knew it to be the truth. She knew also that he remained because he needed to talk to her. Jake would have sent her information and instructions and Warren, because he was a lawyer, would be the conduit. Also, by remaining close to Grayce, he'd be close to Carole Ann and Angie. Tommy, the ex-cop and current security specialist and "muscle," would be Roberta's protector . . . and Luisa's.

Carole Ann shivered. She hadn't thought of Luisa in several hours and the sudden acknowledgment of the woman's day-long absence inspired a chilling discomfort. Something about Luisa was very wrong, Carole Ann was certain. She considered the possibility that the grandson was holding her hostage, and had only partially convinced herself of the absurdity of such speculation when she realized that Tommy had been speaking to her and that she hadn't heard him.

"I'm sorry, Fish. My mind was wandering."

"Yeah, and what else is new?" he growled at her in a most uncharitable fashion.

"That's not fair!" she exclaimed, truly wounded.

"Whatever," he said, dismissively and defensively, and she understood that she had wounded him.

"Fish," Carole Ann said, taking his arm and walking to the door with him, away from the crowd, "I'm sorry I wasn't listening. I was thinking about Luisa. Worrying, really."

He put an arm around her and his handsome features scrunched into a frown. "Me, too. Why isn't she here? I thought you said your mom and her three pals were the glue sisters."

Carole Ann giggled and squeezed his arm and gave him an abbreviated version of the grandson story, which creased his facial features even more deeply.

"I don't like the sound of that worth a damn," he said, and then quickly changed the subject. "Jake says we gotta get your computer and discs and files out of that car trunk ASAP. Where can we go at daybreak that won't arouse suspicion?"

"Jogging, then to the gym for a workout," Carole Ann answered without hesitation.

"Good. See you at seven," he said, and planted a kiss on the top of her head. "That's from Valerie," he said almost shyly. "She said she misses you and to hurry home."

Carole Ann hugged him tightly, not trusting herself to speak. Jake was right. Damn him! Jake always was right. It didn't matter where she was. What mattered were the people in her life.

**By the time** she'd been listening to him for the better part of an hour, Warren Forchette had frozen all her warm, fuzzy feelings. It was almost two o'clock in the morning, she was meeting Tommy at seven, and here was Warren explaining to her in crystal-clear legalese why her actions of the previous night were indefensible.

"I take one look at Aunt Grayce and know I would have done exactly what you did. I think of my own mother, of my sister, of Tante Sadie, and know that I would kill without hesitation to protect them. I look at the fact, however, that you deliberately, intentionally, and with forethought, determined not only to conceal your crime, but to tamper with the crime scene and the evidence."

"Dammit, Warren, I explained to you—"

"I know what you said, C.A.! And I understand what you were thinking and feeling. What I'm trying to get you to see is that we're capsized in the bayou and the gators are aroused."

"So now I'm fish bait," she snarled at him, and only just caught his suppressed grin and chuckle. That he could find humor in her situation worried her, frightened her, and upset her very delicate equilibrium. She began to shake, to shiver, suddenly freezing, and she could not stop. She wrapped her arms around herself and compressed her lips to quell their quivering.

Warren jumped up from his almost horizontal position on the floor and grabbed her into a tight, warming embrace. She resisted initially, tried to pull away. But he held on and after a few moments, she ceased her struggle. She released into him and lost sense of time and place, though she remained very aware of the thudding of her heart and the shaking of her body. He held her without speaking until her body calmed itself.

"I . . . I'm sorry."

"For what?" he snorted, amazement full in his tone. "For not having taken the time to grieve?"

She backed out of his embrace and rapidly rubbed her hands together, aware that she really was cold. "What on earth are you talking about, Warren? Grieve?" She made no effort or attempt to disguise the contempt in her voice. "I'm exhausted and I'm cold."

"You're emotionally distraught, C.A., and you're feeling the effects of not having grieved for your husband."

"Oh, shut up, Warren! You don't know what you're talking about! All I've done for the last thirteen months is grieve!"

He took a deep breath and measured the weight and space of his words. "What you've done, C.A., is mourn, and you haven't done that consistently. Two months after Al's murder you were in New Orleans looking for his killer. In the process, you took the kind of beating some people don't ever recover from. In fact, you almost didn't."

"Stop it! The truth is painful enough without embellishment."

"The truth is, you almost died. Why do you think Tante Sadie sat by your bed for forty-eight consecutive hours?" He was standing looking out the window, his back to her, his hands stuffed into his pockets. "Then there was the media fallout after Leland and Larry were arrested. Then it was Thanksgiving, Christmas, and the New Year, time you spent in airports, running from your mother's house to your brother's house to Dave's house to Lil's house. And now here you are, a year after Al's death, in the middle of another traumatic situation—you saved your mother from being beaten to death—and you haven't dealt with the first trauma yet. You're on the verge of collapse, C.A."

"And how do you know so much about it?" she asked him, feeling that he really did know something that she didn't.

"I've been there," he said.

"So," she said with studied nonchalance, "tell me all about it and then I'll be as cool as you, Mr. Cucumber."

He raised an eyebrow at her—she'd never seen him do that and was quite impressed—and lowered his already basso profundo into even lower reaches. "Tell you for free what it cost me three years and enough in therapists' fees to buy a new fishing boat? Not a chance, kiddo," he said. Then he grinned at her. "Oh, all right. I'll tell you one little thing. And it's this: Grieving is a process. Doesn't happen all at once. Sometimes, you don't even know it's happening. But it's like negotiating a minefield. Some days you blow your ass to Kingdom Come, and some days you tiptoe through the tulips."

Strangely enough, his silliness lightened her mood. "So, Counselor, what am I gonna do?"

"See a therapist," he said, so surprised that she laughed at him.

"About my legal, criminal predicament, Warren, not my emotional one," she said.

"Oh. That. We're gonna throw ourselves on the mercy of the best criminal defense attorney on the West Coast," he said, and stifled a yawn. "Do you know Addie Allen?"

Carole Ann shook her head.

"Well, she's the West Coast version of you, only meaner."

"I'm not mean!"

"The hell you're not," Warren said matter-of-factly. "But she makes you look like the tooth fairy." And he told her everything he knew about Adelaide Allen, his classmate at Howard University Law School, which was considerable. And formidable.

"I don't think I want to meet this woman," Carole Ann said almost meekly.

"You're gonna do more than meet her," Warren said, this time not bothering to stifle the yawn. "You're gonna hire her." And he kicked off his shoes, removed his shirt, lay down on the couch, pulled the blanket over him, and fell deeply asleep.

# ⌇ *t e n* ⌇

Tommy was comfortably at ease behind the wheel of the silver Benz. He'd adjusted the seat and the mirrors; had inserted a compact disc into the player (he'd brought his CD carrying case because he just *knew,* he said, this car would have a CD player); had donned his designer sunglasses and studied himself in the mirror; and had studied the map so he wouldn't need to rely on Carole Ann for directions. He drove quickly and surely out of the Jacaranda Estates front gate, showing only the slightest interest in the activity on the playground.

He glanced frequently into the rearview and side-view mirrors but it wasn't until he powered the car forward onto the freeway that he announced, nonchalantly, that they were being followed.

"Don't turn around, C.A.!" he snapped, even as she caught herself just before making such a silly error.

"Who do you think it is?" she asked.

He raised his eyes to the rearview mirror again. "Cops," he said, a little dryly, she thought, knowing that he still smarted at having been dismissed from the D.C. police department. "It's a decent tail job. You probably wouldn't have picked it up," he said casually, then glanced sideways at her to receive the evil eye he knew would be directed at him. And he laughed when she obliged.

"What should we do?" Carole Ann asked, fighting off the urge to turn around and search out who was following them.

Tommy shrugged. "Nothing we can do. This isn't TV, C.A., where you make one-hundred-eighty-degree turns on the expressway to lose a tail. We'd just get a ticket. Besides," he said, slightly increasing the volume to the Marvin Gaye tune in the CD player, "I don't care if they know where we're going. But I sure as hell would like to know *why* they're on us."

They rode in silence briefly before discussing how they would transfer Carole Ann's files and computer into the empty gym bags they'd tossed into the trunk for that purpose, then Tommy used the remainder of the crosstown drive to explain the inexplicable: why he and Jake believed that the L.A. police department was working some kind of undercover operation at Jacaranda Estates.

"That's the only plausible explanation for them ignoring serial homicides," he said.

"There can be no plausible explanation for ignoring serial homicides, Tommy," Carole Ann said dryly. "And you can tell Jake Graham I said so."

She felt him stiffen beside her. "You may not like it, C.A., but there can be lots of explanations, plausible or not. What's not acceptable," he said, raising a hand to halt the objection she was preparing, "what's not acceptable is the failure to protect the people. That means, Jake says, that whoever is running the undercover op is doing it half-assed. Either it's off the books or it's so secret that nobody can be trusted to know about it."

Carole Ann frowned. "What could be that secret?" she asked, her imagination failing to conjure up a top-secret or undercover operation with Jacaranda Estates as its location.

"Jake came up with a couple of possibilities, but they don't really fit the scenery." And after she listened to him talk about gun running and drug smuggling and fencing stolen property, and sounding so much like Jake she had to keep sneaking sideways glances at him to make sure it was Tommy, she was more wary than before.

"Jake really thinks something like that is going on here?"

Tommy nodded. "He says it's the only explanation for the LAPD to look so shaky. You know Jake. The last thing he wants to hear is that the police department is corrupt."

She nodded. She knew Jake didn't miss the stress of being a cop; but she also knew that he'd forever be a cop in his heart. "Let's play out one of his scenarios. How would it work?"

"The crime itself wouldn't happen there, if that's what you're thinking," Tommy said, looking in his mirrors and shifting lanes. "In the case of gun running, for instance, there'd be some upstanding resident of Jacaranda Estates who would go to work, go to church, go shopping—all as usual. Be pleasant to the neighbors. Walk his dog. Whatever. All the while stockpiling weapons stolen from military bases. Until it was time to deliver. Then he'd back a truck up to the door late one night, load all the guns under cover of darkness, and off he'd go."

"And the undercover cops, who'd been watching and waiting for this night, would spring their trap," C.A. reasoned.

"You got it," Tommy agreed. "And those undercover cops who were waiting for this night would dare anybody or anything to get in their way. This location would be hands off. Do you know how much time and work go into setting up an operation like that?"

"But logistically, something like that could never work at Jacaranda Estates," Carole Ann said.

"Right," Tommy said with a terse nod. "Same thing with fencing: no way to get the merchandise in and out without notice. And a drug smuggler would be too noticeable."

"Let's suppose, though," she said slowly, forcing her thoughts to slow their pace, "that there is some kind of an undercover operation under way. Wouldn't a couple of murders make somebody nervous enough to shut it down—even for a short while—and at least pay lip service to an investigation of those crimes?"

"In Brentwood or Bel Air or Beverly Hills, yeah," he said, with a coldness of tone that chilled her. "But not in Jacaranda Estates."

Carole Ann rode the remainder of the way to Venice Beach in empty silence, unwilling still to confront the truth that she had been avoiding for weeks: that her mother and the other Jacaranda Estates residents were twice victims—of the violence that was destroying their community, and of a system that denigrated them for the color of their skin and their lack of material wealth.

While she ran beside the Pacific Ocean in the early-morning chill and fog, she assessed her agreement with Jake that the only possible explanation for the casual attitude of the LAPD was that a task force investigation would ruin an established undercover operation. She could even imagine that Jacaranda Estates would be a perfect location to conceal a crime of some kind, and for a secret police surveillance. The question was, what kind of crime? And how important could it be that the police would allow citizens to believe that their safety was being ignored?

**Carole Ann** was tense, edgy, and distant when she and Warren arrived at Addie Allen's office later that afternoon, and only noticing that the two gym bags that she and Tommy had left with Robbie at the gym—the bags containing her computer and files—now resided on the floor in a corner of the lawyer's cramped and cluttered office, helped her ease out of what she knew was an unnecessarily bad attitude. She, of all people, knew that meeting one's attorney for the first time in a combative frame of mind could only be disastrous.

Because she thought she'd had no preconceived notions of what to expect, Carole Ann was shocked at how surprised she was to discover that Addie Allen was tiny when the lawyer came from behind her massive desk to greet her newest client. Barely five feet tall, no more than one hundred pounds, she was dressed exactly like a friend of Warren's would be dressed—in baggy, faded jeans, a white tee shirt beneath a crisp, starched white oxford shirt, and white sneakers. Large, black-framed glasses dwarfed her tiny face, and Carole Ann expected that they were a prop, a shield, a defense. And a mechanism to make her appear older, for she wore her silver-streaked hair in a long ponytail that cascaded down her back, and without the props—the desk and the glasses—she'd look like a kid pretending to be grown up. There also was something vaguely familiar about her, Carole Ann felt. Nothing tangible. Just . . . familiar.

The two women shook hands and Addie Allen resumed her position in the chair behind her desk, opened a yellow legal pad, and looked expectantly at Carole Ann, who was annoyed to find herself nervous. She sank down onto the sofa next to Warren. He touched her arm gently, then pulled away. Carole Ann could feel him retreat, leaving her alone with the woman who was her attorney. With the woman who was meaner than herself. She began talking.

Addie wrote and listened for as long as Carole Ann talked, which was for almost an hour. She then asked three simple, blunt questions about the fatal fight and her responses, and Carole Ann thought, without the slightest rancor, *She's better than I am.*

"I'm sure I don't tell you anything you don't already know when I say, Miss Gibson, that our challenge is to retain your license to practice law in California. I'm not worried, nor should you be, about any lasting criminal charges or penalties, though the short-term repercussions of your actions will be a pain in the ass to deal with. But the bar association here, like bar associations everywhere, prides itself on having and following its own lead."

She paused and fixed Carole Ann in a penetrating stare, one as intimidating as her own, and Carole Ann almost blinked. "I'm honored to have you as a client, Miss Gibson. But let there be no misunderstanding: you are the client. If we're going to work together, we do it my way. Understood and agreed?"

Carole Ann did blink now. And inhaled deeply as reality set in. She was the client and Addie Allen was her lawyer. The other woman eyed her steadily, her face as impassive and expressionless as a granite carving, and her body as still.

"Yes," Carole Ann replied finally. "On both counts." And she heard Warren exhale.

"This is a lot of shit to carry all at one time, I know that," Addie Allen said, and Carole Ann, for the first time, heard the South in her voice. "But I don't figure you for the bending or breaking kind."

Carole Ann shook her head ruefully and managed a sideways grin. "I've learned quite a bit about bending in the last year or so, but you're right. I don't break."

"Good, 'cause we got a lotta work to do. Decisions to make. Strategy to devise."

Carole Ann nodded and felt a pang of something—loss? regret?—because someone other than herself was in control, was managing a case that were it not her own, she'd love to be managing.

". . . when and how we're gonna turn you in," Addie was saying, and Carole Ann realized she'd missed something salient, though she'd heard enough to intuit the intent.

"Can you buy me another forty-eight hours?" Carole Ann asked, and explained that she wanted to find and talk to Arthur Jennings. "There's something about the history of Jacaranda Estates that's related to what's happening today and I need to know what it is," she said, not needing to add that when she turned herself in, she risked her passport and her freedom to travel outside Los Angeles County.

They talked among themselves for another quarter of an hour until, Carole Ann noticed, Addie stole a glance at the clock on the bookcase across the room. Understanding fully the implications, Carole Ann reached into her purse for her checkbook.

"Already done, C.A.," Warren said, shaking his head.

"What's already done?" Carole Ann asked, frowning.

"Jake hired Addie. Or rather, his company did. You're a client of Graham Investigative Services, and Addie is its attorney, ergo, Addie is your attorney."

Carole Ann stifled her annoyance at losing control of yet another facet of her life, but capped her protest, shrugged, and raised her palms and eyes to the ceiling. Then she laughed out loud, aware that suddenly she felt like the "heavy load of shit" had been lifted, or perhaps merely lightened. "Where are you from?" she asked her attorney.

"North Carolina," Addie Allen said softly. "Up in the Smoky Mountains, near the reservation. You should visit if you haven't," she said, longing heavy in her voice.

"I haven't and I will," Carole Ann said, and meant it, realizing that the familiarity she'd first noticed in Addie Allen was that she reminded Carole Ann of Robbie and Millie: Addie was a mutt. Part Native and part Black and part something else Carole Ann couldn't identify; but the woman clearly was all advocate, and that inspired within Carole Ann a level of trust and confidence that surprised her. Not only had she learned in the last year to bend, but she'd learned to trust. Both sensations were new enough that she was not yet proficient at them—her bending sometimes felt like breaking, and trusting was terrifying—but both were preferable to standing alone.

**"Not bad,"** Warren said, wiping his fingers on a napkin, and Carole Ann knew that it was a major compliment to the meal, coming as it did from a Louisiana native and epicure. "I think this is only the second time I've eaten Pacific Ocean fish, but it could stop me being such a Gulf Coast snob."

"I doubt it," Carole Ann said dryly, and they both laughed, grateful for the levity.

Carole Ann was recovering from the news that Warren was leaving town on a flight in three hours. He'd not revealed his plans, he said, until he was certain that she would accept Addie as her counsel. "And what if I hadn't?" she'd growled at him. "Would you have postponed your trial to hang around out here babysitting me?"

"Yes," he'd responded simply, quietly, and she'd felt like an idiot for being unpleasant.

"Thank you, Warren. Thank you and Jake and Tommy. This is a hell of a mess I'm in. But even if I get cleared, I'm not certain we'll have all the answers to all the questions." And that was the really scary component. They had no better idea, after several extensive brainstorming sessions between Addie and Jake and Tommy, after all of them compared notes and ideas and theories, what the hell was out of whack in Jacaranda Estates; only that something definitely was. Four people were dead and a fifth, Mrs. Asmara, still lingering in a coma, would be better off dead. And the LAPD, it seemed, knew who was responsible for two of the deaths. And perhaps even why.

"Call me when you get to Anguilla," Warren said.

"Oh, not you, too!"

"Oh, not me, too, what?"

Carole Ann rolled her eyes at the ceiling and sucked in her breath. "First Jake, then Tommy, now you, making me report in like a kid. Or a criminal on parole." She stopped herself midsentence and giggled. She *was* a criminal, one who'd be lucky to be on parole. "I'll call as soon as I can, Warren."

Carole Ann had given Jake the information that Jennings lived in Anguilla and it had taken him exactly an hour to produce an address and telephone number. Carole Ann had called and been so warmly greeted by the sound of an old man's voice that she almost felt guilty about her mission; for she felt very strongly that what she needed to ask Arthur Jennings, and what she needed to tell him, would destroy his peace. Arthur Jennings remembered her—as a small child, in his words—and remembered her mother and his "dear friend" Roberta. "Come right away," he'd said, not bothering to ask why she wanted to see him. Carole Ann, as a result, was leaving on a 6:00 A.M. flight to Miami.

Which gave her time tonight for hurried visits with two longtime residents, especially since Warren had adamantly refused her offer to drive him to the airport, and for a lengthy brain-picking session with Tommy.

Nobody had lived at Jacaranda Estates as long as Grayce and Angie and Bert and Luisa, but Mrs. Philpot had been there long enough to know some of the ancient history, and Mr. Grimes was a big enough gossip to know almost as much as someone who'd been around a long time. He also was a good gossip, the kind who asked for and retained the minutiae of situations and circumstances. And since Mrs. Philpot lived across the street from Luisa, that would provide Carole Ann with the casual opportunity to pop in on the both of them without needing cause or reason. Mrs. Philpot also had been so genuinely moved by the fact that Carole Ann remembered her that the old woman no doubt would receive her at midnight or at dawn had she appeared at those hours.

She could tell from twenty yards away that Luisa's house still was empty, but she knocked anyway. Before she could decide whether or not to jiggle the door handle and peek into any of the windows, she was hailed from across the street. She received from Mrs. Philpot the information that Luisa, indeed, was not at home, along with the desired invitation to "come visit with me for a little while." Since pumping people for information was Carole Ann's job, she didn't feel the slightest guilt at settling herself on the woman's living room couch, crossing her legs, and getting down to business.

Yes, indeed, Mrs. Philpot certainly remembered Mr. Jennings. Mr. Jamilla, too. Nice, polite gentlemen the both of them. And Carole Ann listened to her reminisce for a while about "Mr. J" and "Señor J," as she called them with a chuckle. She also remembered the trouble stirred up after Mr. Jamilla died but she "paid that kind of foolishness no mind. There's always people who want something for nothing. And it wasn't like the man didn't provide for his family. Left 'em more'n a million dollars. But it was Mr. Jennings worked side by side with 'im, and it was Mr. Jennings deserved to get back the other 'J' of J and J Contracting." Mrs. Philpot was on a roll, fueled by the righteous indignation of the frequently correct.

She shook her head vehemently at the mention of *Dame Que Es Mío*. "I want what's mine, too," she said with a snort. "You find anybody willing to give back what they stole from poor people, you make sure you call me! I wanna be in that payback line!"

Carole Ann grinned and was about to stand up and take her leave when the old woman's dry humor changed shape and became real, sharp-edged anger. "And that fool across the street! Got the nerve to be using something as serious as payback for past wrongs to cover up his drug smuggling!" She snorted and tossed her head and crossed her arms across her ample bosom and her eyes flashed fire. "Runnin' back and forth down there to Mexico doin' his dirty deeds. He's gonna get his grandma locked up is what's gonna happen, 'cause I don't believe she understands what he's up to."

"Ah, who, Mrs. Philpot?" Carole Ann realized that she'd lost track of the conversation.

"That Nunez fool! If it weren't for the fact that I feel so sorry for his grandma, I'd call the police on him myself. Not that *that* would do a whole lot of good, the way they treat us." She was revved up and ready to roll again when Carole Ann stopped her with a raised hand.

"You're moving too fast for me. Are you referring to Luisa and her grandson? Ricky?"

She nodded emphatically. "That's exactly who I'm referring to," she said with a self-satisfied sniff, barely aware that she'd imitated Carole Ann's precise language. "But then, no reason she should be able to control *him*. She was never able to control his daddy, or those other boys."

"What was that you said about Mexico and drugs? I missed that part," Carole Ann said slowly, hoping to get the whole story from Mrs. Philpot.

It worked. The old woman sighed deeply, then inhaled deeply. "The grandson. Ricky. He runs back and forth to Mexico like he's some kind of diplomat or ambassador. Here's a boy with no education and no job but always got a shiny car and a pocket full of money. Plus, he beats up on his grandma. You think he's not smuggling drugs?"

Carole Ann didn't know what to think and said as much. She wondered whether Grayce and Angie and Bert knew about Ricky's trips, then wondered how Mrs. Philpot knew. "How do you know he's going to Mexico, Mrs. Philpot?"

She cocked her head to the right, toward the wall. "Mrs. Del Valle. She's my next-door neighbor. You probably don't know her, she's only lived here seven or eight years. But she's from Mexico, born down there, and she has a girl about that Ricky's age and he's always trying to get next to her but Mrs. Del Valle just slams the door in his face. Her daughter goes to college and she don't have time to fool around with the likes of Ricky Nunez. Anyway, he tells Blanca—that's Mrs. Del Valle's daughter—about his trips, always trying to impress her. And he gives her presents. Gold and silver jewelry and a TV one time. Mrs. Del Valle made her give it right back! But anyway, she told me herself this time. Asked me to keep an eye on the house—"

Carole Ann's raised hand stopped the flow from Mrs. Philpot's mouth. "Who told you what 'this time'?"

"Mrs. Nunez. Luisa. She went with him this time. That's what I was trying to tell you. And she asked me to keep an eye out for things. That's how I saw you . . ."

Carole Ann didn't try to follow Mrs. Philpot's stream of consciousness monologue and didn't try to halt it. She could only think that Luisa was in Mexico and that none of them had known it.

When had she left? She interjected the question and Mrs. Philpot answered it without taking a breath: three days ago. The day after the attack on Grayce. Carole Ann recalled Luisa's bizarre behavior that night, the way she sat almost catatonic, staring into space. They'd attributed her behavior to shock at what had happened. But the more she thought about it, the more Carole Ann realized that Luisa's response that night had nothing to do with Grayce. Her absence the following day was proof of that. And now she was in Mexico.

Carole Ann stood up. She really did need to leave if she was to see Mr. Grimes. And she needed to think. Quietly. She asked Mrs. Philpot for Mr. Grimes's exact address and Mrs. Philpot gave it to her and described the house in detail, including the fact that the mailbox listed slightly because Mrs. Grimes backed into it last week. "But they're not home," she said finally, after all that. "They're in Las Vegas. They go the third weekend of every month. They win, too!"

It was just as well, Carole Ann thought. She didn't think she possessed the mental strength to process any more information, especially if it contained more surprises. She felt true shock at learning that Luisa was in Mexico. Shock tinged with worry and a creeping unease. She was wondering whether or not to tell her mother when she noticed Jennifer Johnson's silver 2002 was parked at the curb. The driver's side door opened as C.A. approached, and the young reporter got out and walked toward her.

"Hi, Jennifer," C.A. called out in greeting.

"Hi, Miss Gibson," Jennifer replied, in a subdued, almost shy tone.

"Why are you sitting in the car? Isn't my mother at home?" She hadn't considered that possibility until now and it worried her.

Jennifer seemed to read her worry for she held up her hand. "Your mother's home, Miss Gibson. And her friends are with her."

"Thanks. And it's C.A., OK?"

Jennifer offered a rueful smile and shake of her head. "I looked you up," she said, and shook her head again. "I guess I do need you more than you need me."

Carole Ann had forgotten their earlier confrontation and now dismissed its revival with a wave of her hand. "No time for that, Jennifer. We need each other. As equals. How about we go to Espresso Express and share some information."

**Jacob Graham** looked out into the Washington, D.C., night and saw too many shadows. He'd purchased a block-long, dilapidated warehouse in an inconvenient and unposh section of town to house his investigative business. Partially because the price was right; partially because the area was isolated; and largely because of his plan, now realized, to construct a private patio on the roof of the main building where he could sit alone with his thoughts. Tonight was clear, with a sky full of moon and stars. But he saw shadows.

Much about the situation in Los Angeles annoyed him: that his client and friend was in bigger trouble than she ever would admit; that Tommy Griffin had too much for one operative to do; that he hadn't yet established a reciprocal relationship with a Los Angeles agency; that Los Angeles was so damn far away. But annoyances rarely became problems, and so Jake shrugged off the minor stuff to focus clearly and completely on the two aspects of the L.A. situation that really worried him: the LAPD and Luisa Whatever-her-name-was.

Jake was a cop even though he no longer wore a badge or collected a paycheck from the D.C. police department. He'd done that for twenty-six years—almost half his life—and still would be doing that had not a bullet in the back last year forced his resignation. And, in truth, Jake was grateful for and happy with his new life; and he was downright giddy about the money he was making. For the first time ever, he was able to buy really fine gifts for his wife, and that pleased him. To be able to do it, and to witness her enjoyment.

Also, for the first time, he was able to live a normal married life: to be able to have coffee with his wife every morning, and to be able to actually see her awake every night—even to be able to share dinner with her several nights a week. In the almost twenty-five years they'd been married, he'd never before done those things on a regular basis. Not that she'd ever complained; he'd been a cop when they married, and she had understood what that meant. But to see and feel her joy at having him present in her life, it was worth the bullet that had paralyzed him for nine months. He didn't miss the badge. But no matter what changes he'd gone through, Jake Graham still felt like a cop and still found it excruciating to think about dirty cops.

Still, he knew there was something or somebody dirty in L.A. and the evidence was pointing at the cops and it didn't matter whether Jake liked it or not.

"Shit," he muttered, and stood up. He strolled to the railing that encircled and enclosed the roof-top deck, leaned on it, and looked down. He counted ten vehicles in the parking lot, including his own. Eight of them, he knew, would be there overnight, and as he was watching, one of the computer experts crossed the lot, got into some round-looking car that looked like every other round-looking car on the road, and drove slowly to the end of the lot. Jake watched as an arm protruded from the car and inserted the security card into the metal box. After three seconds, the gate slid silently open and the car drove away, faster now, though not fast enough to be out of sight before the gate slid closed and locked. "Shit," he said again, and returned to his seat and to his thoughts.

Luisa Whatever's disappearance bugged him almost as much as the thought of dirty cops. It was Jake's experience that "normal" people didn't vary the routine of their lives unless there was a reason. "Normal" people, to Jake, were people who weren't criminals, people who had a rhythm and a pattern to their lives. For Luisa to abandon her best friends during a crisis was abnormal. If C.A. was right and the grandson was holding the woman hostage, Jake could simply send Tommy to kick the little punk's ass and that would be the end of that. But Jake didn't think it was anything so wonderfully simple. Nobody did. That's why he was paying a small fortune to a lawyer he didn't even know named Addie Allen. That's why Warren Forchette walked away from an impending trial on a moment's notice. That's why Tommy Griffin was playing boys in the 'hood in west L.A.—as dangerous an undertaking as anything Jake could imagine, and more dangerous than young Tommy knew. That's why Carole Ann soon would be on a plane bound for the Caribbean to see a man she didn't remember knowing. There was nothing simple about any of this and Jake Graham didn't like it a damn bit.

# ❦ *eleven* ❧

Tommy Griffin didn't like it that he was limited to being the guardian and protector of Grayce Gibson, Roberta Lawson, and Angie Arroyo. Not that he resented watching out for them. He genuinely liked each of them and gladly would defend them to the limits of his abilities. What he resented was being limited to that function, even if it was only until Carole Ann returned from Anguilla in two days. Jake had been adamant on that point. But there was more Tommy wanted to do; more he could do in forty-eight hours. Like rid the playground of the thugs . . . if they *were* thugs. C.A. had told him no one had seen any drug dealing or other obvious illegal activity taking place on the playground.

So if those gang-banger look-alikes weren't dealing, what were they doing? He'd seen them and his split-second assessment was that he'd seen tougher in his time. Tommy had grown up in a neighborhood in Washington, D.C., that now had the reputation of being not only one of the worst places in that city, but of being one of the worst and most dangerous places in any city. But it had not always been so. When he was growing up, the neighborhood was typical of any working-class neighborhood: the houses and apartment buildings were small and unostentatious but clean and well maintained; most of the men worked two jobs and a good number of the women were homemakers; kids went to school, played sports, graduated from high school and joined the military (like Tommy himself) or got married. Then the thugs had taken over.

Tommy remembered explicitly and vividly that they'd begun by occupying the playground. Initially, many of the mothers had ignored their presence and attempted to utilize the equipment in spite of them. When that became too dangerous—for the women and for their children—community leaders complained, first to the police, and then to their elected officials. Those efforts brought no useful response. So, the people shrugged and turned to prayer. Within a year, the playground was completely destroyed. And the location had become a favored recreation area for drug dealers and users. Then the crime began in earnest—the burglarizing of homes, the stealing of cars, the purse snatchings, the armed robberies, the rapes, the murders. People who could afford to leave, left; those who could not leave barricaded themselves inside their homes, becoming simultaneously prisoners and victims.

Tommy had looked into Grayce Gibson's battered face, into the still defiant but weakening resolve in her eyes; he had studied the way Angelique Arroyo's quiet bravery was being eroded by fear, and how Roberta Lawson's ingrained pride was being forced to learn compromise; and he knew that one trip to the playground would make all of them, himself included, feel a world's worth of better. But he had been ordered to stay away from the playground. He couldn't even knock on Luisa Nunez's door and ask her what the hell was her problem.

"Dammit, Jake," he muttered to himself, "I can't just sit here!" And then he had a brilliant idea: Jake hadn't told him he couldn't go for a walk. At night. Late. In the direction of the playground. Just to see for himself if he shared C.A.'s and her reporter friend's suspicions about the activities on the playground.

♦ ♦ ♦

**Carole Ann** recalled her concern of just over twenty-four hours ago that her mission to Anguilla would prove disruptive and painful to the aged Arthur Jennings, and she marveled anew at what seemed to be a newly discovered facility for misreading cues and misunderstanding the obvious. She opened her eyes to find Arthur Jennings's age-clouded ones staring at her with concern.

"I hope you're not angry with me for dumping all this on you, young lady," he said.

"I'm extremely angry, Mr. Jennings, but not with you. Though I would be had I been in communication with you every day for the past thirty-five years and you'd said nothing of all this," Carole Ann replied bitterly.

He patted her hand and poured more coffee into her cup. "Then I beg you not to be too angry with your mother. Or with Roberta and the others. You know, our generation is different from yours. You young people discuss everything. We old-timers discuss nothing. We keep our own counsel."

Carole Ann looked out at the Caribbean Sea, well aware of the old man's implicit direction that she refrain from judging him, or her mother. The sea was a color of green that defied description and resisted all attempts at artificial simulation of its unique hue. She knew there were waves, yet the surface appeared as smooth as glass. She could feel the water's warmth from her vantage point on Arthur Jennings's terraced villa on a cliff above it, though deceptively close, and she longed to be in it, surrounded by it, soothed by it. She also wished that she liked Arthur Jennings less so that she could ignore his warning and sit in judgement of him and her mother and Bert and Angie. Damn them!

But within seconds after being met by the man at the island airstrip, Carole Ann understood why everything she'd read, heard, and learned of Arthur Jennings had been positive. He was a delight. Still tall, though slightly stooped, he retained the vigor of a man who had earned his living by using his body. What little hair he had remaining was white and wispy, as were his eyebrows, mustache, and a rakish goatee. He hugged Carole Ann as warmly as if she were a cherished friend, and immediately asked how Roberta and Grayce and Angie were. Carole Ann noticed that he did not inquire about Luisa, and assumed she'd learn the reason for the omission later.

Jennings drove an ancient but well-kept International Harvester, and he drove as if he were newly eighteen instead of nearing eighty. He talked the entire hour from the airport to his home, giving Carole Ann a fascinating and informative history of the island, revealing to her during the monologue that he initially moved his family to the island specifically to escape what had become for him an increasingly uncomfortable situation in Los Angeles. It was as easy to listen to the man as it was to like him, and the more she listened, the more she liked him. The anger flowed from her until she no longer felt the need to judge.

"I understand privacy, Mr. Jennings, and I respect it."

"But what, young lady?" he said, and patted her hand again.

"Secrecy . . ." she said, and could not complete the sentence or the thought that instigated it.

"Ummm, yes," he said slowly. "Secrets are different, no doubt about it. That's why I told you everything right off. I've been carrying the burden of these secrets for a long, long time and I guess I just got too old for all that weight. Besides," he added, a hint of humor in his voice, "you're the first person to ever ask me about any of that ancient history. So, I guess you had it coming."

"Thanks a lot," Carole Ann said dryly, and the old man rewarded her with an equally dry chuckle. Then he quickly sobered.

"Do you really think any of this old stuff has anything to do with what's going on there now?"

"It's the only thing that makes sense, sir," she said, "to the extent that any of it makes sense."

And what sense could be made of the things Arthur Jennings told her last night and this morning of Jacaranda Estates, the place she called home: a rape, a murder, and an almost race riot. What sense could be made of the fact that her mother and Roberta and Angelique and Luisa knew everything and had never hinted that there could be an underlying cause of the current mayhem and destruction? Unless, in actuality, there was no current connection to the past evil. And logic refused to allow Carole Ann to believe that. Bizarre as events were, past and present, there were sufficient similarities of theme to warrant a game of connect the dots.

"I wish you didn't have to leave so soon. I don't get many visitors these days, and I don't mind telling you I'm a little lonely," Jennings said quietly, looking and sounding very much like an old man. His wife was dead and his children were spread, literally, across the globe—one in Europe, one in Africa, one in New York, and one in L.A. And his grandchildren were equally widely dispersed. "Can't you stay another day?"

Carole Ann shook her head. She hadn't told him the full extent of her involvement in current events at Jacaranda, and she told him now and watched his eyes first grow wide in awe, then fill with horror, then narrow, and she couldn't read what was there, so she waited for him to tell her. It took a while. She watched him think and remember, saw him retreat into the past, and he seemed to age, to become fully all of his years in those few moments.

"I didn't tell you everything, either. I kept one secret. It was Enrique's secret, really, and after all this time, I didn't think anyone needed to know. He never wanted anyone to know. He was ashamed. . . ." The old man's voice, barely more than a whisper now, trailed off, and he rubbed his hands together as if for warmth, the sound reminding Carole Ann of the rustle of leaves against the sidewalk in winter. As his body slumped in the chair, she began to worry that she'd pushed too hard, too far.

She touched the old man's hands, stilling them. "I don't want to cause you any more distress than I already have, Mr. Jennings, and I'm truly sorry."

He gripped her hands with one of his, the strength of his grasp surprising. "You've got nothing to apologize for," he said almost harshly. "None of this is your fault."

He continued his grip on her hands but he said no more. She waited and felt his silence grow deeper. She imagined that he was remembering. Finally he released her hands and spoke so quietly that she had to lean closer to hear him. "I can't see how it can make a difference after all this time. It *can't* make a difference." That last was more a plea than a declaration of fact.

"It would help if I knew what it was, sir."

He shook his head. "Help who? Help what?" He shook his head again. "It's too late to help."

"All the secrets but one. You've told me all the secrets but one, Mr. Jennings." *Don't stop now!*

"Will you have to tell anybody? Who else will have to know these things?"

She thought for a moment, understanding that he meant would she need to tell her mother or Angie or Bert or Luisa. "My attorney will need to know everything that I know, Mr. Jennings. And if it can be proven that a current crime is a direct result of a past event, then perhaps the police."

He sighed. "Is it true what you see in the movies, that there's no time limit on murder?"

She frowned at him. "Are you referring to the statute of limitations?"

He nodded. "That's it! A murderer's never safe, is he?"

Carole Ann shivered in the heat and shook her head. What in the world was this old man harboring? "Please, Mr. Jennings. Tell me."

"Don't tell your mother," he said. "I don't care if you tell the lawyer or the police. But don't tell your mother and Roberta and Angelique. Promise me that!" He made it a demand.

She nodded. "I promise."

"Hector Nunez was his brother. Enrique's brother. That's why he was living at Jacaranda. A loud-mouthed, mean drunk with no job who beat his wife and kids. He's the one who did the rape. Him and a couple of his no-account drunk buddies." He was breathing hard and fast, too hard and too fast, Carole Ann thought, and she tried to stop him from talking for a moment so he could regain his breath, but he refused to be stopped. The words spilled from his mouth in torrents, freed after too long a confinement behind a wall of secrets. "They raped her because she was Black, and because she was . . . she was . . . they weren't just friends or roommates, you know what I mean?"

Carole Ann did not know but when she asked him what he meant, it seemed to confuse him. "Who were roommates, Mr. Jennings?"

"No!" he shouted at her. "*Not* roommates. More than that. More than that. Don't you understand?" he begged, now sounding more embarrassed than angry.

"Lovers?" Carole Ann asked. "You're speaking of two women who lived together as lovers?"

He sighed, caught his breath, nodded. "That kind of thing, back then . . ." He sighed again. "But we didn't care about that, Enrique and me. They were good women. They were the kind of people we wanted in Jacaranda. Better than that damn Hector and Luisa! And one was Black and one was Mexican. They were perfect. And so good. And so beautiful." He sighed again, and wiped away a tear from the corner of his eye before it could drip down his face. "I'll bet she's still beautiful and still good, isn't she?" he asked, his tone of voice making it a wish more than a question.

And when Carole Ann didn't respond immediately he turned to her, fear and worry competing for control of his features. "What's happened to her?"

Carole Ann consciously suppressed the wish that the old man had no more secrets to reveal; of course she wanted to know everything and for him to tell more than that, but she was becoming increasingly concerned about the effect on his health. She took his hands again and spoke gently. "I don't know who you mean, Mr. Jennings."

"Yes, you do!" he snapped. "Angelique, her name is. Angelique Arroyo."

Images of Angie danced through Carole Anne's mind and memory—beautiful, gentle, and, yes, good Angie. This woman she'd known for all but two years of her life. This woman she'd loved like a mother. This woman had survived a tragedy as horrendous as her own. She recalled Angie's words to her upon hearing of Al's murder: "I can't come to you, my little girl, because I would be no help to you. It's too much." And Carole Ann had hung up the phone too immersed in her own grief to wonder at the meaning of Angie's words. Now she understood. And with a start, Carole Ann recognized Angie's tragedy as worse than her own; for Al had been murdered, yes, but he had not been violated. Carole Ann tried to imagine the feeling of knowing that one's lover had been tormented in such a fashion, and her heart broke for Angie.

"Did she know, Mr. Jennings? Did Angie know what happened to her . . . what was her name, Mr. Jennings? The woman Angie loved, what was her name?"

"Dorothy was her name, but everyone called her Dottie. And yes, she knew what happened to her. Everyone knew. But she didn't know who did it. Enrique felt it was his duty to protect his brother." He paused and allowed Carole Ann's brief explosion of anger, then continued as if she hadn't spoke. "He knew it was wrong. I knew it was wrong. But we didn't think we had a choice. Everybody thought we were crazy anyway, building a community for middle-class Negroes and Mexicans. If word had gotten out that a woman was raped and murdered . . ."

He shuddered and pressed his temples with his fingers and gave Carole Ann a history lesson that made modern-day intolerance pale by comparison. Difficulties obtaining permits, permits lost, records of tax payments lost or destroyed, a racist attack on the ground-breaking ceremony that was thwarted at the last minute only by the threat that the Blacks and Mexicans were armed and would retaliate.

"You know why Angie lives next door to your mother? Because I asked your folks if they minded living next door to . . . to . . ."

"Lesbians," Carole Ann said, and the old man blushed and ducked his head.

"It was a different world back then. People like your folks were not the norm, I'm sorry to say."

"So my parents, my mother, knew—knows—that Angie is gay?" Recognition was dawning on Carole Ann in degrees. "Did she know that Luisa's husband . . ."

Arthur Jennings was shaking his head back and forth, faster and faster. "No, no, no. I told you. Nobody knew what he did but his wife, and even that wasn't enough to make her hate him, and God knows she had reason without that. The woman was a zombie then and I'll bet you good money she's still a zombie, walking around like she's in some kind of daze. Am I right?"

She couldn't reply. For the second time in less than a week someone had referred to Luisa in such negative terms, and what bothered Carole Ann was that both times the reference had caught her by surprise. How could she not have seen? Who was Luisa that she would accept the abuse of husband and son, and conceal a horrible truth from a cherished friend? Carole Ann had perceived Luisa as a little silly, perhaps—overreligious and unsophisticated. Not a zombie or a doormat. And not as cruel. But she must be to have withheld the secret of Dottie's murder for almost forty years.

"Do you know that Langston Hughes poem? All we were trying to do was build a temple for tomorrow. We wanted to leave something good and strong and true, something that reflected who we really are, not who they say we are. And now look what's happened. After all this time they've been proved correct."

He sagged, body and spirit. His eyes closed and his chin dropped to his chest and he took several deep breaths. Carole Ann opened her mouth to speak and he raised a hand to silence her; and with what she hoped wasn't obvious relief, she accepted Arthur Jennings's pronouncement that he was "finished talking about Jacaranda Estates and people and things and memories that hurt too much." She felt torn between wanting to hear and learn every scrap of every detail, and wanting to stop her ears, to stop hearing things that were destroying this place she'd called home.

The Caribbean Sea rescued her from herself. She spent her remaining hours in Anguilla on the beach, absorbing the sun and floating in water warm and gentle enough to make her wonder how the Pacific ever earned its name, given its wild and raucous nature. Her host served her lunch at an umbrella-covered table on the sand—fresh bananas and mangoes and coconut and crispy conch fritters and fragrant yam muffins and sweet ginger beer. And Carole Ann promised to return for an extended visit once matters were resolved at home. The old man's pleasure was so great that Carole Ann found herself wishing that she'd known him for a long time; and he was so moved when she told him how she felt that tears filled his eyes.

**Carole Ann** wanted nothing more than sleep on the plane ride from Miami to Los Angeles. Her body simply collapsed, and her brain could register nothing but how deceived she felt by the place she called home and the people she called family. And of how foolish she felt when she recalled that she'd escaped to Los Angeles and home seeking a definition of herself from the only place she felt qualified to offer it. Then irony raised up and pointed a gnarly finger at her consciousness and reminded that she had, in fact, achieved a new definition of herself: she was a killer. But finding herself unable to enjoy, even perversely, the dark humor of the situation, she retreated again to drowsiness and unrestful sleep and the promise, made too many times to herself and to Al, to learn how to meditate. If she could meditate, she knew, she would be relaxed right now, and not the helpless victim of painful thoughts and memories.

Thomas Wolfe was correct: one couldn't go home again. And she toyed, only slightly half-heartedly, with the notion of a compilation of memoirs entitled *Fools Who've Tried.* Then she drifted into sleep.

A rocky, bump-and-grind landing at LAX jolted her awake and out of ennui, and by the time she retrieved her luggage and met her driver at the gate, she was almost in the proper frame of mind to meet Addie Allen and allow herself to be surrendered as a fugitive. She was grateful that her driver, after he inquired pleasantly about her trip, lapsed into a respectful silence and concentrated on getting off Sepulveda Boulevard, out of the airport, and onto La Cienega Boulevard, which, he told Carole Ann, he preferred to playing bumper cars on the 405 Freeway, if Carole Ann didn't object. When she assured him that she was in no real hurry to reach her destination, he nodded his complicity and switched on the radio. Back-to-back tunes by Cassandra Wilson, Eryka Badu, and Me'Shell Ndegaocello served to lull Carol Ann into a false comfort zone, so that she actually felt betrayed when, at the top of the hour, the announcer's voice promised the up-to-the-minute details on "a murder and an arrest at the troubled Jacaranda Estates community in West Los Angeles."

"This is Jennifer Johnson reporting live from Jacaranda Estates, where eighty-year-old Hamas Asmara was arrested early this morning and charged with the murder of an unidentified undercover police officer. Mr. Asmara's wife, seventy-six-year-old Fatima Asmara, was attacked and beaten in front of the couple's home two months ago, and remains in a coma at the Charles Drew Medical Center in east L.A. Mr. Asmara himself was attacked three weeks ago. Last night, returning home from his daily vigil at his wife's bedside, Mr. Asmara was attacked again. This time he was prepared. The veteran of the Ethiopian Army's campaign against the invading Italians in the 1930s so far has refused to make any statement to the authorities. He told a neighbor, Mrs. Grayce Gibson, that he would cooperate with police when they cooperate with Jacaranda Estates residents by opening an investigation into the rash of felonious assaults that has left two women dead and his own wife comatose. Mrs. Gibson told me that there is no police investigation into the murders, assaults, and vandalism that have plagued this community for more than six months. The LAPD would not comment on the nature or extent of any investigation of any crimes at Jacaranda Estates."

**Carole Ann** opened the door to Addie Allen's office and looked into the grim, unsmiling face of Warren Forchette and felt dread rise up in her like floodwaters after a storm.

"What," she said to him, and it was not a question.

It was Addie who responded and Carole Ann turned to face her, unable to read anything from or into her expression. "Warren has something to say that you need to know that may or may not affect our work together."

Carole Ann turned back toward Warren, dimly aware that she liked Addie Allen's use of the word "our." Then she became fully aware that she didn't like how Warren was looking at her.

"What," she said to him again, and again no question was contained in the word.

"Griffin called me yesterday to tell me that Roberta told him that she killed one of the 'hoodlums,' as she calls them, and that she planned to confess and turn herself in. I hopped the next flight, knowing you were due back today."

Carole Ann knew they were watching her, assessing her reaction and response, only there was nothing to assess. She was numb. Her brain had shut down, had ceased to process information. She looked at Addie Allen and knew, without having to think about it, that she'd been wondering whether Carole Ann had known about Roberta's action and concealed that knowledge, and now was satisfied that she had an honest client. Carole Ann looked at Warren and saw a reflection of herself: he was motionless and expressionless.

"How?" she asked, only marginally certain of what, exactly, she was asking.

"She shot him," Warren replied, deciding the nature of the question for both of them. "The gun is in that box over there," and he pointed to a shoe box on the bookcase across the room. "It's an old S&W revolver that belonged to her husband."

"When?" Carole Ann asked, and realized that she knew when even as she uttered the word. The memory returned and she welcomed it, because it signaled the return of her functioning brain. Even as Warren was pinpointing the date, Carole Ann was remembering her return from San Francisco. She'd arrived to find a cluster of people discussing the shooting of "the hoodlum." She tuned in to Warren's words and again experienced another jolt. Damn, but she was sick and tired of shocks and surprises!

"Who was walking her home, Warren? Somebody was with her when she killed the guy. Who?"

Warren stood up and walked to the bookcase and stood beside the shoe box that contained the gun Roberta Lawson had used to kill a man. Walked away from her. He folded his arms across his chest and looked at Carole Ann for a long moment, something in his eyes unreadable. "They were all together, C.A. The four of them."

Carole Ann jumped to her feet. There wasn't room to pace, but since cussing didn't take much space Carole Ann stalked the room in a tight circle and cussed long enough and well enough that her two colleagues were suitably impressed. Even Jake Graham would have been impressed. But Carole Ann was beyond noticing. She was too focused on the fact that her mother had witnessed a murder and had kept silent. Her mother and Angie and Luisa. And Roberta had committed a murder and had kept silent. Had they tampered with that crime scene, too? Carole Ann didn't ask. She didn't want to know.

"Why is she ready to confess now?" And she realized as soon as she asked the question that she already knew that answer, too. Hamas Asmara had been arrested. Carole Ann soon would be arrested. It would be uncomfortable for Roberta to continue to conceal her own culpability and to continue to enjoy her freedom. Suddenly, Carole Ann no longer was angry or frightened or even exhausted. She reached into her purse and retrieved her checkbook.

"I'd like to retain your services, Miss Allen, on behalf of Roberta Lawson."

"Not necessary," the lawyer said with a slight lifting of the right corner of her mouth that Carole Ann took to be the beginnings of a grin. "It's taken care of."

"Jake didn't . . ." Carole Ann began, then saw Warren shaking his head and a wide, mirthful grin creasing his up to this point solemn visage.

"Addie and I work alike," he said. "We bill the rich early and often so that we can represent the poor for free."

"Graham Investigative Services will pay me more than enough for your fee to cover Miz Lawson's representation," Addie said, the South in her voice more pronounced than before; and then she changed the subject, from Roberta's status as a fugitive to Carole Ann's own, and she learned that she was about to become a pawn in a well-crafted though noxious scheme to lay the blame for three deaths at the front door of the Los Angeles Police Department, and to use the notoriously suggestive local news media to facilitate that objective.

"Your Jennifer Johnson has already gotten us off to a good start. They're not ignoring her stories anymore," Addie Allen said smugly.

"She's not 'my' Jennifer Johnson," Carole Ann snapped.

"Glad to hear it," Addie replied, " 'cause starting now, no more exclusives for young Jennifer. We need to have the heavy hitters swinging their bats at the LAPD."

"So now that 'young Jennifer' has served her purpose, we toss her aside like last week's newspaper?"

Addie was shaking her head. "That's not what I'm saying. My point is that we selectively control media access to you and the others, and that you can't talk just to Jennifer. You'll be on every television news program, every radio news program, in every newspaper."

Carole Ann wanted desperately to fight Addie and Warren, to argue with them, to plead against the tactic. But they were right and she knew it. In her case, it was not mere hyperbole that a good offense was the best defense, it was fact. Every action she'd taken since she'd killed the man who attacked her mother was indefensible. And while Addie was confident of her ability to secure exoneration for Carole Ann, the protective net needed to be wide enough to provide protection for Roberta and Hamas Asmara. While both could claim self-defense, the fact that they each were in possession of a concealed weapon, the purpose of which could only be to inflict harm, minimized their claims. And the fact that Mr. Asmara's victim was a cop . . .

"What do we know about this undercover cop?" Carole Ann asked.

"Not nearly enough," Addie replied with a frown and a growl. "They're stonewalling us. Tommy Griffin has been nosing around and has picked up enough bits and pieces to confirm the presence of undercovers, which makes our case all the stronger as far as I'm concerned. If there was a police presence over there and they ignored multiple attacks on senior citizens, then it is the cops who are to blame. For everything. Including the death of their own man."

The lawyer in Carole Ann now was wide awake and fully functioning. "Who's representing the old man?" she asked, and Warren pounced before she'd closed her lips on the words.

"Oh, no, you don't!" he hissed at her through almost clenched teeth.

"What?" This time she made it a question, full of innocence.

Warren stepped over several piles of folders and boxes to reach her, and when he did, he leaned over and brought his face in close to hers, close enough that she got a whiff of his aftershave. "Who's *not* representing the old man is you. You got that, C.A.? Dammit, your ass is in a sling and you got the nerve to be thinking about—"

"You don't know what I'm thinking about!" She pushed him away and began circling again. To her surprise, he followed.

"The hell I don't! But you can't forget, even for a second, that you're in trouble, girl. So is your mother. So is Roberta. And Angie. And Luisa. And for that matter, so am I because, as an officer of the court, I'm guilty of concealing knowledge of a crime. I'm also probably guilty of improper representation of a client. I shouldn't even be here! I've got a major trial starting in less than forty-eight hours. I should be home, holding my client's hand, instead of here holding yours."

So many currents of feeling and emotion coursed through Carole Ann that she didn't know which to respond to first, didn't know what to think or feel or say or do. She'd actually forgotten about her mother's injuries; or, perhaps more correctly, she'd ceased to think about Grayce for a while. Until Warren mentioned their names, she'd forgotten what she just learned about Angie and Luisa, and that knowledge returned with the force of a storm gale and slammed into the walls of her consciousness. Her anger at Warren ebbed. He was right in exactly the same way Jake was right: always.

She turned to Addie, seated behind her massive desk, behind her too-large eyeglasses, seeing and hearing and knowing everything, certain of herself and the power of her ability. The way Carole Ann once had been.

"What do you want me to do?" Carole Ann asked her attorney.

"Put on your happy face and your kick-ass attitude. We're going to turn you in."

# ❧ *twelve* ❧

Based on her experience in Washington, in New York, in Philadelphia, cities in which she'd tried cases that had garnered healthy media attention, Carole Ann believed that she knew what to expect from the Los Angeles media when Addie released the details of her involvement in the death of the still-unidentified man. She could not have been more mistaken. Nothing in her experience had prepared her for L.A.'s media monster. Not even the media feeding frenzy that surrounded her discovery of Al's murderer.

It had happened a year ago and it felt like last week. For days on end the major television networks and the major national newspapers devoured and regurgitated the details of the fall of the Louisiana congressman and his lawyer brother—the lawyer brother who just happened to be half Black and had been passing for white all of his adult life. Graft, corruption, greed, natural gas and oil deposits beneath the bayous, environmental racism, and, oh, yes: race. How unusual was it to find half-breeds in Louisiana these days? One of the networks had rushed into production a movie of the week that was more disgusting than the true story. But the media had done the job that needed doing.

No member of Congress wanted to impeach a congressman, even if he was a murderer. Even if he had killed Al Crandall, a prominent D.C. attorney and husband of another prominent D.C. attorney. No member of the bar wanted to disbar a lawyer, even if he was corrupt. Even if he had set up his own law partner, Al Crandall, for his brother the congressman. No DA wanted the case. It was too hot. So the reporters stepped in and got the job done. And they had indeed, in the process, made a shining star of the grieving widow, who'd used her skills as a criminal defense attorney to bring the criminals to justice. But she hadn't really cared about all that; she'd cared only that Al had been avenged.

This time was different. First there were the stories about Carole Ann herself: her crime in defense of her mother; her bringing to justice her husband's murderer; her professional success; her personal wealth; her expertise in the martial arts. These stories then spawned untold numbers of side-bar articles: other instances in which children had defended parents and parents had defended children and one spouse had avenged another; profiles of other successful Black female criminal defense attorneys, including Addie; profiles of unsuccessful Black female criminal defense attorneys; stories on the martial arts, including interviews with Jean Claude Van Damme and Jackie Chan—L.A., after all, was home to Hollywood—and other famous and infamous practitioners of the arts, and detailing the historically deadly potential of the martial arts.

Grayce reluctantly shared the spotlight. Unwilling, initially, to be the subject or focus of any news item, Grayce allowed Addie to convince her to cooperate with just one television interviewer. Who made the mistake of asking, "Why does your daughter, if she's so rich, allow you to live in such a dangerous neighborhood?"

Out of the still swollen mouth of sixty-seven-year-old Grayce Gibson flew the words, "Nobody allows me to do anything!" followed by a recitation of the highlights of her life: widowed by a man who gave his life in service to his country, mother of two young children, whom she raised alone on a teacher's salary, "in a neighborhood nicer and better than any neighborhood in this city and I dare you or anyone to call me a liar!" No one did. But every reporter in the city called her for an interview, and in the process, the media produced an embarrassing number of stories on Jacaranda Estates, several of them concluding that Grayce was not too far off the mark in her estimation of her neighborhood, current difficulties notwithstanding.

Carole Ann alternated between relief, because she no longer was the focus of all the media attention, and the fear that some enterprising reporter would probe deeply enough beneath the surface to uncover the ugly history that she believed was the root of the current evil. She shared her concerns with Addie, who magnanimously made available to reporters Roberta Lawson and Hamas Asmara, newly represented by a friend of Addie's. When it became known that Roberta's crime occurred the same night that Mr. Asmara was attacked returning home from visiting his comatose wife—an attack witnessed by all the members of Grayce and Roberta's bridge club—the feeding frenzy intensified.

Mr. and Mrs. Asmara, refugees from the historic ethnic struggles between the Somalians and the Ethiopians, generated half a dozen stories on that topic, which, in turn, gave birth to stories on Ethiopian and other African restaurants in the city. But the real focus of the final wave of stories was the Los Angeles Police Department.

Mrs. Asmara, Sadie Osterheim, Peggy Hendricks—all of them victims before Carole Ann or Roberta or Mr. Asmara had retaliated. And where was the LAPD? Why was there no response to months of complaining from Jacaranda Estates residents? The media turned the screws and the police department responded—by arresting Angie and Grayce and charging them as accessories after the fact in the murder of yet another unidentified man.

And then all hell really broke loose.

Elderly people from all corners of Los Angeles County—from the desert to the ocean to the mountains—showed up at Parker Center and confessed to having been present when Hamas Asmara pulled the trigger. At least three claimed to have done the deed, thereby exonerating Mr. Asmara; and one gentleman, three years older than Mr. Asmara's eighty years, claimed not only to have shot that victim, but Roberta's victim as well. Half a dozen seniors arrived with their attorney, an eighty-year-old former prosecutor, and submitted signed statements confessing to having been present, along with Grayce, Angie, and Luisa, when Roberta's crime was committed, and demanding to be arrested and charged as were the others. When the police refused, they filed a charge of reverse discrimination against the department.

The newspaper and radio and television stories divided and multiplied, until a *Los Angeles Times* reporter zeroed in on the fact that two of the victims, the ones killed by Carole Ann and Roberta, remained unidentified, and that a third, reported to be an undercover police officer, had yet to be identified by name, and his presence yet to be explained. And while the reporter never said it directly, he implied that the unidentified undercover might actually have been up to no good. Which gave Addie Allen something to do that really interested her.

When the same reporter revealed, a week later, the identity of that undercover cop—Pedro Gutierrez—along with the information that at the time he was killed he had been assigned to patrol duty in Echo Park and therefore had no business in Jacaranda Estates, Carole Ann breathed a heavy and grateful sigh of relief. Addie's plan had worked. Carole Ann and Jacaranda Estates and the people who lived there no longer were the meal of choice of the insatiable media feeding monster, which meant that Carole Ann was free to conduct her own investigation without being observed by press or police. Those two monstrous entities were too busy butting heads to care very much about what she did, as long as she didn't leave town to do it. And as Addie had expected and predicted, the bar association did suspend her license pending a review of her case, which she had sixty days to prepare. And by that time, she believed, she would have unraveled enough of the threads of some near-forty-year-old secrets that her life and livelihood no longer would be in jeopardy.

**What are** you, a shit magnet?" Jake had been in worse-than-usual-temper ever since Carole Ann's return from Anguilla, and the three weeks of media mania had done nothing to improve his disposition. He'd been as taken aback as she by Arthur Jennings's revelations, and now was deeply concerned that the amount of media attention was doing more harm than good—that opinion from the leading proponent of letting the press shake the information tree to see what fell. She held the phone for several long moments, listening to him think and breathe, not unmindful of what she was doing to her mother's telephone bill.

"I feel like worse than that. It's five in the morning, in case you forgot. I take it that by your terms of endearment you mean you don't have anything new for me."

He muttered something Carole Ann couldn't quite decipher, but because it was Jake, she trusted her assumption that it was cussing. Then he said, quite intelligibly, "I got nothin', C.A. No new leads, no new information, no nothin'. It's like these people ceased to exist. With the exception of Arthur Jennings, there's nothin' on any of 'em. And if you hadn't given me a place to start, I'm not sure I'd have found him. There's something screwy about this whole thing. Man like Jennings: why would he disappear into nowhere? He's got nothing to hide, nothing to be ashamed of—"

"And everything to protect," Carole Ann injected. "I told you he said he retreated to his island paradise to escape claims of the *Dame Que Es Mío* people—"

"That was then, this is now," Jake snapped. "Why is he still hiding out all these years later?"

"He's not hiding," Carole Ann challenged, feeling oddly protective of the old man. "His wife's dead, his kids are living their own lives—"

"Whatever," Jake snapped, cutting her off. "It doesn't account for the fact that Jamilla is a ghost, and so are the Nunez people—him and her. And I won't be able even to look for anything on that Dottie without a last name, or an exact date of death." He cut himself off with a sigh, and she pictured him seated behind his big desk, body still as death, face a panoply of scowls and grimaces. "It still makes no sense, but I think you're right about the past being the key to this current mess," he said grudgingly, and Carole Ann smirked and wished he could see her. How dare he call her a shit magnet! "What's your game plan?" he asked, creating an unexpected and unwelcome series of conflicting emotions. She was both pleased and angry that he didn't give her an arm's-length list of what to do and when and how to do it.

She was gratified that he was learning to trust her instincts. And terrified that she didn't know the first thing about conducting a criminal investigation. She was a lawyer. She knew about the law and how it worked and how to use it to benefit clients. Hell! He was the investigator, the homicide detective. But if she were pushed into offering an opinion it would be that the murder of Dorothy—Dottie—Somebody was the key that would unlock the door where all the skeletons lived.

As if he occupied a chair on the front row of her brain, he asked whether she'd told anyone yet about her trip to Anguilla and about what she learned there. She was, at that moment, wondering how to approach Angie for information about Dottie, since no one knew she knew about Dottie. She'd thought it wise not to further upset and worry her mother and the others; now she knew they'd definitely have been worried about her talking to Arthur Jennings, but not for the reasons she'd believed. And when she contemplated the scenario in its entirety, she grew angry with new vigor.

"You think I like listening to you breathe?" he snapped, snatching her back into the moment.

"I listen to you breathe all the time," she snapped back, then added, "and Tommy and I are trying to figure out that playground scenario. Tommy thinks they're cops. And no, I haven't told anybody anything about Anguilla and I don't know how I'm gonna backtrack a woman who's been dead for forty years, whose last name I don't know. Unless I ask Angie what her name was, and I'm not ready to do that."

"You may have to get ready," Jake said, no charity in his tone. "Or ask your mother when exactly she was killed. Then you can check the death certificate."

Now she was irritated. With herself and with him. "Yeah, yeah, yeah. I know what I can do. Thanks," she said after a grudging beat and was relieved when he accepted her half-assed apology without comment. "Do you really think those guys on the playground are undercover cops?"

She heard him grunt. "Looks like it. Tommy saw what you saw, which is they're not dealing drugs or doing anything else, except they leave in shifts at specified times. Tommy tried following a couple of them but had to give it up."

"But, Jake, if those guys are undercover cops, how—"

"I can't answer that, C.A.!"

"And if they're undercover cops, then how did it happen that old Mr. Asmara shot one of them?" She heard what resembled a snarl, then she heard a dial tone. It served as another reminder of how difficult it was for him to understand or accept bad police work. If, in fact, that's what it was. Perhaps they weren't cops at all. But if they weren't, who were they and why were they there? And because she knew no answer could or would be forthcoming, she put herself back to bed.

◆  ◆  ◆

**What she** wanted to do upon waking up three hours later was talk to Tommy, but she couldn't find him and nobody knew where he was. Grayce hadn't seen him since the previous evening, when he'd treated her and Carole Ann to dinner at a Chinatown restaurant. Able to eat only soup, Grayce finally, reluctantly had acknowledged the need for a dental surgeon, and Carole Ann could see that something major had shifted within her mother with that admission. She was less vigorous. She'd resumed her yoga and tai chi classes and was growing stronger physically every day, but spiritually, she was still in pain.

Carole Ann knew her mother could not tell her what she knew about the ugly secrets of Jacaranda Estates. Yet.

Roberta, calmer and quieter than Carole Ann had ever known her to be, hadn't seen Tommy since seven that morning, when he left for the gym.

"What gym?" Carole Ann asked, senses on alert.

"You'll have to ask your friend, Robbie. All I know is it's in Inglewood," Bert said, conjuring up for Carole Ann a hazy image of yet another solid, middle-class neighborhood being taken on a slalom ride to hell by gang-bangers and drug dealers; and along with the image came a tingle of disquiet. Tommy in Inglewood. The more she felt the thought, the less she liked it. She also didn't care much for the way Bert looked. Like Grayce, she was hurting inside. She brushed off Carole Ann's attempts to discuss her case, and grew strangely silent at efforts to open discussion of any aspect of Jacaranda history.

Carole Ann was surprised when there was no answer at Luisa's, and she stood ringing the bell and knocking on the door longer than common sense dictated. Mrs. Philpot had called a little more than an hour earlier to say that Luisa had returned from Mexico, and that the police had been looking for her. She walked around to the side of the house and tried peeking into a window, aware for the first time of the sorry state of the property. The paint was weathered and peeling, the windows were streaked and dirty, the grass was brown and patchy—the whole scene showed years of neglect. And absence. The place looked and felt as if no one had lived there for a very long time.

She strolled back to her mother's, head down, hands stuffed into her pockets, worried and fearful. The police were looking for Luisa. Where was she? *Who* was Luisa? Who were any of them, for that matter? What secret did her own mother harbor, and under what circumstances would it be revealed? She felt anger replace fear and worry, and she had worked herself into a fairly nasty frame of mind by the time she unlocked and opened the door. But the house was empty and she was relieved. She didn't yet know how to confront any of them with what she knew. Her need to talk to Tommy was becoming acute. She called Robbie to ask what gym he'd sent Tommy to, and instead was directed to come immediately to his studio. "There's somebody here you need to talk to," he said, and hung up on her.

**Watching** the karate class under way in Robbie Cho Lee's studio was like seeing a bunch of professional athletes in class with the Alvin Ailey Dance Company: there was no grace, no finesse, no respect for craft, no inherent artistry. There was only raw power, and too much of that. Robbie would demonstrate a stance and a throw and one of the students—if they could be called students—would lumber forward, grab his opponent, and try to kill him. Carole Ann couldn't imagine why they bothered, unless the study of martial arts now was *très chic* in *el barrio*. And since it now was chic for drug dealers and gang-bangers and other varieties of hoodlums to drive Volvos, why not learn the ancient martial arts?

She winced inwardly at the look on Robbie's face, a mixture of several emotions, including fear, and wished she could do something to help him. But as she had no wish to repeat the experience of hand-to-hand combat with a member of an L.A. street gang, or someone who passed convincingly as such, she contented herself with observing from the sidelines.

It took several moments but what she saw, she realized, were two distinctly different groups of young men: four true gang-bangers and three other guys who, as far as she could determine, were merely of Mexican descent. All three were tattooed and two of them wore earrings, but there was nothing evil in their behavior or demeanor. Their lack of grace in stance and throw was just that; it was the other four who were defiant and aggressive and desirous of inflicting harm upon Robbie and one another.

She sat up straighter, her back flush against the wall, her knees pulled forward into her chest, her arms wrapped around and her chin resting on them, and searched the combatants for signs of recognition. Had one of them been involved in the attack on her mother? Had she seen one of them on the playground at Jacaranda Estates? She strained for some sign of familiarity. She raised her eyes and saw the multiple images reflected in the many mirrors lining the walls. None of the combatants was officially or correctly clad. Two of them wore sweatpants and were topless, the others wore jeans and tee shirts, and Carole Ann considered the inappropriate attire at least partially responsible for the awkward postures. That's what she was thinking when the energy shifted like the barometric pressure before a storm.

One of those Carole Ann believed to be a true gangster cursed at Robbie and swung at him. Robbie backpedaled and raised his hands, palms out and facing his would-be attacker. Carole Ann couldn't discern his words but his tone was calm, conciliatory. The other guy wasn't having it. He swung at Robbie again, and then lunged. Robbie threw him so hard the floor shook as if experiencing the aftershock of an earthquake. One of his compadres stepped into the breach and Robbie tossed him, too—hard and fast. They lay side by side on the gray carpet and neither of them moved.

Robbie stood still, arms at his sides, waiting to see what the remaining two would do. She saw Robbie's chest lift and fall when they bent over and each one grabbed the arms of a fallen friend and began the tedious process of dragging dead weight across a carpeted floor.

Carole Ann quickly lost interest in their exit and, when she returned her attention to Robbie, she found that he was beckoning for her to join him. Quickly she untied and removed her sneakers and padded toward him.

"How're you doing, C.A.?" he asked, and she was surprised at the concern clouding his face and giving his voice an unusual huskiness.

"I'm fine, Robbie. Really, I am," she said, and smiled and squeezed his arm.

He nodded and introduced her to the three remaining students and she confirmed her earlier assessment, made from across the room, that these three young men might be streetwise but they weren't gang-bangers. They also were not as young as she'd imagined from a distance—all three were well into their twenties. She watched them watch her as Robbie explained that he'd introduced her to karate "a lot of years ago, when you guys were little babies," and told them she would assist him in demonstrating several stances and throws. He didn't check her reaction to the information that the three young men belonged to a political action group called *Dame Que Es Mío*, "often mistaken for a gang."

"I'm not properly dressed, Robbie!" she complained, aware of how recently she'd mentally criticized the other guys for their improper attire; though in sweatpants and a tee shirt, she could more easily and comfortably execute than in her jeans. She hoped her protestations concealed her surprise. At least she now knew why Robbie had asked her to come on such short notice.

He waved off her objections, bowed to her with a sly wink, and assumed the stance. She could but follow. He led her through the moves and positions he'd been trying to teach earlier, explaining and defining each component of each move to a now fully attentive audience. And before she knew it, Robbie had skipped several chapters ahead and they were engaged in sophisticated, advanced maneuvers, and Carole Ann stopped thinking about the three young men and their political action group and concentrated fully on not having her head handed to her. She was unimpeded by the clothes she wore, and she fought with an intensity that surprised her and Robbie. She was reliving the attack on her mother, this time without the fear or the anger, but certainly with the determination not to be defeated.

The demonstration was blessedly brief and Robbie and Carole Ann bowed to each other and then to the students, who did nothing to conceal their awe at the performance. They stood open-mouthed and speechless for several seconds. Then one of them, short and stocky with a residual case of teen acne, narrowed his eyes at her and nodded his head.

"You gave that dude 'xactly what he deserved," he said in a voice so soft as to be almost feminine. "Although if I hadn't just seen it for myself, I'd still be sayin' no way a bitch could off a dude with her bare hands."

Carole Ann flinched. "Please don't call me a bitch."

His eyes widened, then narrowed again, and he shrugged and grinned at her. "You're right. That's a bad habit." He extended his hand to her. "My name is Ray. My partners are Jose and David." Head gestures to the left and right sides identified the partners, and Carole Ann shook all three hands and received firm, honest, you-can-trust-me handshakes accompanied by steady eye contact. She was one of those who judged a lot of characters based on handshakes and eye contact.

Jose, on the left, surprised Carole Ann by asking, "How's your mama?" and all three nodded their heads and offered mumbled messages of goodwill when she briefly and succinctly described Grayce's recovery, and Ray once again opined that Grayce's deceased attacker deserved to be deceased.

"I wish it hadn't happened," Carole Ann said, looking Ray directly in the eye. "I'm not proud of what I did."

"You're not proud of saving your mama's life?" This from Jose.

She shook her head. "I'm not proud that I needed violence to do it."

"You don't like violence but you do karate?" Ray made no attempt to disguise the disbelief in his voice.

Carole Ann was forced to smile. "Karate is about as close as I've managed to get to meditation. And it's art and sport. I didn't learn it to hurt anyone and I don't ever want to again."

"Suppose you have to?" asked Jose. "Suppose"—

She cut him off. "I can't think like that. All I can think about now is how to find out what's causing the violence in my neighborhood and put a stop to it." She paused to look hard at the three young men. "Will you help me?"

Confusion and distrust struggled for control of Ray's face, and Jose and David looked at Carole Ann as if she'd suddenly sprouted a new appendage in an unlikely place. She quickly explained to them the history of Jacaranda Estates and the nature of the recent violence and watched understanding dawn. Just as Ray was about to explode in anger she raised her hand and her voice.

"I'm asking you for help. I'm looking for information. I'm not accusing or blaming."

"Bullshit!" Ray spat at her.

"Truth, Ray," Carole Ann said, holding his eyes with her own, not blinking for as long as he didn't blink. "Do you know Ricky Nunez?" she asked, and when he didn't respond or blink, she said, "He tells people he belongs to your organization. And he might be connected to the attack on my mother and those other women."

Ray's shoulders relaxed and his fists unclenched and he blinked.

Slowly. "We're a cultural and political organization. Not a gang. We don't beat up old ladies. Or young ladies. Or nobody else. You understand me?"

Carole Ann nodded. She believed him. She'd known as soon as she saw the three of them that whoever they were, they weren't her mother's attackers; but she'd hoped they could lead her, point her in some useful direction. Now that hope faded. She thanked them for listening to her, apologized to them for any misunderstanding they might have had interpreting her words, and wished them well in their study of karate. She turned to Robbie, who'd been standing and listening, and thanked him with her eyes, and started across the room to retrieve her sneakers. She heard Robbie tell Ray, David, and Jose to call and schedule an appointment but she didn't turn to catch a final glimpse of them. Had she, she'd have seen the three of them standing as if their feet were glued to the carpet, their stares at her back reflecting off the mirrored walls.

# ᘓ *thirteen* ᘔ

From her vantage point under the canopy on the side of the restaurant, Carole Ann enjoyed an unobstructed view of the pedestrian traffic in both directions on the boardwalk, as well as that on the narrow, cobbled side street, without seeming to be engaged in any activity other than drinking ginger beer and people watching. Her mission was to observe Tommy's approach and arrival and to determine whether he was being followed. It was his suggestion—and she and Jake had agreed—that they limit their Jacaranda Estates contact with each other. That way, Tommy more effectively could be Roberta's nephew from D.C., a body-building homeboy whose questions about people, places, and things would arouse no more interest or ire than those of any other newcomer. To Tommy, if anybody asked, Carole Ann was just his aunt's friend's daughter, some rich, crazy lady who just happened to have killed some dude. That she also was from D.C. was of no consequence to Tommy. She didn't hang out with his crowd. She was too old.

He spent his days helping his "auntie" and her friends—running errands for them, repairing odds and ends around their homes, taking them to lunch and dinner, meeting and talking to their neighbors. He'd learned that there was, indeed, an undercover police presence in Jacaranda Estates. " 'Cause I know a cop when I see a cop," he'd growled, Jake-like, when Carole Ann had pressed him about the certainty of his information, and they didn't appear to have any connection to the group on the playground. One of them was a young Mexican woman who lived with her aunt and uncle, the one who spoke out against retaliating against the violence and whom none of the other residents knew; another was a Black guy named Bobby who'd thwarted the attack on old Mr. Asmara.

He'd also learned that for the past four days Luisa had been staying with her daughter in Van Nuys, in the San Fernando Valley, north of Los Angeles, waiting for the bruising and swelling in her face from her latest beating to recede. Which is why Carole Ann couldn't find her after her return from Mexico. And he'd learned that Mr. Asmara was moving to Glendale, to live with his son, apparently having accepted that his wife's coma was permanent. And he'd learned that a new family would be moving into the Asmara home some time in the near future.

Carole Ann looked beyond the throng skating and jogging and strolling on the walkway before her, out to the ocean and on to infinity. There was no hint of the ugly smog that so frequently draped itself over the L.A. basin that a sunny day was an anomaly. Growing up here, she mused, every day had been bright and sunny and perfect. Every day had been the fairy tale that untold millions sought as their truth. She studied the people around her—a universe of people—and felt, for a moment, normal. Felt as if she belonged to a world where sitting at a cafe a hundred yards from where the Pacific Ocean glistened and rippled in the sun was normal and natural behavior. And in feeling that sense of belonging, she shed, for an instant, the aura of alienation that had clung to her for the past month.

She looked quickly around as self-consciousness snuck up on her, waiting to be recognized as the "karate lady from TV." Then, relaxing and grinning, she noticed that the tables around her contained real television personalities: names she didn't know but faces she recognized from small and large screens. All of them relaxed and calm and pretending an unawareness of the fact that all around them, people were pretending an unawareness of their existence.

She returned her gaze to the ocean and there was Tommy, strolling loosely and easily, lips pursed as if whistling, his eyes concealed by a pair of sunglasses. He wore a body-caressing tee shirt and the loose though sensually suggestive slacks favored by body-builders, and some leather sandals Carole Ann hadn't seen before. She studied the people surrounding him as he deliberately walked past the restaurant. Carole Ann thought herself as adept at recognizing a cop as Tommy, and satisfied herself that no undercover police presence preceded or followed him.

He stopped suddenly at the table of a tee shirt vendor and nobody stopped with him. He studied the shirts for a few moments, holding up one and then another, before turning back toward the restaurant, where he paused to peruse the hand-lettered menu on the board outside the door. When he entered, he brushed quickly past the hostess, through the front patio, and around to the side where Carole Ann sat.

As soon as he removed the dark glasses that had concealed half his face, Carole Ann knew something was wrong. Reflexively she hunched her shoulders and closed both her hands tightly around the glass in which all the ice had melted and created puddles of water on the glass-topped table. Tommy banged into the table as he attempted to fold his bulk into the too-small chair, and water dribbled over the edge into her lap. She didn't care. She was too intent on trying to read meaning into the look on Tommy's face.

"Can the news be that bad?"

"Couldn't be much worse," he said.

"Well," she said, and cleared her mind of the clutter of speculation and wonder.

He took a breath and blew it out like a whale. "LAPD is turning
its back on Gutierrez. Their story is going to be that whatever he
was doing at Jacaranda the night he got offed, he wasn't doing it for
them. He'd already been suspended without pay for an infraction
they won't specify."

"But what about the others? They can leave Gutierrez dangling
but they can't keep pretending the others aren't there."

"Sure they can," Tommy said with a shrug. "The LAPD hasn't admitted it's running an undercover operation—" He was stopped by
an expression on Carole Ann's face. "What?"

"Suppose there are two undercover ops, Fish. The young woman
who lives with her aunt and uncle, and that Bobby—they're one;
and the playground guys are another."

Tommy scratched his chin and nodded his head. "It's possible.
It'd be a real screwed-up way to do things, but it's possible. Makes
sense, even, considering . . ."

"So, how can we prove it? How can we push back against the
LAPD?"

"We can't." Tommy was shaking his head. "They're the biggest
gang in L.A."

Carole Ann understood the futility of her objection even as she
made it, yet could not stop herself. She understood as clearly as if
the words had been engraved on the concrete walkway in front of
her the implications of Tommy's words: the L.A. police had heaved,
shrugged, and dropped the weight of the murder of their obviously
corrupt undercover cop right back on the shoulders of Jacaranda Estates and its residents, three of whom, at least technically, were
murderers. In fact, had upended Addie's defense strategy, leaving
all of them exposed and vulnerable—Carole Ann, Roberta, Angie,
and Grayce. All except Luisa. She muttered an almost audible curse
and then shook her head.

Then she shrugged and a self-deprecating grin spread over her face.

"Damn," Tommy whispered, and reached into his waist pouch and retrieved a tiny cellular phone.

"Who're you calling?" Carole Ann demanded to know, still grinning.

Tommy arched an eyebrow at her, pursed his lips, opened the phone, and commenced dialing. "Jake," he muttered between punches at the phone's keypad. "He needs to know that you've gone completely around the bend." His seriousness increased her humor and she was laughing out loud when she reached across the table and snatched the phone from him.

"I'm perfectly fine, thank you. In fact, I'm finer than I've been in quite a while. And if you want to tell Jake anything, tell him I just remembered his first rule of survival: Don't get mad, get even. I've spent the last couple of months yo-yoing between being frightened and being angry. It is now get-even time. Tell that to your boss when you talk to him."

**Carole Ann** rehearsed her words to Angie. Rehearsed as she would a summation to a jury. Not just the words she'd say, but the tone of voice she'd use, and the pitch, and the pace. And she worried whether to sit next to Angie and hold her hand or face her across a divide, putting distance between them—between the strength of their relationship and the potential damage Carole Ann was about to inflict upon it. For she could no longer not press Angie for details about Dottie: who she was and how she was murdered.

Carole Ann had called Angie to say that she wanted to talk and to set a convenient time. Puzzlement heavy in her voice, Angie had said come now. And now Carole Ann was standing outside the door that was downstairs from the door she'd called home all of her life. Angie's door, one at which she'd never before knocked. She stood there, hand raised. The door swung open and Angie welcomed her, as always, with a smile of love and warmth and welcome, and she knew this was no time or place for a speech. Angie was no jury.

She entered, closed the door, and accepted Angie's embrace, turning it into a brief, fierce clutch before releasing. She followed the older woman into the home that always spoke in a language of the past. The combined living and dining room reflected the truth of who Angelique Arroyo was. Several richly colored hand-woven rugs covered the floors, hand-woven baskets adorned walls and, at various intervals about the room, held articles of need and interest. The dining table and coffee table were of hand-hewn north-woods planks, as was an armchair with a stretched, tanned hide. The sofa and complementary ottoman were commercially produced and looked as if they weren't, being of some fabric natural enough to blend in with the decor.

She followed Angie to the sofa, where, on a rough table in front of it, a bottle of seltzer water and two tumblers waited on a woven reed tray. Angie poured water and Carole Ann drank. She was ready.

"You remember a few weeks ago, Angie, when I was out of town for a couple of days? Before all the media madness? I went to Anguilla to see Arthur Jennings."

Angie's eyes widened slightly but held no question, and she waited, hands folded in her lap, for Carole Ann to continue.

"He told me about Dottie."

For several seconds Angie registered no reaction. It was as if the words either had no meaning when they reached her brain center, or there was a short circuit that prevented their meaning from registering immediately. And when she responded, it was not in the way Carole Ann had anticipated, for which she had steeled herself. Angie tilted her head slightly toward the left and her eyes narrowed slightly.

"Why?" she asked almost lightly. "Why would he talk to you about Dottie?"

Carole Ann released breath she wasn't aware she was holding

and explained her theory connecting the present-day mayhem at Jacaranda Estates to something in the past. Angie reclined back into the embrace of the sofa, tucked her feet beneath her, and closed her eyes. Her breathing was even and her body was perfectly still. She could have been meditating. Except that after less than a minute, she opened her eyes and looked at Carole Ann. Without speaking, she unfolded herself, stood, and walked briskly to the bedroom, bare feet whispering on the floor where there was no rug. She returned almost immediately with an ancient black leather briefcase, the kind preferred by professionals of another era. It was an accordion case—it opened on hinges and was wider at the bottom than at the top.

"This was Dottie's," Angie said, placing the case in Carole Ann's lap. It was heavy. It also was clean and the leather was gleaming and pliable, as if this case was polished and buffed regularly. And, Carole Ann knew, it was.

"Tell me about her, Angie. If you don't mind. I don't mean to be rude, to pry. But I'd like to know. It hurts me that I never knew before."

Angie smiled and shook her head. "I don't mind. I wish you could have known her. She was beautiful. And funny. And very smart. She was a bookkeeper for the government. She worked for the immigration department. That's what it was called back then. It was a good job for a Colored woman to have, but she couldn't really take pride in it because she was being used against other Colored people. You see, they wouldn't let Mexicans or Chinese or Japanese work for immigration. Not in office jobs, like Dottie had. And they used the Negroes against the other Colored. If Dottie wanted to keep her job, she had to uncover so many illegals every month." She stopped talking and Carole Ann misunderstood.

"Angie, don't talk any more if it's too painful."

Angie gave her hand a gentle stroke. "I got over the pain long, long ago, C.A. Don't worry about me. I mean it." Carole Ann searched the face before her. There was considerable sadness, and loneliness, and a hint of anger. But no pain.

"If she was a bookkeeper, why was she doing . . . whatever it was she was doing," Carole Ann asked, and realized that she was guilty of a form of transference: she was the one in pain. It hurt to feel the implications of Angie's words. She wanted to hear more, so she stiffened her spinal column and urged Angie to continue.

"They never would let her—any Colored person—do their real job. Not back then. We were lucky just to have an office job. But Dottie didn't feel lucky. She felt dirty. She'd started warning people, especially people with families, that immigration was after them. She was going to quit and go to work for J and J as their bookkeeper. And then she got murdered."

"What's in here, Angie?" Carole Ann asked, stroking the soft leather of the old briefcase, willing the tears now stuck in her throat to remain there. Angie may have released her pain, but Carole Ann still carried a full load.

Angie shrugged. "Whatever was in there when she died. She brought it home from work every night. Sometimes she worked at home, sometimes not. For years, I couldn't bear to look. Then, after a while, it didn't matter what was in there. She wasn't. And nothing in there could bring her to life. I kept it in good shape because I don't believe in waste. If you think it can help, you can have it."

Carole Ann picked up the case and pressed it to her breast. It easily could have belonged to Al.

**Ricky Nunez** called her a nigger and spit at her and she smacked him hard enough to propel him across the room, and across all the furniture that was in the room. Then she made the fool's error of turning her back on him. She was feeling just angry enough to tell Luisa to stop with the screaming and the goddamn praying when she felt the cold wetness spread across her shoulders. Then she felt the pain and smelled something slightly disgusting. Then she heard shattering glass. Ricky had thrown a bottle of that awful malt liqour at her. Had he been more sober or had a better arm, the bottle would have opened a gash in her head.

He was standing across the room screaming and cursing at her; Luisa was tugging at her arm and screaming and praying at her, the only intelligible words *"Madre de Dios"* and "He's just a baby." In that moment, Carole Ann despised the two of them. She looked at Luisa and heard "doormat." Looked at Luisa and saw a woman who had lived more than half her life with the knowledge that her husband had raped and murdered her best friend's lover, a zombie. Looked at Luisa and saw a woman who harbored a boy who beat her and who might be responsible for terrorizing an entire community.

She felt a fury previously unknown. Not even in the aftermath of Al's murder and the ensuing hunt to bring his killers to justice had she experienced the kind of rage she now was feeling. She stepped over a broken chair to reach Ricky and so quickly grabbed the hand that he'd raised to strike her with, and found the pressure point, that he was on his knees writhing in pain before he fully understood what was happening to him. Anger creased his face, momentarily crowding out the vestiges of drugs and alcohol, and he opened his mouth to speak. Carol Ann increased the pressure on his thumb and he emitted a squeak.

"If you ever touch me again, I will kill you," she hissed into his ear. "And if you ever hit your grandmother again, I will kill you."

"Me and my grandmother is none of your business," he spat back at her, and she found herself slightly impressed that he had either the energy or the courage to mount a protest. But only slightly. She bent the finger back toward his wrist and the breath left him in an audible hiss.

She leaned in closer to him, then recoiled at the smell. "I don't give a good goddamn about you, you little piece of shit. But your grandmother was my business before you were born, and she'll be my business when they slam the jail door on your sorry ass, and don't you forget it." She released his hand and stood over him for a long count to ensure that he remained subdued. She didn't approach Luisa again, but at the door she turned toward her and felt all the anger ebb away at the sight. Luisa was a broken woman. A doormat upon which the footprints were visible. How, Carole Ann again asked herself, had she never before noticed? And how, she wondered, could she ever confront this woman, ask her the questions that had begged answers for almost forty years? And she knew she could not. Would not. Should not.

Ignoring the cobblestone pathway, she trudged across the grass, angling toward Roberta's house. First Angie, then Luisa, then Bert, and finally Grayce. That had been her planned order of confrontation. So far, neither encounter had proceeded as expected, and Carole Ann found herself apprehensive about facing Roberta. She'd thought she knew these women, had thought she understood them, understood their motivations. She now knew that she was mistaken. How, then, would Bert react and respond? With anger? With pain or sorrow or regret? With resentment toward Carole Ann for her intrusion? Would she even acknowledge the facts of the history? Bert, Carole Ann reminded herself, was the most obstreperous of the group, the real hardhead. Bert was tougher even than Grayce, and Grayce Gibson was plenty tough enough for Carole Ann.

She was grateful for the grin she could experience at the sight of Tommy's new car parked at the curb in front of Bert's house. It was "new" only in the sense that it was a recent acquisition. The car was a 1966 Bonneville convertible, gleaming white with black leather interior. It had been lovingly and perfectly restored beyond its original magnificence, and Tommy was so proud of it his chest visibly expanded when he was in its presence. He was, she mused, becoming a bit too acclimated to the California lifestyle. What in the world would he do with a L.A. muscle car in D.C.?

She was wondering whether it was wise or not to attempt to tackle Bert in Tommy's presence when he opened the door and stepped out onto the walk. He spied her and immediately came toward her. He stopped several feet away and compressed his face into something quite unattractive.

"You smell like you fell into a bucket of piss!" he all but shouted at her. "Where have you been?"

She bristled at his tone and his attitude until she got a whiff of herself, and recalled the source of her aroma. She told him what happened and instantly regretted it, as she hung on to his arm, preventing him from rushing to Luisa's.

"Stupid little bastard! I'll break his fuckin' arm!"

"I already did, Fish! Will you settle down? Please?"

"Why is it little punks like him are always punching out women? Why don't they ever take a swing at a dude?" Tommy clinched and unclinched his fists and gradually calmed himself. Then he wrinkled his face again. "You do stink, C.A. Go change your clothes."

He followed her home, but not into the house. He sat on the front steps while she went in, stripping as soon as the door closed behind her.

"What is that odor?" asked Grayce, wrinkling her face á la Tommy, even as she was reaching for the tee shirt and bra Carole Ann already had removed. Grayce waited for the jeans and panties and hurried through the kitchen to the laundry room, holding the bundle arm's-length away.

When Carole Ann stepped out of the shower, she heard Tommy's voice downstairs and knew he'd have told Grayce how she wound up smelling like a brewery. She sighed heavily, dried herself, quickly dressed, and, en route downstairs, prepared herself for her mother's admonitions. She received, instead, another surprise.

"What's that?" Grayce asked, pointing toward the black bag she'd left beside the sofa.

Carole Ann hesitated only briefly. "Angie gave it to me. It was Dottie's," she said quietly. And waited, watching.

Something deep within Grayce stilled. Her eyes closed and the breath caught in her throat. She sat unmoving. Then she opened her eyes and the tears spilled out. Carole Ann was beyond amazed. She'd expected tears from Angie, not from her own mother. She'd expected stunned shock from Angie at the mention of the murdered Dottie, not from her mother. And yet it was Grayce, folded into her favorite armchair, rubbing her hands together as if for warmth, tears streaming down the face that still bore the marks of the beating she'd sustained.

"Dottie." She whispered the word and managed a smile. "She was my best friend. We grew up together. Went to elementary school and high school together, began college together, but Dottie had to drop out. Her parents couldn't afford the tuition and it became too much for her, working full time at night and keeping up with her classes—" Grayce choked on a sob and Carole Ann rushed to hold her. Tommy went into the kitchen and returned with a glass of water and a box of tissues.

They hovered over Grayce, watching her anxiously. They both knew that Grayce's recovery had been slower than anticipated, primarily because she'd not managed the emotional trauma as efficiently as she, and they, had assumed she would. Consequently, everyone around her had made every effort to shield her from upset of any kind. She and Tommy exchanged glances over Grayce's head, Tommy's accusing and Carole Ann's defensive: how was she to know that a woman she'd never heard of had been her mother's best friend?

"I introduced them," Grayce was saying, smiling through the abated tears. "Shocked the hell out of both of them. They couldn't believe that I knew. After all, we didn't discuss that kind of thing back then."

"You knew Angie before you lived here?" Carole Ann could not contain her surprise.

"Not as well as I knew Dottie, of course," Grayce replied matter-of-factly, as if she'd not just revealed another secret as old as Carole

Ann herself. "A friend of Mitch's was sweet on her and we'd double-dated with them a couple of times. I can't recall that fella's name now, but he was crazy about Angie and couldn't see that she was barely tolerating him." Grayce's eyes closed as she looked back into her memory, and she smiled slightly. "She was so polite to all of us whenever we were together, but I could tell she was bored to tears. Anyway, I convinced her to meet me for lunch one Saturday. I was kind of pushy back then."

Both Carole Ann and Tommy snorted and Grayce subdued each of them with "the look," the one Carole Ann had inherited.

"Anyway. As I was saying, I bullied Angie into meeting me for lunch at the Santa Monica pier. And, of course I'd arranged for Dottie to be there. And after we'd talked for a while, I left them there. They didn't even pretend to be sorry when I said I had to leave." Grayce chuckled softly to herself as the tears began again.

Carole Ann touched her mother's shoulder. "Arthur Jennings said he asked you and Daddy if you minded living next door to Dottie and Angie."

"So you've talked to Arthur," Grayce said, wiping away tears. "Such a kind man. Yes, he asked, not knowing that we already knew."

Tommy cleared his throat more loudly than was necessary. "Ah, if it's not too much trouble, could one of you tell me who Dottie is?" he asked.

"Angie's lover and Jacaranda Estates' first murder victim," Carole Ann said, and instantly regretted the words as Grayce sobbed. She and Tommy again exchanged accusatory stares as they worked to calm and comfort Grayce. They prepared a light supper for her of carrot soup, yogurt, and toast, brewed a pot of tea, and arranged her before the VCR with her favorite film, *Glory*, ready to be viewed for the dozenth time.

Outside, strolling through the grass, Carole Ann told Tommy everything she'd learned from Arthur Jennings, and asked if he wanted to help her sort through Dottie's briefcase. He whistled at the thought.

"Forty years of untouched memories. Yeah, I'd love to, C.A. But I can't. I'm meeting a friend of Addie's at the gym. Ex-LAPD guy. Got tossed out on his ass for violating procedure, kinda like me. He does some off-the-books private stuff for Addie while he's waiting on his PI license."

Carole Ann frowned. "Why is she just making this guy available? We've been sweating bullets for over a month now, and she's all of a sudden got a cop contact?"

"Oh, come on, C.A. You know you don't give up an inside source to every joe who comes along," he chided.

"Every joe?" She bristled. He laughed at her and she was working herself up to some real annoyance when suddenly she remembered something this ex-cop could do. "Ask him if he can run a tag for me, Tommy," she said, recalling the number of the license plate on the badly restored El Dorado she'd noticed parked in the alley behind Robbie's studio the last two times she'd been there. She hadn't liked the looks of the car or of the four homeboys inside it.

"You want me to ask the dude for a favor the first time I meet him?"

"Damn straight," she snapped, her thoughts already on Dottie's black bag and what secrets it might hold. For Carole Ann was certain that there would be more secrets.

**She spent** the entire night tossed and buffeted by images of the past. Not dreams, but real images, memories, long forgotten but which surged into her consciousness with a shattering clarity. First there was Hector Nunez at ten or eleven years old.

        🙦 🙖

*A group of perhaps two dozen people, adults and children of all ages, dot the landscape of Grayce and Angie's yard, back, side, and front. Several barbecue grills are going at once. There are two long tables for eating, and half a dozen card tables for games. Brightly colored blankets and towels gleam in the sun in exquisite contrast with the deep green of the grass. It is a Fourth of July celebration! Carole Ann is certain of it. She can hear the music—someone has placed the stereo speakers in the windows—and several of the kids are dancing. The adults will dance later, on the concrete carport under the soft glow of colored lanterns, when the younger children are sleeping and the older ones have drifted away from the adults to pretend their own maturity.*

*But while it is still bright and hot, the children compete with one another for food, for toys, for attention. And, of course, tempers flare. A child cries. Then another. Then a voice is raised in hateful anger:* "You stupid nigger! Leave me alone! I hate you! I hate all niggers! Why don't you go back where you came from!" *So quickly does silence envelop the festivities that the blare of the music is deafening, when previously it was barely audible. It is Marvin Gaye. But nobody notices. All eyes and ears and hearts are resounding with* I hate all niggers! *Who said it? Hector. Hector Nunez. And he was speaking to Grayce, who has turned to Luisa for help. Luisa, this is yours to handle, says the look on Grayce's face. But Luisa does nothing. Does not move, does not speak, does not acknowledge the transgression. No one moves or speaks. Marvin continues to ask,* "What's going on?" *Then young Mitch Gibson rushes Hector, knocks him down, falls on him, and begins pounding. Grayce grabs her son and Luisa, finally in motion, grabs her son. And hugs him to her breast, weeping and praying.* "He's only a baby," *she says, rocking him.*

*Then the images shift and though it is the same place, it is a different time. Carole Ann is a college freshman and proud of her adulthood. She lives on campus, even though her campus is across town instead of across the nation. Her roommate, a pre-med major from San Francisco, immediately is a friend and confidante. The first two secrets are that she's unbelievably homesick and that she's a lesbian. No problem for Carole Ann, who has a mother with enough space in her heart—and in her kitchen—for another daughter, and with an intolerance for intolerance. The image is so clear:* "Mommy, Marge is a lesbian," *she whispers. After all, Marge is upstairs, in the bath-*

*room. "I know, dear." She is shocked. How could she know? Did Marge tell her already? "Set the table, please. Do you think Marge would prefer biscuits or cornbread?" They have a wonderful weekend and when it ends, Grayce envelops her new daughter in a hug and whispers, "You must tell your mother! You must! She will love you no matter what!"*

⁂

**Carole Ann** arose at six-thirty, just when she thought that finally she could sleep. But it was too late to go to sleep. She showered and dressed and marveled at the memories that had kept her awake, at the subtle machinations of the mind. Would she ever have remembered Hector's outburst had his son not called her a nigger that day? Or was it Luisa's reaction that triggered the recall? *He's only a baby.* Would she have remembered her mother's ready recognition and acceptance of Marge without the knowledge of Grayce's long-term friendship with Dottie?

Dottie. She sat on the edge of the bed and caressed the briefcase. It hadn't taken very long to sort through the contents, but the effects would live forever in her heart and mind, most especially the unopened letter from Enrique Jamilla. She easily could imagine Angie opening the mailbox two or three days after Dottie's murder, finding a letter addressed to her, being too distraught to open it, even to care what it contained. And tossing it into the briefcase. And forgetting about it.

The letter was dated March 12, 1964. The ink was faded and the creases in the paper tore when Carol Ann opened the pages. The writing was careful, almost childlike, the language simple—the language of one for whom corresponding in English was an unperfected habit. It read:

Dear Miss Miller. I am sorry for not trusting you. I do not trust many, and no one with this secret. How could I think such help

**183**

to come my way? Thank you from the bottom of my heart. I will warn my brother and his family. I know you can not destroy their records, and I do not ask it. It is funny, you know, that I do not think I am illegal here. After so many years and so much hard work I feel American. Like California is my home. Why does the immigration care after so much time? No matter. Please take the job. We want you to work for J and J. Not as a payback. I so sorry I say that to you. You do a good thing for me and I thank the Virgin for you. Please. Let me do good things for you. No more working for the immigration. OK. You working now for J and J as bus. manager. You don't worry what to say to Hector and his family. I tell them and make all the plans. They go home to Mexico and soon come back with legal papers. The house we take care for them until they come back home. Thank you my friend. Your friend E. Jamilla

# ❧ *fourteen* ❧

Jake didn't call her a shit magnet again, but he did opine that Jacaranda Estates could enter "the worst mess in the history of homicide investigations" record book and be a real contender for an award-winning position.

"I'm gonna quit worrying when I don't hear from you for a couple of days because every time I *do* hear from you, I find myself knee deep in another pile of shit! I'm running out of shovels!"

Carole Ann found herself in uncomfortable agreement. She wasn't pleased at Jake's description of Jacaranda Estates as a "shit hole" and its residents as "New Age assholes." This, after all, was her home, and the people her friends and neighbors. Her family. Yet, she could not escape the reality that with each new revelation, the place seemed more sinister than idyllic; the people more layered and complex than the simple, working-class, family-oriented heroes and heroines of her memory. Memory was selective; that fact was proven to her last night.

Jake readily concurred with her belief that Dorothy Miller had been raped to obscure her murder, and not the other way around; and that Hector Nunez murdered her to prevent her from reporting him and his family to immigration. That was the easy part for Carole Ann to digest. Much more difficult to manage was the knowledge that Luisa and Hector were illegal residents; that Enrique Jamilla was willing to sacrifice his brother, Hector Nunez, in order to maintain his own position of prominence; that Luisa must have known at least some of these facts.

And, she wondered, had Arthur Jennings told her the entire truth? Had he really not known that Jamilla was an illegal? And what of Dottie Miller's belief that she was to go to work for J and J Contracting? Was that Jamilla's idea and he just hadn't gotten around to discussing it with his partner, or had Jennings chosen not to mention it? Carole Ann was feeling the need for a shovel herself. And a long, hot shower. She also was feeling restless and agitated and tired of sitting in one place.

She gazed across the room to the clock on top of the bookcase. One twenty-five. She was still waiting for her noon appointment meeting with Addie to prepare for her upcoming arraignment; "prepare," in this case, being a euphemism for "praying for a miracle." She had much to tell Addie, none of it particularly useful in structuring a defense. Carole Ann had uncovered no proof to support her theory that Jacaranda Estates' past was responsible for its present troubles, only threads of information that wove a lovely cloth of supposition.

She stood up and began to pace, then plopped back down on the couch. Addie's office was a mess. There was no room for pacing. Every few steps or so there was a pile of folders, a stack of books, a box. Carole Ann had to admit that the piles were neat, each of them was labeled, and several were numbered. Upon reflection, it actually was quite impressive for a solo practitioner, which is what Addie Allen was.

Warren had mentioned that Addie once had been a rising star in a major L.A. firm, but had seen burnout all around her and opted to save herself before she ignited in a pyre of self-incineration. She now worked alone, accepting only those cases that interested her. She was good enough that clients with deep pockets sought her talents, and she accepted enough of those clients, like Carole Ann via Jake, to support her efforts on behalf of the nonwealthy.

Carole Ann stood again and contemplated the room. Perhaps, she mused, if Addie arranged her piles along the walls, there would be sufficient space in the middle for pacing. . . . The door opened to admit one of Addie's two secretaries, the one who Carole Ann thought appeared barely old enough to be out of high school. Her face wore the look that signaled to Carole Ann that she'd just wasted an hour and a half waiting for someone who wasn't coming.

"I'm terribly sorry, Miss Gibson. Miss Allen just called again. She's been detained. She asked if you'd be kind enough to call her at home tonight. Late." The young woman paused on the word "late" and took a breath. "After midnight," she said with a wry smile, one that indicated that this was not an uncommon message.

Carole Ann smiled and nodded. "As long as I don't get in trouble with the judge."

The young woman's smile faded and her hackles rose. "Your arraignment has been recalendared, Miss Gibson. Miss Allen will give you all the details. She's very busy, but she never neglects a client's needs."

Put properly and impressively in her place, Carole Ann recovered those pieces of her dignity not in tatters and left Addie's office, a suite on the top floor of a low-rise building on the low-rent end of Olympic Boulevard. She wondered, and knew the answer immediately, whether Addie had deliberately maintained an address on the same street as her former office in a high-rise on the other end of Olympic Boulevard in Century City, where the rents were as high as the buildings.

The heat was bordering on oppressive, the glare of the sun so intense she had to turn her back and allow her eyes to adjust, even with the protection of sunglasses. By the time she reached her car, in a parking lot two blocks away, her blouse was sticking to her back and her throat was parched. She turned on the engine and the air-conditioning and, while waiting for cool to happen, she called her mother. If she rushed, she could get home in time to take Grayce to the dentist's appointment she'd been dreading.

"Tommy and Bert and Angie are taking me," Grayce said, and Carole Ann knew she was more than dreading the experience; she was terrified.

"I'll meet you there, Ma—"

"You can't, C.A.," Grayce said, cutting her off. "You're to call Robbie right away. Something important, he said."

"When did Robbie call?" Carole Ann frowned at the clock on the console of the Benz. Robbie taught four karate or tai chi classes between seven-thirty and one every day, at two different locations. If he had taken the time to call her, there certainly must be urgency involved.

"Not five minutes ago. I gave him Addie's number. . . . Where are you, anyway, C.A.?"

Carole Ann explained her situation, wrote down the address of Grayce's dentist, just in case, and made an appointment to have dinner with her mother. Silly as it felt, if they didn't schedule specific time to be together, their encounters often were brief, and rarely, unless very late at night or early in the morning, private. "And, Ma? Everything's going to be just fine. You're going to be just fine."

"You really think so?" her mother asked, the slightest tremor in her voice.

"I know so. I love you too much for any other thing to be possible," the daughter replied.

**Carole Ann** eased the car out of the aggressive traffic on Washington Boulevard and into the parking lot of a dingy and congested strip mall. She backed into a parking space, facing away from the sun, and, leaving the engine running to keep the air-conditioning going, she opened the *Thomas Guide,* the invaluable street map of Los Angeles that was the size of the telephone book of a small city, and began the search for the address Robbie had given her. Either she'd copied his directions incorrectly or he'd given her incorrect directions, because she could not find the address and she'd been riding in circles for fifteen minutes and she was becoming frustrated. Besides, if she didn't find the location in the next five minutes she'd be late. And she had the feeling that late would send the wrong message.

She jumped at the sound, tapping on the car window, and recoiled when she turned to find a face staring at her, only the glass separating him from her. She forced herself into a quick recovery and pressed the button that lowered the window.

"Yo, *mami.* You lost?"

Carole Ann peered into dark glasses that reflected her own image. "As a matter of fact, I am," she said, grateful that she sounded calm and relaxed. She proffered the paper on which she'd written the address Robbie had given her. "Do you know where that is?"

A tattooed hand, strangely graceful and attractive, received the paper. The body straightened and the face vanished, leaving in Carole Ann's sight line the tops of a pair of jeans, several inches of bronze washboard abs, and the fringe of a cut-off white tee shirt. Then the face reappeared, sans dark glasses and wearing what might have been a smile, which revealed three gold teeth beneath a needle-thin mustache.

"This ain't far. Left at the light and left again at that old school building. Down a few blocks. Then there's a church, Saint Camilla's. That's the street you lookin' for. You have to find which way to turn, right or left." He grinned and gold glinted.

"Thanks very much," Carole Ann said. "I appreciate your taking the time to help."

"No problem, *mami,*" he said, face still in the window.

Carole Ann nodded, forced a smile, and pressed the button to roll up the window. Only then did he stand up and back away. Backed up, angled left, and leaned against the ugly El Dorado she'd seen parked at Robbie's. The one she'd asked Tommy to ask his contact to run the plates on. Had he followed her from Addie's? He must have. She turned slightly for another look at him and was certain that he was no undercover cop. He was the real thing: a Los Angeles gang-banger, and he was still standing there, leaning against his car, when she eased hers into gear and forward out of the parking lot and into the stream of traffic.

She kept a vigil on the rearview mirror, then wondered why: he didn't need to follow her this time; he knew exactly where she was going. And the thought frightened her. Whoever he was, he was a full-fledged gang member. Nothing pretend about him. And she was en route to meet a group of men who probably were not gang members but about whom she knew precious little beyond what they'd told Robbie: that they had information for her regarding Enrique Nunez. That had been sufficient when she talked to Robbie an hour ago. Now, checking her mirrors, she was uncertain. Was she endangering them by bringing whoever was in the El Dorado to them . . . or was she entrapping herself?

She slowed as she approached the abandoned school building and contemplated the nature of waste, peculiar to the American culture. Americans tired of things, or outgrew them, and tossed them out. Or allowed them to rot. She thought of Angie polishing Dottie's briefcase, preserving the leather because she didn't believe in waste. She alone among the masses, for the bedraggled school was surrounded by waste and neglect, by a neighborhood of dead or dying houses. What could be said of the people who had lived in them? What could be said of the ones where there remained signs of life? Or what masqueraded as life. For certainly the neighborhood still was peopled. There were cars and bicycles in the hardscrabble

yards, and scraggly, scruffy dogs and cats ambling about in the brais-
ing heat. The several people Carole Ann saw appeared ancient—
the reason, perhaps, for the demise of the elementary school.

St. Camilla's was only slightly less shabby. It must once have been
a lovely structure. Small by California church standards, reflecting
perhaps the reality that this neighborhood never had been more
than modest, the Moorish-influenced design nevertheless was regal
and graceful. Its once alabaster exterior now was a dingy, dirty,
crumbling gray. The formerly elegant wrought-iron fence that surrounded it sagged and gaped in places, though the front gate was
closed and apparently locked. Why, Carole Ann wondered, when a
child could have pushed the side fence to the ground?

She reached the corner and looked in both directions from the
church. More sad houses to the left, a park with a ballfield and what
appeared to be warehouses beyond to the right. She looked at the directions Robbie had given her. "Across from the park," she'd written, and she turned right.

This end of the block could have been the other side of the world.
The houses here, and the yards, were immaculate. The park was a
community garden, the largest Carole Ann ever had seen. She could
not identify everything that grew, but she knew enough to recognize
healthy fruits and vegetables when she saw them. She counted eight
people working the rows, and another six resting in the grass. She
parked and got out of the car and looked across the street toward
the warehouses. Only they weren't warehouses.

She crossed the street and stood directly before the building upon
which was written, in red calligraphy, DAME QUE ES MÍO CULTURAL
CENTER. Next door was a small grocery store with a table of fresh
produce in front. Next to it was a medical facility that, according to
the block lettering on the window, housed a women's clinic, an AIDS
clinic, a dentist, a podiatrist, and a psychologist. Next to it was a
barber shop. There was a steady stream of foot traffic into and out of

all the doorways to the building, and while there were cars parked on the street, Carole Ann could not discern the source of so many people.

The door before her opened and she stood face to face with Ray, David, and Jose. Though she was expecting to meet them, she was startled by their sudden presence. Her fear returned, then abated just as quickly.

"Thank you for coming," Ray said with a slight bow.

"Thank you for inviting me," Carole Ann said, returning the gesture. Then, with a slight grin, "But you knew, of course, that I would?" She deliberately made it a question.

Ray smiled and lifted his shoulders slightly and dropped them. "I don't claim to know anything for certain, but, yes, I thought the message would bring you."

Carole Ann looked around her, taking in everything she'd so far seen. "The message got me here, but now that I'm here, I'm almost more interested in these surroundings that in Ricky Nunez."

Now he smiled a real smile and stepped aside with a gesture that indicated she should precede him into the door from which the three of them had exited. She did and they followed. Then she stood aside to allow Ray to lead the way down a hallway, which opened into a room that could have been a gallery, were it not for the presence of computers and video equipment and maps and other indicators that it was a place of work.

The walls were covered with cultural artifacts—masks and tools and weapons and baskets and full-body costumes and pipes and drums. It was as if somebody indiscriminately had emptied a museum collection. There were clay items, and straw, and metal. A ten-foot-tall tepee occupied one of the rear corners of the huge room, and in the adjacent corner was an adobe hut. Photographs of indigenous peoples' ceremonies covered that wall space not otherwise occupied—red people and brown people and black people. She traversed the room, awed by the sheer magnitude, the amount and scale, of the collection. And she realized that she felt transported. She also felt a sense of familiarity, as if she'd been here before.

"This . . . this is . . ."

"Not a gang headquarters."

"If it is, sign me up," Carole Ann said. "I'll pay my dues and proudly carry my card. Or wear my colors."

"You already wear your colors," Jose said solemnly, and Carole Ann was reminded of her reason for being in this place.

"What do you know of the history of Mexico and California?" asked Ray.

She considered his question and her answer. "What I learned in school, I suppose," she said, realizing that it hadn't been very much. Her hosts agreed with her.

"Then that's not much, and the part that's not lies is probably just flat-out wrong," David said with a sigh.

"Did you know that Spanish is not the language of the indigenous people of Mexico?" asked Ray, and when she frowned, he recited the date of the Spanish invasion and Carole Ann understood the impact of this brief history lesson. "The reason we display culture the way we do here is because none of us can ever be sure who we are. You can't really call yourself an African American because you can't ever know for sure not only where in Africa your ancestors might have come from, but what they might have mixed with along the way. And you'll never know the language of your ancestors, just as I'll never know the language of mine, only that it wasn't Spanish."

Carole Ann listened with real interest as they explained that the name of their organization referred not to any sort of land reclamation scheme but rather to a reclamation of culture and mores and language. "Not only wouldn't we want to reclaim the parts of California and Texas and Nevada and Utah that once belonged to Mexico, we wouldn't know what to do with it if we could. The Anglos have made a mess of the land!"

Reflection was shattered by the arrival of what felt and sounded like a million schoolchildren, though there could have been no more than thirty of them, second or third graders, Carole Ann guessed, shepherded by three teachers. Their sudden presence reminded her to ask the question she'd pondered outside earlier: given the absence of cars and the relatively inconvenient location of the place, where did all the people come from? And she was as impressed with the answer as with the entire setup.

"We've got four shuttle buses and we bring people from all over. We only have to do it once. They make the return visit on their own. Same with the schools. We have to convince them to bring the first class." He pointed to the tour in progress. "That's the fifth class from that school."

"I am truly impressed." More than that, she was overwhelmed. And puzzled. And curious. "I apologize in advance for my rudeness, but where did the money for this come from?"

The question surprised them and the answer surprised her.

"City of Los Angeles via the LAPD," said David, and explained how the three of them had been arrested seven years earlier while walking in the Westwood section of L.A., a ritzy enclave of expensive homes not far from Malibu and the ocean. It also was UCLA's neighborhood, and the Strip in Westwood was a convenient and popular hangout for students, which Ray, David, and Jose were then. But to the police, they didn't look like UCLA students. After all, they were Hispanic and they were dressed in baggy jeans and tee shirts and their hair was long and they sported earrings.

After thirty-six hours and a couple of beatings, they were released. They never were charged, never were processed, never were given a reason for their detention. The city settled quickly and quietly.

"Not many young people would have invested their riches this way," Carole Ann said, waving her arm around to encompass everything from the artifacts on the walls to the produce garden across the street.

"When he was twenty-eight, Langston Hughes wrote an essay challenging his peers. He told them to stop worrying about what others thought of them and to build temples for tomorrow. We had temples, once, your people and my people and all the ancient people. And they were destroyed."

Carole Ann twitched as if she'd received an electrical jolt. "What did you say . . . who said what about temples?" She was hearing Arthur Jennings say those exact words.

"Langston Hughes—"

"Don't get him started," Jose interrupted with a grin, punching Ray on the shoulder. "No matter what you might think, she didn't come to hear one of your lectures. She came to hear how Enrique Nunez is a bigger scumbag than we thought. Speaking of which," he glanced at his watch, "I'm on in about ten seconds."

Carole Ann watched him hurry toward the student tour group and was aware that both Ray and David were watching her watch Jose. He was speaking now, hands moving about, body and face animated. Giving a lecture. Her emotions registered.

"Jose is a cultural anthropologist," Ray said slyly. "I'm an ethnologist, and Dave here is a sociologist. And now that we've enjoyed our revenge, this is what we brought you here to tell you," Ray said, immediately relieving Carole Ann of her chagrin and embarrassment.

Angered that anyone would use the name of their organization to perpetrate violence, the three of them decided to launch a major search for Ricky Nunez. They called on every possible source of information, cashing in a few IOUs along the way. After all, they were products of *el barrio* and counted among their childhood friends, not to mention a brother or cousin or two, the members of several gangs. It hadn't been difficult to locate people who knew Ricky . . . or to ferret out why he chose to say he was down with the *Dame Que Es Mío* organization.

"It makes a perverse kind of sense," Ray said when he'd completed explaining what he knew of Ricky Nunez and his activities.

"Here you have a guy who, on his best day, is a fuck-up, and somebody sets up a deal where he can run back and forth to Mexico like a *jefe mejor* and get paid big bucks for his trouble. You think he cares if it's dangerous or he could get busted? He only cares that he makes enough cash to stay high and pull girls. As for the rest of it, he may not even understand what he's doing. And he sure as hell wouldn't have enough sense to figure out that what he's doing has no relationship to *Dame Que Es Mío.*"

Carole Ann agreed. And most certainly it could be the link between past and current evils in Jacaranda Estates. She easily could fathom a connection to Dottie Miller. But how to explain the attacks on Fatima Asmara, Sadie Osterheim, and Peggy Hendricks? How did they tie in? And why hadn't Arthur Jennings told her this piece of information? He'd been so forthcoming—why conceal this? Unless he hadn't known.

So engrossed was she in trying to forge and weld connections between past and present, between fact and speculation, that she was unaware that Ray had spoken.

"I'm sorry, I didn't hear you. What did you say?"

Ray's demeanor was more serious than before and Carole Ann gave him her full attention. "I was saying that Enrique Nunez is a loud-mouthed, pot-smoking, beer-guzzling idiot. The people he's involved with are not. They are mean, greedy bastards, and if you plan on getting in their way, you better be careful."

She acknowledged the warning and thanked the three of them—Jose had returned with whispered thanks that it wasn't his job to teach eight-year-olds all day long. They shared a brief moment of levity, and Carole Ann prepared to take her leave. She was stopped by Ray's hand on her arm.

"What are you going to do?" he asked, looking grim.

"Try to extricate myself from the pile of crap I'm buried under," she replied equally grimly, "and try to bury Ricky and his cohorts under an even deeper pile in the process."

"I told you, those people play rough. I don't think you know how rough."

She considered the body count, including Dottie Miller, and added the emotional and psychological toll, including her own. "I think I've got a pretty good idea," she said, and turned toward the door.

"Miss Gibson!"

She turned back to them. Jose had his hand raised as if to ask a question in class. "Carole Ann," she said. "My name is Carole Ann."

"Carole Ann," Jose said. "When the bar gives you your license back, we need ourselves a good lawyer. Even in the old days, the temple builders had themselves good lawyers."

She studied them for a long moment, nodded, turned, and walked toward the door, thinking that the sense of familiarity she experienced when she first entered the room stemmed from the fact that it reminded her of Angie's home.

**Tommy** had been as fidgety and wiggly as a four-year-old while she'd talked on the telephone to Arthur Jennings. He crossed and uncrossed his legs; tied and untied his sneakers; scratched his head, ears, and nose; got up and sat back down; picked at his fingernails. She was beginning to learn his behavior, and when he was excited or nervous, he fidgeted. They both felt they were close enough to the truth of Jacaranda's buried secrets to warrant excitement, but Carole Ann was a seasoned pro at concealing all emotion, while Tommy either wore his emotions on his face or on his sleeve. Or he fidgeted.

"No, Arthur Jennings hadn't known that Enrique Jamilla was an illegal," she said, hanging up the telephone, "but given that information, and the involvement of Hector Nunez, and the probability that Jacaranda Estates itself is involved, he points the finger at the management company. The one we can't find."

"Yes!" Tommy jumped up and pumped his arms as if he'd just scored a three-point jumper from midcourt. "It all makes sense. What's his name? The management company guy?"

Carole Ann perused her notes. "Pablo Gutierrez . . ." She stopped short and whispered a curse and looked at Tommy, waiting for him to make the connection.

He instantly sobered when understanding dawned. "That's the name of the dude old Mr. Asmara offed," and when she winced, he apologized for his choice of words, but began to fidget again. "They've gotta be related. Gutierrez. Pablo and Pedro."

"Not necessarily. Gutierrez is as common a name as Smith or Jones. So are Pablo and Pedro. It could be coincidence—"

"Bullshit! We both know better than that." He jumped up from the sofa, almost upending the low table in front of it, and reached the front door in two giant lunges.

"Where are you going?"

"To Bert's, to change clothes. I'm meeting Robbie at the gym. He set me up a face-to-face with a dude who's done some dealing with Ricky Nunez."

"I don't like it, Tommy. Anyway, we know all we need to know about Ricky Nunez and his dealings—"

"No, we don't. Ricky is too stupid to run an international operation by himself, and that's what we're talking about here: smuggling undocumented Mexicans into California, supplying them with driver's licenses and visas and birth certificates, not to mention a place to live while the paperwork is being processed. That's the definition of an international operation. I've seen Ricky. He couldn't organize a two-hot-dog picnic."

She stifled the giggle starting in her throat and gave him an evil look. He was sounding, and behaving, more like Jake every day. "Ray and Dave and Jose said their informants told them that 'an old dude' ran the operation, and that Ricky was his 'right hand.' Their words, not mine," she added quickly when he snorted. "So maybe the 'old dude' is the management company guy, or . . ." The words froze in her mouth as the thought that sent the chill took shape and form. "Oh, my God."

Tommy hurried himself back to where she sat and knelt next to the chair. "What, C.A.? What!"

"Hector. It's Hector. That's what keeps Luisa involved and contained. Hector in Mexico and Pablo Gutierrez here . . ."

"And Pablo's—what? son?—in the LAPD keeping a lid on everything? I'll bet everything I have—except my wife—that Pablo and Pedro are related and in on this scheme. And a hell of a scheme it is, too," Tommy whispered, almost admiringly. Then he got up and headed toward the door again. "I'll be back late. Wait up for me."

"I'll be up. I've got a phone meeting with Addie at the stroke of midnight." The dryness of her tone scraped like sandpaper.

He laughed. "And people criticize the hours cops keep." He closed the door behind him and she heard him whistling and as the sound faded, so did her excitement. Whatever joy she'd felt in having unearthed the truth about the long-forgotten Hector Nunez's involvement in a human smuggling ring—and she was convinced of her correctness—paled compared with the knowledge that Luisa Nunez certainly would go to prison. For certainly she was his accomplice. Still.

Shuddering at the thought of what she was doing to her mother's telephone bill, she called Jake and told him everything.

"Well, I'll be goddamned!" he said in an almost reverent tone.

"You sound surprised, Jake."

"Surprised?" he snorted. "I'm damn near speechless!"

"But it's exactly what you speculated was happening: that Jacaranda was a cover for some large-scale illegal activity."

Jake whistled something tuneless for a few seconds before speaking. "This is one time, C.A., when I could have done with not being right. You know anything about the smuggling of human beings?"

"Only that it's illegal," she said with a grimace.

She heard him sigh. "I guess L.A. cops know a lot about this kind of thing, but it's not something I've ever seen and it's turning my stomach." He was silent for a moment. "But I'm about to find out all there is about the subject and I'll call you later with what I know."

"OK—" she began but he cut her off.

"You *will* be home later, won't you, C.A.?"

"Yes, I will be home later," she answered through clenched teeth. Damn, but he annoyed her sometimes. "I've got a midnight phone meeting with Addie."

"You lawyers keep worse hours than cops."

"That's what Tommy said."

He asked where Tommy was and she told him. Then he asked whether they'd had any success figuring out the playground guys.

"We tried following them, Jake, a couple of times. But there's no place to surveil from here. Nothing but wide-open spaces. But we've watched and they do the same thing: hang out, talking and smoking, and every couple of hours, they peel off in groups of three and go do we don't know what."

"I thought it was in pairs," Jake said, the frown evident in his voice.

"They changed to threes last week."

"Cops," Jake said. "They're undercover for sure, although why they're running an op so half-assed puzzles the shit out of me."

"Suppose they wanted everybody to think that they were responsible for all the violence. That they wanted people to stay inside and away from the playground."

"Then they failed miserably, wouldn't you say?"

Something stirred in Carole Ann's memory. "You remember me telling you that I thought there were three of them the night my mother was attacked?"

"Yeah," Jake said slowly, drawing the word out until it became a question.

"Suppose one of them was one of the undercovers."

"No cop attacked your mother!" Jake yelled into the phone.

She held up a hand he couldn't see. "Will you let me finish?" And when he didn't respond, she continued. "Suppose he was on his round, doing his patrol duty, and stumbled upon the attack on Ma. What I thought I saw as I drove up was someone running toward my mother and one of the others—"

"And your arrival scared him off."

"Makes as much sense as anything else."

"None of it makes sense," he snapped. "This is the biggest pile of shit I've ever seen! And the more we dig, the deeper it gets! This is giving me an ass ache!" And he hung up.

She took a moment to laugh at the miracle of creation that was Jake Graham, then rewound in her brain and replayed the conversation with Arthur Jennings. His surprise at learning of his partner's immigration status had been complete. He'd believed that both Hector and Enrique had been born in California, and that it was their mother who had been born in Mexico and who had immigrated north as a young woman.

He remembered little about Pablo Gutierrez except that Jamilla had liked him. He retained him to manage the land of Jacaranda Estates, Jennings said, because he had no reason not to. He wasn't surprised that there was not a listing in the telephone directory or elsewhere for Gutierrez; most likely, Jacaranda Estates was his only business. He lived on the property, rent free, and spent his time caring for it. It paid well enough that if he didn't require luxury, he didn't need other work.

Two points reverberated in her consciousness: That Pablo Gutierrez lived at Jacaranda Estates; and that he lived an almost anonymous existence. For she'd never heard of him and had no idea where he lived.

**The only** single house on the property," Grayce said, chewing gently but with gusto. Her visit to the dentist had served to allay all her fears and restore most if not all of her brash spirit. It had taken Carole Ann weeks to understand that for her mother, having reached the age of sixty-seven with her original teeth healthy and intact was a source of enormous pride and self-gratification. The thought that she'd lose her teeth as a result of the attack was more of an assault on her spirit and pride than on her body.

"But where is it, Ma? Why haven't I seen it? Why don't I know where it is? And why don't I know who *he* is? This Gutierrez character?"

"I don't know why you don't know where the maintenance sheds are, C.A. They're where they've always been, on the business side of the complex. And that's where Mr. Gutierrez lives as well. His house and all the maintenance sheds are the boundary markers for the end of the property. And you don't know him probably because he keeps to himself. He always has. His English isn't very good, and he sees himself as an employee, so he doesn't socialize." Grayce's eyes narrowed and she ceased her chewing. "And I haven't seen him around in quite a while, now that I think about it."

"Maintenance sheds? Maintenance sheds! Yes! How damned convenient! And pretty damn smart, too."

Grayce put down her fork with a determined clatter and fixed her daughter in the glare that had, from the very beginning, solidified the mother's position of prominence and authority. Carole Ann put down her fork, gently and silently, wiped her mouth on her napkin, and began to squirm.

Annoyed with herself for her regression, she jumped up from the table, pointedly ignoring her mother's reaction to her profanity—Grayce abhorred cursing—slouched into the living room, and collapsed onto the sofa. "Come have a seat, Ma, while I tell you a little story."

Grayce sat in silence for a long time after Carole Ann finished talking. Then she sighed deeply and shook her head. "Those poor people. They bring them here and lock them up in those little sheds? How cruel!"

Carole Ann raised her hand. "This is all speculation, Ma. It's what we think is happening. We have no real proof."

"It shouldn't surprise me, I suppose. So much about this smuggling business has changed in recent years."

She looked at her mother in open-mouthed wonderment. "Ma, what could you possibly know about smuggling? About smuggling human beings, for the love of Christ!"

"Watch your mouth, C.A. I don't want to remind you again. And quite a lot. Smuggling human beings is big business in this part of the world, and the news is full of it. Especially when there's some kind of tragedy involved. Like the time a bunch of them were found dead in this van—"

Carole Ann called time out. "How many is a bunch, and are you talking about Mexicans smuggled over the border, and how did they get dead?"

Grayce showed her annoyance. "A bunch is twenty-something if I recall correctly," she snapped at her daughter. "And yes, I'm talking about Mexicans brought illegally into the States. I thought that's what we were discussing. And they got dead from carbon monoxide poisoning and heat stroke and starvation and only God knows what else. And to make matters worse, most of them were women and children."

Carole Ann wanted to ask many more questions but held back because she felt overwhelmed by what she'd just heard. And because she knew Grayce was annoyed with her. So they sat in silence, thinking and feeling and wondering at the perversity of human nature.

"There was a time when just working, family men found their way across the border. They'd get established and then send for their families—wives, children, parents, other relatives. Then women began coming alone in great numbers and following the same pattern: work, get established, send for the family. Well, now they're bringing in the hoodlums. Anybody who can pay the price, the mules will bring in. And these days that includes some pretty rough customers—"

She was interrupted by the ringing of the phone, which Carole Ann answered in the middle of the second ring.

Jake began talking before the "hello" was out of her mouth. "People smuggling is damn big business, C.A. And damn dangerous. More for the people being smuggled than for the damn smugglers! And the really bad news is that some really nasty fuckers are being brought in along with the honest citizens, who're just looking for a chance for a better life."

"That was quick," she said, not having the heart to tell him that she'd already just heard the same thing from Grayce.

"So how 'bout this for a scenario: all the bad stuff that's been happening in Jacaranda, including the murders, is the work of some of these smuggled-in hard asses. That's why the one who Roberta shot hasn't been ID'ed, or why the one you . . . that one still hasn't been ID'ed. They're illegals."

He finally wound down and they listened to each other breathe for a moment.

"Can we prove any of this?" she asked.

"I don't know about proof," he said, and she could see his shrug. "But this points us in the right direction of which trees to shake. And if we start shaking trees, something's bound to fall out."

"But will that be good enough for . . . good enough to—"

"To get your ass out of the sling it's in? We'll make sure it'll be good enough," he said, and hung up on her again.

**When it** got dark, she took a long, slow jog around Jacaranda Estates. Twice. Each time taking a long, slow look at Pablo Gutierrez's house and at the eight maintenance sheds, painted the same color as the house, as was the trim around the windows and doors. Nothing unusual about the house itself unless one looked at it long enough and carefully enough for it to register that, unlike its neighbors, it was neither a duplex nor a triplex. It was a single, one-sto-ried house, architecturally identical to every other house in the de-velopment. And the maintenance sheds closely resembled garages. Nothing unusual about them, either, unless one stopped to ponder why one house would have an eight-car garage. And why they would have windows. And why those windows would be open.

She called Arthur Jennings again, to inquire what one might ex-pect to find inside the sheds, and was annoyed with herself that she hadn't reached what should have been a logical conclusion: lawn mowers and rakes and water hoses and sprinklers and grass seed and fertilizer and paint and paintbrushes and tools, whatever might be required to maintain the grounds and buildings of an estate. As an afterthought, she asked whether Pablo Gutierrez had known Hector Nunez. And through his surprise at the question, he recalled that Pablo had been a closer friend to Hector than to Enrique.

She envisioned the sheds and imagined them empty . . . or empty of maintenance materials and equipment. Each shed contained more than enough space to secret human beings long enough for forged documents to be delivered to them. She envisioned cots or, more likely, sleeping bags lined up on the concrete floor, and quickly abandoned the exercise when attempts to imagine how the people would eat, and then relieve themselves, made her, by turns, angry and ill.

It was easier to recall the shabby condition of the Jacaranda Estates grounds and imagine that the reason was that Pablo Gutier-rez was otherwise occupied. And to imagine the bolder of the sheds' occupants breaking away from captivity for a stroll around the grounds, encountering unsuspecting old ladies carrying purses and grocery bags.

# ❧ *fifteen* ❧

Carole Ann could hear Addie's excitement. She'd had no difficulty jumping to the conclusion that Pedro Gutierrez, erstwhile L.A. cop, was a trafficker in human beings. And it looked as if the LAPD had known it. "If the DA wants to take you and Mrs. Lawson and Mr. Asmara to trial and risk having me run that flag up the pole for all the world to see, I'm ready to bet the farm it'll be a mistake they'll regret longer than they already regret Rodney and O.J."

Addie was as alert and excited as if it were noon instead of half past midnight; and while Carole Ann shared the excitement, she also was exhausted and she wanted to sleep. Addie wanted to hear the details again. Especially the tying in of Hector Nunez to the operation.

"I'm speculating, Addie, and extrapolating. No one's seen Hector in thirty years—"

"But it all makes sense, C.A. It's a perfect plan. And it's probably been working perfectly for a good many of those thirty years. Until something went wrong. That's what we have to figure out—what screwed up the plan?"

"Losing control of the merchandise," Carole Ann said thoughtfully. "Pablo or Pedro or whoever is in charge here lost control of their . . . what do you call smuggled human beings?"

"So, you're saying the thugs on the playground didn't kill Sadie What's-her-name, or beat Mrs. Asmara senseless?"

"I'm saying the thugs on the plagqround aren't thugs," C.A. replied, barely stifling a yawn. "I think, and Tommy and Jake think, they're cops."

"Then how and why in the hell did they allow people to be beaten and killed! I can't buy that part, C.A. I know the LAPD has done some pretty sorry shit, but this I can't accept."

Carole Ann, fighting fatigue, struggled for enough clarity to share with Addie thoughts she had yet to share with Jake or Tommy. Because she hadn't completed the processing of them. "What I think, Addie, and this may be totally off the wall, is that the cops on the playground were there to watch the smuggling operation. And the two other undercovers, the ones living in Jacaranda, were put in to curb the assaults and the vandalism. But they had to stay out of the way, keep low profiles."

"So the renegade illegals are responsible for all the vandalism? The broken windows and stolen cars and turned-over grills—"

"I think so. Listen, Addie, if I don't get some sleep—" Carole Ann was interrupted by the call-waiting beep. "Who the hell," she muttered, before asking Addie to hold and clicking over to the other line. "Who is it?" she snapped into the phone.

"It's Robbie, C.A. They've got Tommy."

It took several seconds to process those few words, to reconcile them with the time of night and with her expectation of who might be calling so late and why. Seconds in which she shifted mental and emotional gears. Seconds before the fear took hold. "Who's got Tommy, Robbie? Where are you?"

"At the gym. Tommy met me here. We were gonna meet another dude, only he didn't show. We waited for a while, then went across the street to a burrito place and ate, then came back to the gym. I went inside to see if anybody was waiting or if anybody had left a message. Tommy was leaning against his car. He's some kind of crazy about that damn car!" Robbie's voice caught and stuck in his throat and he coughed. "The gym is on the second floor. It's got those one-way windows. Look like mirrors outside, you know? Anyway, I was standing there talking to Pete, the owner, when this rocket ship pulls into the parking lot—"

"When *what* pulls into the parking lot?" Carole Ann had regained some sense of herself, enough to pose a question.

"That's what I call it. It's an old Caddy convertible painted this ugly orange."

"I know it," she said, and felt a cold wave pass through her.

"Two dudes jumped out and grabbed Tommy before he could even think to protect himself. C.A., they got him!"

Carole Ann could not protect herself from the panic she heard in Robbie's voice. It invaded her and spread, poisoning her system like a killer disease.

"What are we gonna do, C.A.!" Robbie screamed at her.

"I don't know, Robbie. I'll call you back." She pressed the button, cutting him off and returning to Addie. "They've got Tommy," she said to her lawyer, the same way Robbie had said it to her. And she waited. And when Addie didn't respond, Carole Ann told the story the way Robbie had told it to her. "I have to find him, Addie. And you have to help me."

"I don't know what I can—"

"You'd better figure it out." Something unfamiliar reigned within Carole Ann. Something cold and fearful and rigid. And whatever it was, it spoke a language Addie Allen knew.

"I'll call you in thirty minutes," she said, and severed their connection.

The thing within Carole Ann transformed her. Nothing she felt or thought was familiar. She could think of nothing to do, to say. Nothing useful. To call Jake or Warren would accomplish what? To wake her mother? To get in her car and search for Tommy? Where? What? Why? How? She was shivering the way she had the day War- ren held her and told her she was grieving . . . Warren! No. Call Warren and say what? That she'd lost Tommy? Besides, he'd already saved her life once. He and Jake and Tommy.

And there it was, announcing itself. The thing that had invaded her: terror. And the fear of it.

She'd lived the past year with the terror she'd felt when she was abducted by Leland Devereaux and transported, bound and beaten, deep into a Louisiana bayou where, she was certain, he'd planned to kill her. Until Jake and Tommy and Warren and Warren's cousin, Herve, had saved her. She'd lived a year in fear because the worst had happened and she was terrified that it could happen again. And it had. To Tommy. She'd save him. She had to. He'd saved her. She owed him. She owed Valerie more than a year with the husband she adored. Al was gone, but he and Carole Ann had had more than a year. So should Tommy and Valerie.

"Addie?" she said, snatching up the phone in the middle of the first ring.

"Listen carefully and do exactly as I say."

**She'd followed** Addie's instructions to the letter, but she was find- ing it difficult to leave the keys to the rented Benz on the floor be- neath the mat. Even if the car was parked in a brightly lighted area of the arriving-passengers parking lot of LAX, near the security checkpoint. She inhaled deeply, held the breath, then released it in a loud puff and dropped the keys to the floor. She'd been willing to trust Addie with her own life. Trusting her with Tommy's life was a different matter. But she was without options.

Addie had told her to dress in dark, functional clothing—black, if she had it—and to drive to the airport. She'd told her to park in the arriving-passengers lot, as if she were meeting someone, and leave the car keys and the parking ticket under the mat on the driver's side. Carole Ann lifted the mat and placed the keys and the ticket beneath it.

She strolled toward the terminal. Addie had said not to rush, to appear as if she'd arrived in plenty of time to meet the plane. She stopped at the first baggage carousel she reached and looked for the overhead monitor that displayed flight arrival times. It was where Addie said it would be and she stood reading it for several seconds. Then she looked at her watch. Then she rode the escalator up to the airport lobby. She looked right, located the symbol for the women's bathroom, and followed the arrow.

She was holding her breath when she entered the bright, empty space, and released it when she realized she was alone. No contact person here. She checked, pushing open each of the stall doors. She was wondering what to do when the door opened. Again Carole Ann released breath. An airport security guard.

"Miss Gibson, I'm Gloria Jenkins. Thank you for helping my mother."

Carole Ann studied the woman before her. She didn't recall how Gloria Jenkins looked, but she did remember declining Jake's invitation to a reintroduction. This woman was her height, though not as thin. Her hair was cut short and streaked with silver, more salt than pepper. Her eyes were dark and steady. The silver identification bar on the breast pocket of her starched, light blue shirt read, "E. Killian." There were three stripes on the sleeve of the shirt.

"Sergeant Killian," Carole Ann said. "I'm glad I was able to help, though I regret the need for it."

Something flashed for an instant in her eyes, and was gone. "My son saw Tommy Griffin yesterday. He ran a license plate for him," she said, and waited for Carole Ann to make the connection.

"How old is your son?" Carole Ann asked, and the woman who had been Gloria Jenkins those many years ago smiled; for that woman's children had been five and seven years old when they entered the witness protection program thirteen years ago. Not old enough now to be running license plates for Tommy Griffin.

"Anthony was my lover's son. We were raising our children together. He was thirteen when his mother was killed. He was with his father the night . . . everything happened. He spent one weekend a month with his father. He wanted to go with us, with my children and me, when we left. When we entered the protection program. His father didn't object. He knew Anthony loved me and that I loved him and would take care of him. Anyway. One weekend a month was as much of a father as he wanted to be."

Carole Ann nodded her acceptance of the explanation and marveled at the turns the woman's life had taken. Marveled at the twists and turns of so many lives she'd recently learned of. Marveled that people managed as well as they did.

"Have you been here in L.A. since . . . for the last thirteen years?"

She nodded. "They got me this job. I thought it was some kind of joke at first, the government's brand of humor. But I learned to like the work. Can't say I was pleased, though, when Anthony decided to become a cop. But he loved it. Then they turned on him."

"Is that how you know Addie? From your son's trouble?"

"What business is that of yours?" Her tone was so calm as to be devoid of emotion, but Carole Ann did not miss the potential for hostility that was there.

"It isn't, certainly. I only ask because of the incredible coincidence: that I should be connected to you through both Jake and Addie."

Her eyes flashed another message and Carole Ann rushed into the breach and changed the subject. "Did he find a match for the plates?"

She nodded and compressed her lips and seemed to be thinking of something more to say when the radio clipped to her gun belt crackled. She unhooked it, brought it to her mouth, and said her name.

Then she put it to her ear and listened for several seconds before acknowledging the message and signing off. "Anthony is waiting for you at Gate Eleven. You have a tail. Two of 'em—skinny white dude with long hair, beard, ragged jeans, and a woodwork Black dude: khakis, loafers, and a white oxford shirt. The type who could blend in anywhere. He's at the phone kiosk just outside the door. Skinny is in the gate area across the way pretending to be asleep beneath a newspaper. There'll be a crowd at the gate when you get there. Full flight just in from JFK. Walk directly into the mass like you're meeting someone. Anthony will take it from there. He looks like Marvin Gaye and he's dressed like a flight attendant." Her radio crackled again and her body language abruptly changed. As she bolted for the door, hand on her holster gun, she said, "Don't notice me when you see me at the gate," and she exited the ladies' room at a fast trot.

By the time Carole Ann emerged several seconds later, Gloria Jenkins, aka E. Killian, was not in sight. She looked both ways, taking in Skinny and almost missing Woodwork, who had blended so well into the scenery that he almost was invisible, before turning left and toward Gate 11. She felt the crowd's energy a split second before she heard the cacophony of voices as the first passengers off the plane spilled out into the main passageway. She immediately could sympathize with the feeling of freedom after the five-hour coast-to-coast flight. She had never enjoyed the New York to Los Angeles trip, had always felt like a kid let out of school for the summer when the door of the plane opened.

Following instructions, she reached the gate and waded into the crowd, swimming against the tide. She recoiled when she was bumped from behind, and she almost reacted defensively when she felt the pressure on her arm. Then she heard, "It's me, Anthony," and she allowed herself to be steered toward the plane's jet way. Suddenly she heard a shout and people began pushing and shoving. Several women screamed and the man in front of her stumbled and fell. She tried to stop but Anthony pushed her forward, around the fallen man. Out of the corner of her eye she saw an official uniform—Sergeant Killian—and felt the scuffling energy intensify.

Anthony abruptly changed direction, forcing her into a hard left turn. They ducked behind a metal partition and, for an instant, were back in the main hallway. On their right was a steel door with EMPLOYEES ONLY printed in block letters. Anthony turned the knob and the door opened and he pushed her inside.

The room, about ten feet square, was an employee lounge. Several ugly vinyl couches lined the walls. Equally ugly metal tables were arranged before them, and littering the tables were old newspapers and older cups of coffee and cans of soda. Windows spanned the back wall of the room, and there was a door in the far corner. Anthony saw her notice the door and he nodded.

"Your car already is en route to a garage in Ladera Heights. My girlfriend's parents' house. It'll be safe."

"Thanks," she said, thinking that he really did resemble Marvin Gaye. Eerily so. "Do you know where Tommy is? Do you know who has him?"

Anthony massaged his head with both hands. "The 'who,' yes. The 'where,' maybe." He looked at his watch and pressed his temples. "Come on." He was at the door, opening it before Carole Ann crossed the room. The whine of a jet engine rushed in on the night air and caused the room to reverberate. "I don't know how people listen to this noise all day." He said something else she didn't hear, then he pressed his lips to her ear and, as they descended a flight of stairs to the tarmac, he pointed to a white food service truck and told her that was their way out of LAX.

The food service van dropped them at an employee parking lot, where Anthony climbed in behind the wheel of a nearly new Ford Bronco. Carole Ann climbed into the passenger side. She checked her watch as the mechanical arm lifted and they exited the lot. It had been exactly thirty-five minutes since she parked her car in the arriving-passengers lot. She was impressed with the operation and she told him as much. He turned and looked at her, something in his gaze familiar but unreadable.

"Griffin thinks you walk on water. But I look at you and I see the lawyer who defended the piece of shit who killed my mother."

Carole Ann knew what it was she recognized in his eyes: it was the same thing she'd seen in Gloria Jenkins's eyes. Something that if they'd been different people would have been related closely to hatred. Gloria and Anthony did not hate her, but they did, she suspected, hate what she'd done. And suddenly it all reminded her of Hazel Copeland. Juror number seven. What she had seen in Hazel Copeland's eyes is what had prompted her decision to leave the practice of law. Or at least to leave the way she'd been practicing it.

She nodded. "That's a mistake I wouldn't make now."

"I wouldn't be here if I thought otherwise, lady."

Since there was no appropriate response she settled for silence. She watched him drive and watched the traffic ebb and flow around them, unconsciously on the lookout for Woodwork and Skinny, though she was satisfied that they'd be spending the rest of the night explaining to a superior officer how they lost their mark at the airport. Traffic was as heavy as if it were midday. She often wondered where so many people could be going at two o'clock in the morning; and she wondered if any of her fellow travelers wondered at her presence on this road, and speculated about her destination.

Anthony had taken the 105 from the airport, to the 5, and was heading south. He wove in and out of the dense traffic, lane shifting like a maniac. Then, at Anaheim, he got on Highway 91. She sat up and took notice. Her familiarity with this area was vague. This was the way, she thought, to Anaheim Stadium and to Disneyland. He kept driving, fast and steady. The traffic thinned and the Santa Ana Mountains loomed dark and forbidding in the distance and he seemed to relax a bit. He checked his watch and increased the pressure on the gas pedal. The truck leaped forward. She must have dozed because when she looked again for a road sign, they were on Interstate 15. Unless they were going to have a mud bath at the spa in Temecula, Carole Ann couldn't imagine why . . . unless they were going to Mexico.

She flashed back to the journey she'd made in the back of a vehicle similar to this one, about this same time last year. She was bound and blindfolded and in Louisiana. She tried to find comfort in the fact that she was not, on this journey, a captive, a prisoner. At least not in name.

"Are we going to Mexico?" she asked, and concluded from his response that she must have succeeded in sounding barely concerned and extremely nonchalant.

"You don't seem too put off by the notion. Griffin must be a major player in your ball game."

"He saved my life, so I suppose that qualifies him for the majors," she replied, not caring that an undercurrent of nastiness accompanied her words. She hadn't liked what she'd heard implied in his question. Robbie, too, had questioned her commitment to Tommy, but with nothing prurient in his question.

Anthony whistled through his teeth. "No shit," he said. "When somebody steps up to the plate like that, I suppose you do have to pay back in kind. So. To answer your question, we're not going to Mexico. But the smugglers have a safe house down near the border and when they snatched Griffin, they headed in this direction. My source says they lost 'em out of Tustin, so we're guessing about their destination. But it's an educated guess. You know what I mean?"

Carole Ann said she did and she asked him who his source was. He laughed. "Tommy was right about you."

She didn't ask what Tommy was right about. After the silence had stretched into several minutes, he told her that his source was an INS agent he'd worked with for over a year trying to bust up what he called "a big-league people-smuggling ring." It was a joint project, the LAPD and the INS for the first time really and truly cooperating with each other instead of competing. The reason for such a high degree of cooperation, he offered before she could ask, was "a van full of dead people. Twenty-seven of 'em. Eleven children. Jammed into the back of the thing like slaves crossing the Atlantic. All dead but one woman, and she eventually died. But not before giving us the smuggler's name and the deep and skinny on his scam."

"Hector Nunez, Pablo Gutierrez, Enrique Nunez, Jacaranda Estates," she said, and smiled inwardly at the double take he did in her direction.

"How the hell did you piece all that together? It took us months!"

"I thought you were ex-LAPD," she said, emphasis on the "ex," ignoring his question and wondering whether she'd misunderstood, for Anthony sounded and acted like the real thing. But his face told her there'd been no misunderstanding.

"I told you we'd been at this more than a year? It's been closer to two years. And every time we'd get set to spring the trap, they'd be five miles down the road. It finally dawned on us that they were getting inside information. But we didn't know where from. We blamed the INS and they blamed us and the whole thing almost unraveled. Then Gutierrez set me up to take the fall." And he stopped talking and waited for the impact of his words to register with her.

"Gutierrez. You mean the one . . ."

He nodded. "Yep. It wasn't until that old man took him out that the brass knew who the dirty cop was and that it wasn't me. But it was too late. I'd already quit rather than endure an IA investigation and have my whole life dragged through the mud. Besides, Mom—Gloria—didn't need the aggravation. But now that they've got Gutierrez's ass, I can get my record cleared and get my private license and try to live a normal, happy life." He tried a light laugh but the pain in his voice was too evident.

"How'd Gutierrez set you up? And, help me out here, but are you really telling me that a *cop* beat up my mother?" Unlike Jake, Carole

Ann had little difficulty embracing the concept of hoodlums in blue, but even her cynicism was taxed by that thought.

Anthony shook his head and muttered a curse, followed by more mutterings about wearing his heart on his sleeve. "The setup was easy. We were looking for a place to live. Mom, Teresa—that's Mom's partner—Grandma, and the kids, and my girlfriend and me. We wanted to live near each other. Gutierrez introduced me to his uncle, also Gutierrez. This is before we knew the part he and Jacaranda Estates played in the smuggling operation. Anyway, I meet with old man Gutierrez and take a tour of Jacaranda Estates and fall in love with the place in about two seconds. I pay to get on the waiting list for two houses—a big one for Mom and the gang, and a small one for me and my girl. Snitch Gutierrez videotapes the whole thing. When we learn about old man Gutierrez and his part in the smuggling, I say nothing. I've heard nothing from him, I know I wouldn't dare move in under the circumstances, forget about it. Then the suspicions begin and that punk serves me up. And my ass is grass. End of story." He shrugged elaborately, still not doing a very good job of masking his pain.

"Gutierrez obviously was scum," Carole Ann said, wrinkling her lips in distaste.

"Yeah. But I don't think he was beating up your mom. I think he was trying to get control of one of his contraband," he said. "A lot of the guys they're bringing up here now are hard-core criminals and the first thing they do to work off some of their anger is look for somebody to rob. I mean, think about it: they spend days cooped up in some funky old van. Then they finally get here, and Gutierrez locks 'em in those sheds for another couple of weeks."

They rode in silence for a long while, Carole Ann assessing her feelings based on viewing the attack on her mother from a different perspective. Not that she could accept or excuse it, but she thought she could understand it. People who are treated like animals often behave like animals. But what of people like the Gutierrez men? What could one say about them? And what could she say for herself? Where did she fit on the continuum? For an instant she wished that she could trade places with Mr. Asmara, that it had been Gutierrez she'd killed and not one of the contraband. And immediately she regretted being glad she'd killed anyone, and that she'd thought of another human being as contraband. What the hell was happening here?

She must have made a noise of disgust or dismay because Anthony asked if she was all right and she shook her head. But before he could inquire further, she committed a major no-no: She offered unsolicited, free legal advice. "You know, you can do more than get your record cleared. With Gutierrez on the block, you can get reinstated. With pay, benefits, the works."

He gave a funny look, one she couldn't read. "That's just what Miss Allen said. Come to think of it, you're a lot like her."

"Really," she said dryly, fully regretting having opened that door.

"Are you an Addie Allen kind of lawyer? Do you bill the rich early and often so you can help the poor for free?"

She was silent for so long she knew he thought she'd dozed off. But she was wide awake. She was silent because she wanted to answer his question and found that she could not. She didn't know what kind of lawyer she was. At the moment, she was no kind of lawyer. She didn't practice law. And she didn't want to. She thought of what Addie and Warren did and knew that she no longer wanted to fill her days and nights with the technical aspects of lawyering. She recalled the buzz she got when she thought of representing Hamas Asmara. Warren had been right about what she wanted to do. But the feeling had been fleeting. She didn't want to do what they did, not anymore. But she believed in what they were doing. So where did she fit in? Who needed, who wanted, a nonpracticing attorney?

She looked out the window and tried to remember the last time she'd been this far south of L.A. and could recall only that Al had not been with her on that trip; she and Marge had made the drive to the spa and had spent the day in various hedonistic pursuits, chief among them mud baths and massages. The desert was a perfect place for such endeavors. It was too hot during the day to do much of anything but relax, and too cool at night to venture too far from the fireplace and a good book.

**It was** too dark to see the landscape, but she knew what was out there: scrub grass and cacti and the homes of the hardy or the fool-hardy, as sparsely placed as the foliage. Despite years of overdevelopment of the Los Angeles Basin and everything around it, there were sections of the desert that refused to be controlled, where wildness prevailed. Carole Ann always had loved these places and the places her imagination took her as she speculated on the nature of those who chose to live in the wild, and the reasons for their choices. At this very moment, she felt a keen understanding of those motivations.

For an instant she indulged fantasy and imagined herself living in the desert, surrounded by the aloneness with which she had become so familiar in the last year. Out here, she wouldn't be required to be an Addie Allen kind of lawyer . . . or any kind of lawyer. Out here, she could be nobody. Or somebody about whom nobody else harbored expectations.

"You're the lawyer who beat Griffin's dirty-cop rap, aren't you?"

Carole Ann jumped. She'd been so lost in her own reverie, lulled by the vehicular motion and the mesmerizing calm of the desert, that she'd lost touch with the present. She looked over at Anthony, still wearing the flight attendant's uniform, still looking like Marvin Gaye. "Yes, I am," she replied.

"If you beat the charges and got him reinstated, why'd they fire him?" Anthony was looking at her, not at the road. Not that it mattered; nothing out there but jackrabbits, snakes, lizards, spiders.

She hesitated before answering. Her first and natural response would have been to tell Anthony to ask Tommy, that it wasn't her place to answer for him. Given the circumstances, however, she waived client duty and told him how Tommy's walking off the job at Jake's direction to rescue her from certain death at the hands of a venal Louisiana politician created a stink that spread wider and deeper than all the swamps and bayous. Tommy had violated all manner of departmental and jurisdictional rules and boundaries. Terminating him was an infinitely simpler process than explaining or justifying his behavior. So the D.C. police department terminated him.

"Sounds like they had just cause," Anthony opined.

Carole Ann actually grinned. "That they did," she agreed.

"So, first you saved his ass. Then he saved yours. Now you're saving his again. You two plan on going through life saving each other from the clutches of death and disaster?"

This time she laughed out loud, her mirth falling into the "laugh to keep from crying" category; for it did seem that lately she'd been rushing from one crisis to the next. Not that she sought them, or wanted them . . . perhaps Jake was right. Again. Maybe she *was* a shit magnet. She said as much to Anthony and he laughed, too, repeating the phrase to himself a couple of times.

"You know, that's a perfect description of my life the last year or so. But I feel that cycle coming to an end. Busting these asshole smugglers closes a big, shitty chapter in my life." He laughed again. "Maybe I'm demagnetized now. You, too, you know?"

She smiled. "It's a nice thought, Anthony. Thanks."

"You're welcome. And I'm sorry I was rude to you earlier. You're OK, just like Griffin and Addie said."

Feeling no response was necessary, she rode in silence for a while, still peering out into the darkness, straining to see something and wishing it were day so that she could. Then she did see something ahead. Lights. And as she began to recognize shape and form, the truck began to slow and she tensed. Their destination obviously was a tiny gas station ahead on the right. It was closed, she could see that much from the weak glow of the spotlights on the side of the concrete building. As they drew closer, she could also see at least half a dozen vehicles parked in the lot. And as her brain was forming around the situation that was shaping up before her, Anthony turned off the lights of his Bronco, downshifted, and coasted into the exit off the freeway and toward the gas station.

"I'm going to need you to stay put while I explain why you're here," he said in a different tone of voice. A cop's tone of voice. "It's bad enough that I'm unauthorized."

"This is not just about getting Tommy back, is it?"

He shook his head. "Uh-uh. This is about bustin' their asses. Gutierrez is gone, and so is Mrs. Nunez—"

"What!" Carole Ann snapped to attention. "Mrs. Nunez? You mean Luisa? She's gone where?"

Anthony shrugged. "Back to Mexico, I guess. They've felt the walls closing in on them. She's been gone for three days, so she's probably already there. But Gutierrez just left this morning, so we think he's still on this side. At their safe house, where we think they're holding Griffin."

Carole Ann was numb. All of a sudden, this expedition had turned dangerous. Not that she'd expected to walk up to this safe house, knock on the door, and ask if Tommy could come out and play. But she hadn't expected a full assault. She scanned the parking lot and could discern flak-jacketed and helmeted INS agents and components of the LAPD SWAT unit.

Anthony opened the door, stepped out of the Bronco, removed his airline jacket, and tossed it into the backseat. Then he unbuttoned and unzipped his trousers and stepped out of them. And, opening the back door, he retrieved a bundle that, as he unraveled it, presented itself as black combat clothing, boots included. He was dressed in a matter of seconds. He gently closed both doors and walked around to the passenger side. Carole Ann lowered the window and was face-to-face with him as he leaned in toward her. His expression was grave. She'd seen Tommy look like that, and Jake. It was coplike.

"Can you shoot a gun?"

She shook her head.

"I know you're a martial arts expert, but hand-to-hand combat may not be of much use here. But," and he shrugged elaborately, "you never know. Just concentrate on staying back and out of the way." And he walked off toward the cluster of vans at the rear of the tiny gas station.

She sat still in the chilly darkness feeling fully aware of the extent of the danger facing Tommy Griffin, and of the extent of her own fear. For him and for herself. Then she tried to imagine how he must have felt as he embarked on his mission to save her. He was a cop and therefore acquainted with danger, that she knew. But he was a stranger to Louisiana and to the bayous and to Warren and Herve, the men he'd had to trust in order to save her, and that must have frightened him. He must have contemplated the possibility of failure.

"No," she whispered. He wouldn't have. Any more than Jake would have. Or Warren. Or Herve. So, she could not. And as she eliminated from her reasoning the possibility of failure, she felt the gripping fear release its hold on her innards. She felt her chest open and her breath flow. Her stomach ceased its cramping, her nails their skin-bruising attack on her thighs.

She wondered whether Anthony or one of the other cops had an extra Kevlar vest for her to use; and she wondered to what extent it would impede her range of motion and movement. She could not, she decided, kick the shit out of people smugglers strapped into a bulky vest, and therefore concluded that she'd simply have to stay out of the way of stray bullets.

# ❦ *sixteen* ❧

He couldn't see very much and he could understand nothing of what he heard, but Tommy Griffin considered himself to be in much better condition than the people around him. He didn't know all C.A. knew about the smuggling ring—she hadn't had the chance to tell him—but he did know that Mexican citizens were being smuggled into the United States and he surmised that the two dozen worn-out-looking people sharing the locked room with him were not there by invitation of the president. He was almost grateful for the semi-darkness; he could feel and smell the misery around him. He didn't need to see it.

The single, glass-encased candle positioned on the windowsill illuminated the room sufficiently for Tommy to count his companions and to determine their gender: fifteen women, eleven men. No children, though at least three of the females appeared to be quite young—barely pubescent, he guessed—and took the grasp that three of the more adult women had on the younger ones to be confirmation of his surmises. Mothers and daughters. All but three of the men sat near the women, suggesting to Tommy that they were relatives of some kind, husbands, fathers, brothers. The three who sat apart from the crowd also sat apart from one another. Each one a stranger to all.

They all sat apart from Tommy, who, in addition to the fact that he wasn't Mexican, was bound, hands and feet. In any culture, a sign of trouble. They didn't need to be told to keep their distance. He struggled to sit upright and grimaced as a line of pain radiated from his groin down both legs. Ricky Nunez had kicked him, the cowardly little bastard, waiting until he was tied and supine. The weirdo of a grandmother had watched in silence, and Tommy couldn't tell whether her brain was actually registering what was transpiring around her.

He'd also recognized Pablo Gutierrez, though he didn't know his name or his function. He just knew he'd seen the man around Jacaranda Estates. And it occurred to Tommy that there was more than a loose connection between Jacaranda Estates and smuggled Mexicans.

Damn! but he wished he could talk to C.A. To Jake. To Anthony. To Addie. To anybody! And barring that, he wished he spoke Spanish, so he could talk to the poor people locked in this room with him. Though, he concluded, it wasn't likely that any of them would be willing to make a break for it with him. Where could they go but back to Mexico? Who in their right mind would pick up a bunch of Mexicans hitchhiking in the middle of the night? For that matter, who in their right mind would pick him up? He didn't imagine that the Black population in whatever part of California they were in . . . were they still in California?

That thought jarred him, then he settled himself. Certainly they were in California because these people had just arrived, shortly after he did, from Mexico. And he'd heard that asshole, Ricky, say something about not wanting to cross the border until sunup, and Tommy thought there was something cruel in the way he said it. Then he realized how cruel: Ricky was an American citizen with a passport. He could cross the border, legally, in broad daylight, whenever he chose.

He wiggled his toes and flexed his fingers and performed a series of isometric exercises, which caused the pain to jog up and down his legs again. He had to keep his circulation going. He had to be prepared to act when the time came. He didn't imagine for a second that his captors planned to haul him to Mexico. After all, there couldn't be much profit in smuggling Americans into Mexico. He knew they planned to kill him. He also knew he had no intention of making it easy for them. He hoped it was the Nunez punk, but he knew better. The kid was a druggie and a coward. He couldn't kill anything that might strike back.

He closed his eyes, saw Valerie's face, and popped them open again. That definitely was the wrong thought to have. He had no intention of giving in to the maudlin. He was a cop. His wife was a cop. They'd handle whatever they needed to handle. His eyes slid closed again. This time the screen showed his sparkling convertible. He really liked that car! And he hoped Robbie Lee had the good sense to move it from that crummy parking lot.

Poor Robbie. He'd probably called C.A. in a panic. . . . Oh, shit! C.A. in a panic was not a cheery thought. She would have called Jake.

**But she** hadn't called Jake. Addie Allen had called Jake. And had been treated to a first-class Jacob Graham explosion. She had been properly impressed and entertained and had not, until his tirade was sputtering to a close, realized the true nature of his emotion: the man was frightened. She'd never met him; had conducted business with him via telephone on Warren Forchette's introduction; had sent him a contract, which he'd signed and returned with a check; had heard enough about him to know that people she liked and respected—Warren, Carole Ann Gibson, Tommy Griffin—

revered the man. She didn't know that the feeling was mutual. Didn't know that he thought of Tommy Griffin as a son; thought of C. A. Gibson as a blend of all the women meaningful in his life. To contemplate both of them simultaneously in danger was more than he could bear.

"I'm catching the next plane out there."

"No!" Addie issued the command before she could talk herself out of it. So startled was he that she had sufficient time to recover her equilibrium and fashion a more appropriate response. "Mr. Graham." She took a deep breath. "Your coming here would serve no purpose. I promise you that things are as under control as they can be in such circumstances. Miss Gibson is with my chief investigator, who also is ex-LAPD. And both federal and local officers are en route to the location where we believe Mr. Griffin is being held. This situation will be resolved long before you could get here."

Jake felt more helpless than when C.A. was captive a year earlier. Back then, he couldn't walk, so there was nothing he could do. Now, at least, he had use of his legs but still there was nothing he could do. Addie Allen was correct. No point in his rushing out to Dulles Airport and making an ass of himself, demanding to get on a flight, and then spending the next five or six hours sitting down.

"Will you keep me up to date on what's going on, Miss Allen?"

"That I will do, sir, and that's a promise. I'll call you every couple of hours whether or not there's anything new to report."

"I'm very grateful. What time is it out there? Five o'clock?"

Addie glanced at the clock and shuddered. "Barely," she replied.

"You haven't been to bed, have you, Miss Allen?"

"No, sir, I haven't," Addie answered.

"Then I guess I'm not the only one who's concerned. I get carried away sometimes. I apologize for my outburst."

Unexpected tears formed in Addie's eyes and she roughly swiped them away. She understood their source; instinctively she knew that Jake Graham was not the kind of man who apologized to people, and to receive his apology was tantamount to a benediction. "Apology accepted, with appreciation. And Mr. Graham?" She paused and awaited his acknowledgment.

"Yes, Miss Allen?"

She opened her mouth and took breath to speak, but the words wouldn't come. And no wonder: she'd been prepared to say that C.A. and Tommy would be fine. But that was a silly thing to say. For all she knew they could both be dead. Instead she said, "You're not in this alone," and hung up the phone.

**Carole Ann** was received with a mixture of ire and awe among the assembled law enforcement troops, thirty women and men, sinister outlines of shadow lurking in the dark. They all knew who she was. Most displayed indifference to her presence. They didn't object as long as she didn't interfere. Several openly welcomed her, and three were overtly hostile. But since the officers in charge of each squad accepted her presence as long as it didn't extend to participation, she was permitted to remain—if she followed orders. She was to continue riding with Anthony since he, too, officially was little more than an observer. She would not have or use a weapon, which was acceptable to her. And she would obey any direct order, which she agreed to in principle. Certainly she had no wish to disrupt their operation. But it was *their* operation. If they apprehended the smugglers and shut down their trafficking in human cargo, excellent. But her objective was to secure the safe release of Tommy Griffin and she would permit nothing to deter or detract her.

She overheard enough snatches of conversation to learn that a "shipment" of Mexicans had arrived at the house that very night, and that while no one had seen Tommy arrive, the Caddy low-rider that abducted him from the gym was parked in the yard, along with two windowless vans. "Contraband-transport vehicles," the cops called them. Their excitement crackled in the air like August lightning. They expected to capture the leaders of the ring, as well as perhaps two dozen illegal immigrants, with a kidnap victim thrown in for good measure. It would be a productive night.

Carole Ann looked through the shadows for Anthony. Other than herself, he was the only person not wearing an identifying police logo. She spied him huddled with an INS agent, the two of them standing well apart from a larger group and talking with their heads close together. Suddenly there was movement. Energy. It was time to go. She looked at the sky. There was no light on the eastern horizon, but the promise of dawn was in the air. The sun already was up and hot in D.C., she mused, and Jake and Valerie already were up and into the day. She and Tommy would talk to Jake later, and Tommy would talk to Valerie, and she wondered whether they both would tell of the excited dread they felt at the prospect of this new day.

"Ready?"

She hadn't seen Anthony approach and was startled when he spoke. "What's the game plan?" she asked.

"The ground troops pull out now. The choppers'll be here in forty-five. We'll all reach the location at the same time."

Her heart was pounding so hard that she was certain he must have heard. Choppers! This was to be a full-fledged assault on the smugglers. Panic would ensue. People would be injured. Tommy was in more danger now that his emancipation was imminent than he was at the moment of his capture. Fear caused a roaring in her ears and a roiling in her intestines. How could she save Tommy under these circumstances!

"This is not gonna be the shoot-out at the OK Corral," Anthony said dryly, reading perfectly the emotional display on her face. "The choppers are for effect, mostly. They'll scare the shit out of the contraband and they won't try to run. But they'll also provide aerial tracking of the smugglers if they make a run for it. Nothing out there but high desert and low mountains. Somebody familiar with the area, we'd lose 'em fast."

She wanted to believe him but there was nothing upon which to hang an article of faith. She took a long, hard look at him. What was there to reassure her? A steadiness of the eyes and a solidity to the jaw. A proud and confident carriage of the body. Memory of a mother slain because of her courage and sense of justice. Enough courage inherited from that mother to induce him to quit a job rather than hurt the woman he now called Mother. It was nearly enough.

"If you're going, now's the time," he said, holding her gaze. "And unless everything we've learned about Gutierrez and Nunez and the rest is flat-out wrong, this will not be Waco revisited. These people are stupid, not violent."

She raised her left eyebrow at him. "The people at Waco weren't stupid? Locking twenty-three people in a van to die of carbon monoxide poisoning isn't violent?"

His lips crinkled in what could have been a grin and he shook his head with what definitely was a little sigh of exasperation. "I'll rephrase the statement, Counselor. We don't think they have an arsenal and we don't think they have the stomach for a firefight."

She resisted the impulse to point out to him that the size and scope of the operation now in progress suggested just the opposite. Instead, she opened the passenger door to the Bronco. "I'm ready," she said, climbing in and shutting the door firmly behind her. She still was securing her seat belt when Anthony rumbled out of the parking lot, fifth in line behind four other black four-wheel-drive vehicles. They drove, all of them, as if trying to outrun the dawn. Despite the fact that she'd had virtually no sleep in the past twenty-four hours, she felt wide awake and alert. Tommy would call it wired, and indeed she felt as if tiny electrical currents were coursing through her being. The thought of Tommy intensified the charge. She hoped he knew that she was on her way. She hoped he knew how strongly she felt her commitment to him.

"You've got time for a short nap," Anthony said.

Carole Ann shook her head. "It's past time for that. In fact, it's almost time to wake up. Do you mind if we talk?"

"About what?" Wariness crept into his voice and his body. She saw the imperceptible hunching of his shoulders, the tightening of his hands on the steering wheel.

"About Gloria—Sergeant Killian—and her two children and you and how your lives have been. And why you and she risked your protected witness status to help me."

"That last part's easy. She met Griffin in D.C. He handled all the crap with what happened to her mother—he dealt with the cops, even spent a couple of nights there just to make sure that Ricky fool didn't pay a return visit. And Jake Graham told her what it cost you to get protected witness status for the old lady. She's had a stroke, you know." He retreated deep within himself. The silence went on so long that Carole Ann assumed their conversation was finished and lapsed into her own silence. When he spoke again she jumped. "Know what she said? That she'd always wanted to live in California. She's seventy years old and nobody ever knew she had that dream."

"What does she like best?"

He laughed. "The ocean, of course. The way it sounds and the way it smells and the way it never ends. She says she can tell, standing on the beach and looking toward the horizon, that the ocean never ends. She said that feeling tells her she's finally safe."

Carole Ann pondered that, attempted to experience the ocean from the point of view of a seventy-year-old blind woman who'd escaped death only by virtue of an error. An incorrect address. And found that she could not. "She'll like living at Jacaranda. It's as California as the ocean."

"Only if she can hang out with the Wrecking Crew. She was born to mischief."

Carole Ann emitted a bark of laughter. "Tommy told you about them, huh?"

"I'd like to meet them myself," he said with a hoot of his own. "They make me almost glad Grams is blind and paralyzed on one side. Maybe instead of trying to keep up with them, she'll slow them down." Then he sobered suddenly. "But this is all needless and pointless wishful thinking. We're never going to get in there, not after what's happened."

She felt his sadness and did not attempt to lighten the load. She allowed the silence to grow as she contemplated the imminent changes in store for Jacaranda Estates. Tommy had already told her that a new family was moving into the Asmara home. And certainly a new property manager would be hired. And, oh, God! Luisa! What would happen to Luisa's house, for certainly she'd not be permitted to remain? Whoever the new property management entity was, he or she would most likely want to purge the place of all remnants of the reign of terror.

"Those guys on the playground. They're cops, right?"

He looked sideways at her, and nodded his head.

"And there are two undercovers living there."

"Yep," he replied. "Both LAPD. The others are LAPD and INS."

Darkness prevented him from noticing, but her eyes narrowed and her lips tightened. "Then I'm sure," she said through clenched teeth, "that the LAPD and the INS won't mind paying for the destruction to the playground."

He clearly wanted to laugh, but instinct dictated a wiser display of behavior. He said nothing. He watched the road ahead, conscious of her eyes on him, and offered a silent prayer of gratitude when the brake lights on the GMC Jimmy in front of him glowed red, off and on, three times as the driver tapped his brakes: the signal that they were nearing their destination.

Carole Ann felt him tense, saw the signal, and felt the Bronco lose speed as Anthony lifted his foot from the gas pedal. Since there was no vehicle behind them, he didn't need to give the signal. A half mile or so ahead, she saw the first vehicle make a right turn off the road. She saw what looked like a barn in a field. A cloud of dust trailed the lead truck, followed by the second truck and its own dust shroud. By the time she and Anthony arrived and parked, the other sixteen officers were paired and ready to proceed. She took in their vests and their assault weapons and shuddered. For their own sakes, she hoped Anthony was right about the smugglers, hoped that they would not offer any resistance.

As she observed them, several of the troops looked up, and as Carole Ann followed the direction of their gaze, she heard a dull grumble, like half-formed thunder. The choppers. She could not tell from which direction they approached, though the assault team was looking north. Then everyone began moving at once. Anthony grabbed her arm and propelled her forward. Despite the fact that she was wearing lightweight sneakers and they were wearing combat boots, she had to struggle to keep up with the cops. They ran double-time in a low, bent-knee crouch. Anthony followed suit. She tried, and failed, and had to settle for a bent-waist approximation. Within minutes, her nose and throat were coated with dry, powdery dust and she hacked, trying to clear it.

She raised her head hoping to discern their destination, but she saw only an endless expanse of gray-brown, sandy soil, scrub grass, cacti, low-growing piñon trees, all eerily shadowed in the interim between dark and dawn. She knew that hundreds of life-forms were moving in the dimness all around them, and she wished that she, too, wore high-top combat boots with her pants legs tucked in. Carole Ann loved the desert and the beings that lived in it, but she didn't want any of them finding new lodging in her clothes. She was contemplating tucking the bottoms of her sweatpants into her socks when Anthony reached out and grabbed her arm. She stopped at the same moment as he, and she looked where he was looking. They almost were at the front door of an adobe and timber cabin so artfully crafted that it seemed to be of the land rather than on it.

Swift-moving shadows fanned out, in too wide an arc, she thought, merely to surround the structure, which was dark and still. Carole Ann studied it, realizing that it was one of several outbuildings, part of a complex much larger than she'd initially thought. This was much more than a cabin out in the middle of the desert. This was, she was beginning to recognize, an elegant, expensive, and quite extensive compound. The main building's roof was covered with gently sloping hand-crafted tiles of azure. The roof's varying heights and angles guaranteed an eternal match with the sky, whatever its mood. The sandstone-colored adobe and worn timber blended in with the earth. The entire setting was one of perfection, and Carole Ann realized that smuggling human cargo was an extremely lucrative enterprise. And she guessed that this was how Pablo Gutierrez had spent a significant portion of his share of the scam.

A sliver of light creased the eastern horizon and snaked its way toward them, enhancing the magic of the setting by several hundred percent. Gutierrez's morals may have been way out of whack, but his artistic sensibilities existed on a very high plane. Not an uncommon occurrence, Carole Ann mused. Aesthete Thomas Jefferson bought and sold human beings and the Nazis committed unspeakable atrocities upon human beings to the strains of classical music. The thought disgusted her and she shook her head, forcing herself to focus on the moment and what must be done. She wondered in which of the buildings the smuggled Mexicans were being held, and whether Tommy was with them. Would his proximity to them make effecting his release simpler or more difficult?

She didn't have time to reach a conclusion.

The choppers had arrived. Cruising in for on-the-dime landings, the blades churning up the desert and the sound of the Bell Jet engines churning up the spirits of long-gone desert beings; for this must be what was meant by a sound "to raise the dead." She resisted the urge to cover her ears, and her reward was that the noise quickly abated as the engines were cut and the passengers disembarked, joining the scurrying black-clad figures already on the ground.

Suddenly, it seemed to Carole Ann, it was fully light. Day had arrived, obliterating all traces of the night. It was bright, hot, dry, and, for an instant, still. Then people began shouting, and, after several seconds, screaming. And running. The air was charged with panic and anger and fear. She could feel all those emotions and more, emanating from those whose dreams were being so rudely deferred. From her vantage point she could see two women and a man who, after they'd run several feet from the larger of the outbuildings, quietly dropped to their knees. And Carole Ann felt another emotion: despair. So close. They'd come so close to having their dreams realized.

She was galvanized by the sound of a shot that came from within the building. Then she heard the sound of a car engine, followed by slamming doors and rubber racing and churning on dry dirt, seeking to gain traction. On her hands and knees, she crawled toward what she thought was the front of the building. The car, the low-profile, half-assed restoration that she'd seen parked in the alley behind Robbie's studio, careened around the building on two wheels. Two INS agents followed on foot at a respectable trot. When they reached the clearing, they stopped, in unison, and aimed, both of them holding their weapons in two hands and sighting down their arms toward the barrel. Simultaneously they squeezed off shots and the Caddy shimmied, swerved, and rolled over. The scent of burning rubber and the sound of screams contributed to the sense Carole Ann had that the situation was getting out of hand.

Still concerned about the shot fired inside the building, she crouched low and scooted closer to the structure, flattening herself on the ground when she reached the cover of the side of the building. Feeling safe enough, she turned to catch a broader glimpse of the action away from the building. The overturned Caddy now was surrounded by INS agents and LAPD cops, who were pulling two men from it. Judging from their lack of gentleness, Carole Ann assumed that the would-be escapees were not seriously injured. Toward the rear of the building, toward open desert and the mountains, several agents stood guard over perhaps a dozen men and women who were spread-eagle on the ground. Sickened by the sight, she turned away and began inching her way around the building to the door from which all the people had run. When she reached the corner, she peeked around. Two LAPD cops stood several feet away with their backs to the door.

She snatched herself back before they saw her, and wondered how long she'd have to wait for them to find something more challenging to do. Not long, the sound of running feet told her, and when she peered around the building's corner again, the two cops were chasing two men who had a twenty-yard head start. Crawling on her hands and knees, Carole Ann rounded the building, then quickly stood and approached the door. She opened it slowly, carefully.

The odor inside was foul—the smell of perspiration and dirty clothes and dirty bodies and unwashed hair. And fear. There was no furniture in the large, square main room. Mats and cots were lined against the walls, all empty. Three doorways led off the room and she approached them in order. The first opened onto a kitchen of brick and tile and timber and a fireplace, occupying half a wall, that should have exuded warmth and comfort but did not. The room contained no appliances. A dozen Styrofoam chests lined one wall and bags of paper plates, cups, and napkins were piled on the countertops.

Not wanting to see more, Carole Ann backed out of the kitchen and approached the second door and pushed it open. The odor that emanated told her it was the bathroom and she quickly pulled it shut. One toilet for two dozen frightened people. At the third door there was a short hallway and in it, a puddle of blood on the floor. Nausea rose in her throat and she pushed it back down as she stepped over the blood and to the door. She stood listening and heard nothing. She gripped the latch, lowered it, and pushed the door open as she leaned her body away from it. Then she peered inside. A trail of blood led to Tommy Griffin, propped in a sitting position against the wall, eyes flickering open and shut, but not seeming to focus.

She rushed to him, knelt down, and embraced him. He groaned and she uttered a cry of relief. His left shoulder was oozing blood; a quick check revealed a bullet hole in the soft flesh beneath his shoulder and no other wounds. She pulled him upright and he groaned again and opened his eyes and struggled to have them focus.

"Fish," she whispered. "Fish. I'm going to get some help."

He grabbed her hand with frightening strength. "Don't," he managed through lips that barely moved. His eyes fluttered and his mouth opened and closed but no other sound came out. Then his head dropped to his chest. She quickly untied her sneakers and removed them and her socks, which she folded into a pad and pressed against his wound. She then removed the shoestrings, tied them together end to end, and bound the makeshift bandage under his arm and around his chest. When she pulled him toward her, he did not groan and she didn't know whether or not that was a good sign; only that he was not conscious.

"Fish!" she whispered into his ear, gently tapping both sides of his face. "Fish! Wake up now. Come on, Fish! Don't fade on me!" She brought his head forward into her embrace and held him tightly.

He groaned. "C.A.? You . . . ?"

"Yes, it's me. And we've got to get you up and out of here." But she didn't know how she'd get him up and she didn't know why, but she didn't feel that leaving him was a good idea. Why not? It would be for seconds . . . a minute at the most. There was a small army outside the door. She'd run to the door, yell for help, and return immediately to Tommy.

"C . . . C . . ." He tried and failed to say her name. His eyes rolled back and his head flopped down, chin on chest. The two socks, folded together into a thick pad, were saturated with blood.

Carole Ann jumped to her feet and ran out of the room, almost tripping and falling as she remembered too late about the pool of blood in the hallway. She slid in it and stumbled and as she caught herself, she thought she detected movement in the bathroom. The door was slightly ajar, she could smell it. She thought she'd closed it, but she'd been so intent on getting away from that stench that perhaps she hadn't. And anyway, it didn't matter. She sprinted across the wide room and to the door and rushed out into the yard, looking for help. There was no one. She dashed around the side of the building. The Caddy now was upright and listing toward the passenger side, a function, no doubt, of the tires having been shot out, but the INS agents who had disabled it were not in sight.

She ran back around the house. She stopped when she reached the door. Luisa was standing in the doorway holding a gun, pointing it at Carole Ann.

"Luisa." It was a word spoken, not a name called in greeting, because Carole Ann did not know how to greet the person aiming the gun at her. And not because of the weapon, but because this Luisa was unknown to her. The familiar, soft roundness of her body and face had metamorphosed into hard angles. The crinkles around her eyes seemed to have flattened, and the laugh lines around her mouth frozen into hard ridges. Carole Ann searched the mouth for signs that it once had whispered *"Madre de Dios"* a dozen times a day. These lips were straight lines, the fullness drained from them. This Luisa was flat. Like a doormat. And empty, like a zombie. The irony was not lost on Carole Ann, but she hadn't the strength to indulge it.

They stood staring at each other, Luisa framed in the door of the lovely house that should have—perhaps at one time had—welcomed guests, for it was, Carole Ann had concluded, the guest house of the estate. She detected movement in her peripheral vision, off to her left. Luisa, she was certain, could see only what was directly in front of her, her peripheral vision restricted by the door frame. Tommy was bleeding to death, slowly and surely. She had to do something. She took a step backward and Luisa raised the gun a couple of inches. It was an automatic of some kind. Carole Ann didn't know; she didn't like guns. But she could differentiate between a revolver and an automatic. She raised her hands over her head and took another backward step.

"You've already shot one person, Luisa. Don't make it worse."

"I killed him so it can't be worse," Luisa said, and Carole Ann felt a silly rush of gratitude. The voice hadn't undergone alteration. It still was Luisa's slightly sing-song little girl voice, still heavily accented after almost half a century of Americanization.

"Will you kill me, too, Luisa?" she asked, deciding it best to allow her to think she'd succeeded in killing Tommy.

Her answer was a dead stare. There was no light in her eyes. There was nothing remaining of the Luisa Carole Ann had known. This Luisa blinked slowly, like a lizard, and Carole Ann recalled the night that Grayce was attacked; the night that she killed Grayce's attacker. Luisa had sat dead like that in the living room that night. Was that the beginning? For from that night on, Luisa had been absent from their lives, and they had been so engrossed with the effort of preventing those lives from collapsing that they had not forced the issue of Luisa. She had seemed not to want to be involved in their troubles, and they had accepted her right to steer clear of difficulty. After all, Luisa hadn't shot anybody or been beaten up. And even though she'd been charged as an accessory, along with Bert and Angie . . .

"They found out, didn't they? The police. When they charged you but then didn't arrest you. They found out that you were—"

"Say it!" Luisa hissed at her. "Say it! The *policía* find out I'm illegal alien. Illegal. Alien. Wetback border rat. They all want me to confess, to get sent back, so they can keep their business, Pablo and Hector and Ricky. But I say no! If I go back, they all go back, I tell them. All my life nobody ever does what I want to do. Never! *No más. No más.*"

Carole Ann watched the sadness envelop Luisa, and so heavy was the mantle that it caused her shoulders to sag, and the gun lowered enough that she could have chanced an escape. But Luisa looked at her through half-closed eyes and emanated a hatred so forceful that Carole Ann flinched. And when she flinched, the gun inched back up into heart range.

Carole Ann wanted to be able to say something to this woman at whose table she had eaten, in whose home she had slept; for whom she had baked her favorite coconut cakes for her birthday. To this woman Carole Ann could think of nothing to say.

"What happened, Luisa?" she finally managed. "What did we do wrong?"

Luisa's now skinny lips curled as if she were preparing to spit. "They always thought they were better than me, with their good jobs and big cars and new clothes and furniture and bridge clubs and friends. Anglo jobs and Anglo friends and Anglo cars—"

"What the hell are you talking about, Luisa!" Carole Ann forgot to be afraid and dropped her arms. "These are Black and brown women you're talking about, women just like you!"

"Not like me! Never like me! Like the people in the *Ebony* magazine. Black Anglos, caring about nothing but working hard and saving money and sending kids to college." She finished with an anguished wail that spoke of sorrow, ancient and deep; and of regret and loss and anger.

Flashes of movement left and right. She kept her eyes glued on Luisa's gun and her peripheral consciousness attuned to the fact that help was at hand. And grateful as she was, she knew that they would kill Luisa. To them, she was not a mother figure; she was a smuggler, a kidnapper, an illegal alien, and an accessory after the fact in the negligent homicide deaths of twenty-three people. Tears welled up in her eyes and she extended a hand to Luisa, and took a step toward her.

"Let me help you, Luisa. You know I can help you."

"I don't need your help. I don't need them, either," Luisa snarled. "Not anymore. I'm rich, too. I'm going home to Juárez and be rich." Then she fired off a round.

Carole Ann floated to the ground on a wildly rocking wave of pain and euphoria. The pain was searing in its place, and the airy euphoria balanced it. Yin and yang. She smiled. Al would appreciate the reference.

# ❧ *seventeen* ❧

When she opened her eyes the first time, she saw her mother and smiled at her. Her mother wept. She closed her eyes again and wondered why her mother was crying. The second time she opened her eyes, Grayce, Roberta, Angie, Addie, Warren, Valerie, and Anthony were looking down at her. Why were they all here? And where were Tommy and Luisa? She closed her eyes and welcomed the return to unconsciousness. When her eyes opened the third time, they saw Jake Graham.

"Jesus," she mumbled through lips too drugged for proper movement. "What are you doing here?" And he laughed and cried and she laughed and cried with him and he called her the granddaddy of shit magnets and they both laughed and cried until she fell asleep again.

Eventually, after four and a half days, she woke up and remained awake. Her mother was dozing in a chair next to the bed, holding her daughter's hand. When Carole Ann moved, Grayce sat up, wide-eyed and attentive. "My baby," she whispered, a wide grin overpowering the tears. And she held and rocked her daughter for a long, long time. Then, as always, she released her.

Carole Ann assessed herself. She was fuzzy and groggy and hungry. When she tried to sit upright, screaming pain radiated from her left shoulder, down her left side, and around to her back. She sank back into the pillows and began wiggling feet and toes and hands and fingers. She lifted her legs and arms and moved her head from side to side. With her right hand she felt her head and face, and she explored the bandage that all but covered the left side of her torso. To touch herself caused pain, so she stopped.

"Ma. Luisa?"

Grayce inhaled deeply, as if she were doing yoga breathing exercises. "She's dead. Anthony says they shot her after she shot you."

Carole Ann nodded. "Tommy?" she asked in a whisper, and was caught by surprise at the transformation in her mother.

Grayce snorted in a very unladylike fashion. "He's at Bert's, eating everything under the sun and driving her and everybody crazy! That boy is as hardheaded as they come. Won't do a thing you tell him and laughs when you fuss at him. And Valerie lets him get away with it!"

Carole Ann interrupted Grayce's raving. "Tommy's at Bert's eating and laughing and I'm still in here?" She moved to sit up and flopped quickly back into the pillows, stifling the cry of agony in her throat.

"Luisa's aim had improved by the time she got around to shooting you," Grayce said dryly. "Tommy's wound bled a lot, but wasn't serious. The bullet went straight through. You, on the other hand, almost died," and her voice caught on that last word and tears filled her eyes and spilled down her cheeks. "You've got to stop all this, C.A. Please promise me you will."

"Stop what, Ma? This is the first time I've ever been shot."

"Stop this attitude for one thing!" Grayce snapped. "There is nothing funny about what you just did here. Or what you did in Louisiana. I used to worry about you defending all those hardened criminals, but you've been in more danger since you stopped practicing law than when you spent all your time with drug dealers and murderers! You've got to stop it."

Bilious rage arose in Carole Ann and she released it, not minding that it was directed at her own mother. "You talk like I *wanted* to get shot! What was I supposed to do? Let them kill Tommy? I owed him! He saved my life, Ma! Do you understand at all what kind of weight that is? He risked his life, and lost his job in the process, trying to save me. I was obligated to go get him, and I'd do it again. Just like I'd go again to find out who killed Al. That was my obligation to him."

"And what of your obligation to yourself?" Grayce asked, her anger icy and cold, the antithesis of her daughter's. "Do you need to die to satisfy it?"

Carole Ann and her mother locked stares. The mother was the teacher and therefore the master, and so the daughter was the first to yield. She looked away, wounded by her mother's anger and still harboring a sense of betrayal at the secrets kept from her, a justification for her own anger. "I feel like I'm down the rabbit hole," she said.

"The difference being everything you've experienced is real," the mother replied, without anger but still full of parental resolve.

"I think Luisa hated us."

Grayce shook her head in disgust. "Luisa always blamed everybody for her problems."

Carole Ann groaned. Another secret about to be revealed. This was worse than the rabbit hole. Reality always was. "So you're saying you knew how she felt?"

"I knew, we all knew, of Luisa's resentment. But it was her choice to live as she did. She allowed Hector to control her from Mexico—"

Carole Ann was incredulous. "You knew he was alive? You've always known? About everything?"

"Not everything," Grayce replied, shaking her head. "That he was alive, yes. He had to be. How else was Luisa supporting herself and the children? She never earned more than minimum wage and she refused every opportunity we put in her path. And over the years, C.A., there were so many that we lost count. Luisa refused— flat out refused—to study English, to earn her GED, to take any of the skills training courses we set up for her and paid for. She accused us of acting like Anglos."

"She said that to me!" Carole Ann had forgotten and the memory returned with force. "Black Anglos, she said."

"Nigger Anglos, Hector used to call us," Grayce said with a venom Carole Ann never before had witnessed. "Told Mitch he was a fool for being in the Army and told me he was a dead fool after he was killed. He called Bert's Charlie a thief after he bought his own rig. Hector refused to believe that a Colored man could—or would—work long enough and hard enough to afford his own rig. But he saved his real nastiness for Angie. He called her *puta,* and if you don't know what that means, you'll have to ask someone else. Bad enough for Hector that she was a lesbian, but with a Black woman? And after Dottie was dead and he found out that Angie was the beneficiary of Dottie's double indemnity life insurance pol-icy . . ." Grayce forced a bark of dry laughter from her throat that sounded as if the effort had hurt.

"You knew all these things and continued a friendship with Luisa? Why—"

"Because!" Grayce snapped. "We were all she had! Hector was nothing without her and so he held on to her, and she was nothing without us and she held on to us!" She heard all the questions writ-ten on her daughter's face. "She was our friend, C.A. We couldn't turn our backs on her weaknesses and her madness any more than if she had cancer or . . . or . . . diabetes or some other thing that slowly kills the body. What Luisa suffered from—and you'd have to get a name from the therapists—was slowly killing her spirit. Now, if we'd known about the illegal-alien smuggling, things would have been different! We knew that Pablo Gutierrez traveled back and forth to Mexico and that he brought Luisa money from Hector. But that's all we knew, all we wanted to know, and if we did anything wrong, it was that. We didn't want to know more. About Hector and Luisa or about Mr. Gutierrez's trips and his strange visitors. We just wanted . . . to be happy."

"But what a price you paid, Ma."

Grayce laughed, a real laugh this time, though slightly tinged with irony. "Happy always has carried a high price, C.A. That's one of the things we could never make Luisa understand. But I hope and pray that you do. Happiness is so easy to have that people think it's free. But you pay. When you make a painful decision, you're buying your happiness. When you do what's right for you, even if it's not right for somebody else, you're buying your happiness."

Carole Ann grinned at her mother. "Are you sure about that, Ma?" she asked, confident that no trace of the setup in progress was revealed in her voice.

"Of course I am," snapped Grayce righteously.

"Then everything I've done in the past year should be a pretty big down payment on a big bunch of happiness," she said, and winced. Because of the pain caused by the motion of raising her arms in victory, and by her mother's sniffed, "Serves you right."

# ❦ *eighteen* ❧

Summer was in full swing when Carole Ann got back to Washington. It was ninety-six degrees and the humidity was 89 percent. It was not yet ten o'clock in the morning. Whenever D.C. did this, Carole Ann gave serious thought to living elsewhere. They'd been playing this game for more than fifteen years, she and D.C., and D.C. still was the most miserable place in the world in the summer and she still lived in it, almost on the bank of the Potomac River, the muggiest part of town.

From the balcony of her penthouse condominium she could see most of Washington and a good bit of that part of Virginia closest to Washington, the Potomac River the dividing line between the two. Boats sped and bobbed and glided across the placid surface, impervious to the heat.

Despite the protective overhang that shielded her balcony, she was drenched in perspiration. But so grateful was she to be home that she dismissed all thoughts of retreating to the air-conditioned interior. This was her home. This was her view. She had missed it. And she intended to savor it. She leaned over the railing and looked down at the ground. Grass and flower beds trimmed to neat and orderly submission. Not the wild, exotic splendor of Jacaranda Estates—this was azalea and rose and forsythia and pyracantha country. People, despite the heat, clad in full business armor, rushing to and fro; nothing casually elegant or laid-back about them.

She knew that it was both unwise and counterproductive to continue drawing comparisons between D.C. and L.A., yet she could not stop. Everything she saw here with her eyes, her brain compared and contrasted to similar items and objects there: the Potomac and the Pacific; azaleas and bougainvillea; government lawyers and studio executives; Jacaranda Estates and Foggy Bottom; home and . . . home. Different places for different people. She was not now who she had been growing up in Los Angeles, and she had been mistaken to expect that things and people there would have—or should have—remained unchanged. And though she'd made peace with those changes before she left, she would, forever, remember her hurt. And that she knew to be unfair.

She stretched out full length in one of the rattan chaise lounges and removed her robe, exposing her still-healing wound to nature's heating pad. She could not feel the sun directly because of the overhang, but she welcomed the moist heat, so different from L.A.'s crispy dryness.

"You gotta stop this, C.A.," she muttered to herself, doing the work for Tommy or Jake. And back her mind and memory went to Los Angeles, Tommy's new home.

He had fallen in love with the place. Not to mention with his new car, which he'd gone to retrieve immediately upon leaving the hospital, which is what had annoyed Bert and Grayce so. And though Valerie, too, loved the old convertible and the beach and Rodeo Drive, she was enchanted most by Jacaranda Estates. Where they now would live, next door to Roberta, in Sadie Osterheim's house. And Tommy and Anthony would be Jake's West Coast operatives. And Anthony's mother, the former Gloria Jenkins, would be the new property manager at Jacaranda Estates. And Anthony and his fiancée would be the new residents of Luisa's house. All made possible because Carole Ann was the new owner of the land beneath Jacaranda Estates. "The person best equipped to carry on my dreams and my work," according to Arthur Jennings.

Carole Ann didn't know what to believe, or think, or feel about the old man's unexpected—and unwelcome—gift, but she was certain beyond a shadow of a doubt that she did not want to remain in Los Angeles to "carry on" for Arthur Jennings or any other reason, so she'd returned to Washington.

She'd run away from L.A., her mother said, just as Jake had accused her of running away from D.C. Was it only three months ago? She marveled at the effects of the passage of time. She'd gone to L.A. seeking refuge and definition in the secure embrace of her home and family and had found, instead, that everything she'd revered as sacred was tarnished and ugly.

"Preposterous!" her mother had almost shouted when Carole Ann had attempted an explanation of her feelings. "You were loved completely and fully and nothing that happened could ever affect or change that!"

"But why didn't you ever tell me?"

"Because you didn't need to know. Because it was none of your business. Because it was too painful. Because we had to live every day in the present. We couldn't afford to think about or worry about or cry about the past."

"Luisa was the present!"

"And we couldn't waste time and energy on things and people that refused to change, so we dealt with them as they were!"

For the first time ever, Carole Ann and Grayce departed from each other with a splinter of uneasiness wedged between them like a popcorn kernel between teeth, something foreign, an irritant that would fester if left too long. But Carole Ann was in no frame of mind to make amends. Nor was she of the mind-set to go have lunch with

Jake. But she'd promised almost two weeks ago that today, she'd have lunch with him and spend some time with him at his office. And instantly she revised her thoughts and feelings, and questioned why there'd been the reluctance.

She *did* want to see Jake and spend time with him and share his excitement at the growth of his company. She was happy for him that Tommy and Anthony would team up to represent him out West. He was her friend. What then was the source of, the reason for that initial and immediate negative reaction? Warren, she imagined, would tell her she was grieving still. And perhaps she was.

She roused herself from the chaise, and scooted to the sliding glass door, wincing at the effort required to move the door on its track; and with the pain came the reminder that she began her work with a physical therapist the following morning. "Best damn physical therapist on the East Coast," Jake had growled. "She's the reason I'm able to walk today." Carole Ann flexed the fingers of her left hand and lifted her left arm, which displayed a reluctance to take orders from her brain. She'd almost died from the bullet that had ripped open her chest, missing by crucial inches her clavicle and a lung. "That's twice in one year," her mother had said more times than she needed to hear, but it wasn't the near-death experience that troubled her spirit as much as it was the source: Luisa had intended to kill her. Had wanted to kill her. She would be a long time recovering from that knowledge; perhaps she never would.

Jake had said lunch would be a casual affair, served on his rooftop deck, so she donned white drawstring slacks and a white sleeveless blouse—she couldn't manage a tee shirt these days, a real tragedy since they were a staple of her wardrobe—and with her wide-brimmed straw hat and matching purse, she could have been en route to a garden party. "Maybe I am," she mused, and snickered at the thought of Jake hosting a garden party. She tried to imagine him in a seersucker suit and spectator pumps and the snicker became a giggle. Jake was and forever would be a homicide detective. And that, she thought with a warm and loving feeling, was a truly wonderful thing.

**He greeted** her wearing khaki slacks, a pale yellow short-sleeve shirt, and oxford loafers, and Carole Ann thought perhaps she'd been too hasty in consigning him to a lifetime of shiny, ugly police detective suits.

"You look positively gorgeous!" she told him without the slightest hint of mockery. "And this is spectacular," she said, waving her good arm to encompass the rooftop garden, which could easily have been the setting for a spiffy party.

He growled at her. "What you see before you is my wife's vision of how an 'investigative specialist' should look. That is, if he absolutely refuses to wear a suit and tie. Which I absolutely do unless I absolutely have to."

She grinned at him. " 'Investigative specialist?' "

He muttered something she couldn't decipher, then shrugged his shoulders and raised his palms to the heavens. "Since I'm not a cop anymore, I don't know what I am. I'm sure as hell not a private detective or a private investigator! None of that TV shit. Give some thought to it, would you? To what I should call myself? You lawyers are good with words."

She followed him to a corner of the deck, which resembled a merger between the Caribbean and the South Pacific: a series of thick bamboo poles that almost seemed planted into the wood rails and flooring, supported three floor-to-ceiling rattan blinds that not only blocked the sun's glare but actually seemed to cool the area. High-backed wicker chairs surrounded an oval glass-topped table, which held bowls of fresh fruit, pitchers of water and lemonade, a basket covered with a brilliantly colored napkin, and two place settings. An antique black and brass ceiling fan, mounted on a thick beam, turned overhead, gently rocking the half dozen ferns and flowering plants that hung suspended from the beamed ceiling. The mix of cultures reminded her of Ray, Jose, and David, and the *Dame Que Es Mío* Cultural Center. She told Jake as much and he remembered the place from her report to him.

"That place and those guys sound pretty special."

She nodded. "They are. They also want me to be their lawyer, once the bar lifts my suspension," she said, quickly dismissing that subject from her mind.

"Well?" Jake asked after a beat.

"Well what?"

"Are you gonna represent them?" he asked in the tone of voice reserved for the intellectually challenged.

She shrugged. "You think you don't know what to call yourself? What do you call a lawyer who no longer practices law? Especially one whose license to practice in her home state is on hold pending her 'demonstrated ability to conduct herself in a manner befitting an officer of the court.'" She couldn't prevent the bitterness that tinged the words. The DA quickly had dropped the charges against her and those against Grayce, Roberta, and Angie. But the bar association had persevered, as Addie had predicted at their initial meeting.

"Well, I just happen to have a few thoughts on that matter," Jake said, much too casually, and Carole Ann's eyes narrowed as she sat in the chair he'd waved her to. He opened the top of one of two coolers and retrieved a large, brightly colored bowl. "Cold cucumber soup," he said, depositing it on the table with a flourish. And, opening the second cooler and withdrawing an identical bowl, he turned toward her and bowed. "Chinese chicken salad." Like a magician, he whisked the napkin off the basket. "Grace's homemade rolls." He sat opposite her, tucked one of the napkins into his shirt front, and lifted the plate from the soup. "Let's eat," he said.

They feasted. The food was wonderful and plentiful and, as Jake observed, Carole Ann's appetite had returned in full force. Which, he commented, was a good thing since she was looking a bit "scrawny." She gave him the evil eye and he laughed at her. They talked easily about a wide range of issues: how much he'd enjoyed meeting her mother, finally, and the rest of the Wrecking Crew; how sorry he was about Luisa; how excited he was that Tommy and Anthony were building his West Coast operation; how proud he was of her successful rescue of Tommy. "He'd have bled to death if it hadn't been for you, C.A. Or that woman would have plugged him again to finish him off. You did good. A real stand-up effort."

They rehashed as much of the truth as they'd been able to figure out about what had happened at Jacaranda Estates and why, and though Jake was gratified to learn that the LAPD had not simply ignored the plight of the people there, he was alternately dismayed and disgusted by the extent of the tragedy.

"That's too many people dead," he growled. "They should've scrapped the entire operation rather than let that many people die."

Carole Ann marveled at their role reversal even as she spoke. "They had so much time and effort invested, Jake. And they didn't know whether or not there was another spy in the ranks."

"Didn't matter! Citizens were at risk. Legal, law-abiding, tax-paying citizens!"

Carole Ann tried again. "Anthony said they also didn't want to jeopardize the fragile INS-LAPD relationship, and so nobody wanted to be the first to pull the plug."

Jake grinned his crooked grin, the one that made him look sinister, and shook his head. "TV cops. Damn OK Corral mentality. Nobody wanted to be the first to blink."

She studied him and wished that every cop everywhere could be like him. His toughness wasn't macho posturing and his loyalty to his profession wasn't blind. Jake couldn't abide lawbreakers of any stripe, and he railed against the acceptance of mitigating circumstances as a criminal defense. He also couldn't accept mitigating circumstances as a reason for police action—or inaction.

"I guess we should be grateful for the stupidity and greed of youth," Carole Ann said. "Because were it not for Little Hector and Pablo, Pedro and Hector still would be in business, smuggling in decent, hardworking adults instead of anybody willing and able to pay the price."

"What absolutely amazes me," Jake said, "is how long that Gutierrez clown was able to bring those people in and hide them right there on the property!"

That truth opened a wound for Carole Ann and she told him how betrayed she'd felt by Grayce and Angie and Roberta and Luisa; how empty and isolated she'd felt with each new revelation; how, because Warren harassed and bullied her, she'd agreed to talk to a therapist about grieving; how she'd accepted that D.C. was home; how uncertain she was about what she'd do with the rest of her life.

"You could become my partner," Jake said quietly and with a reverence that almost frightened her.

"I . . . don't . . . how? How could I be your partner, Jake? I don't know anything about police work."

"You know more about police work than a lot of cops I know," he said in his normal tone. "But that's beside the point. That's what I was saying earlier. What I do isn't really 'police work.' A lot of it is legal stuff. Sure, we investigate companies and individuals, and we provide security and surveillance for companies and individuals. But we're doing some stuff now, for embassies and foreign governments. . . . I'm in over my head, C.A. Not only do I need your knowledge, your brain, I need your approach. You're a class act, C.A. I'm a street cop."

"Nothing wrong with that!" She bristled in her defense of him, and surprised herself with her vehemence.

He got somber again. "Sometimes there is," he said quietly. "I don't fit in at diplomatic functions. Even in one of those two-thousand-dollar Italian suits I'd look like a cop. You, on the other hand, can put on two thousand dollars' worth of clothes and look like a million bucks. You got brains, C.A., and class, and you're tougher than anybody I know, and you're loyal. I'd go to hell with or for you. And I need you. I honest to God need you, C.A."

He sat back and folded his arms across his chest and looked at her, nothing readable in his eyes. He sat so still and so quietly that Carole Ann wanted to ask him to move, to speak, to do something. But she knew that she could do nothing but respond to his request: yes or no. Nothing else would be acceptable. Anything else would be insulting.

She took a deep breath, held it, and expelled it. She nodded her head. "All right, Jake. But I will tell you that I'm terrified by the prospect. The only thing that scares me more is not working at all."

The grin began and spread, lit his face like fireworks in the night sky. He reached beneath his seat and withdrew a legal-sized envelope that she hadn't noticed before. He took from it a sheet of paper, which he extended across the table to her. Even before she took it, she recognized it as business stationery. Her eyes widened as she read the raised gold lettering on the cream-colored paper: GIBSON, GRAHAM INTERNATIONAL. Before she could speak, he presented another document and she read the words, "Partnership Agreement." She placed both documents on the table and looked at him.

"Pretty damn sure of yourself, aren't you?" She wasn't really angry, but she could not accurately or adequately define her emotions.

He shook his head, the smile only half faded. "Not sure at all. Just hopeful as hell."

She picked up the papers again, appreciating the simple beauty of the design: GIBSON, GRAHAM INTERNATIONAL. Nothing more. And, to the left, in the same gold lettering, her name: Carole Ann Gibson, Esquire, and a telephone number.

"Impressive," she said. "Why'd you put my name first?"

"Well," he drawled, "for one thing, it's alphabetically correct. *I* comes before *r* And it rolls off the tongue better: Gibson, Graham sounds nicer than Graham, Gibson. And . . ." he said, drawing out the word and alerting her to the punch line, "if you take a closer look at the partnership agreement, you'll see that you're putting up the most money." And he laughed out loud. A gleeful, joyful, belly-shaking, little-kid kind of laugh.

It was infectious. She laughed with him. Full and hearty. "Well, shit, Jake," she said when she could talk. "I guess you're right. I guess I am some kind of shit magnet." And when his face showed that he'd finally realized what she'd said, she laughed so hard she cried, impervious to the pain shooting through her chest and arm.

He opened his mouth to say something but no words came, so he sputtered a bit, then gave it up. And he, too, laughed until he cried, his tears, like hers, cleansing waters.